Things We Surrender

A LOWCOUNTRY NOVEL

HEIDI HOSTETTER

Tall Cedar
PRESS

Tall Cedars Press

Seattle, Washington

This is a work of fiction. Any similarities to real people is made up. Some of the places are real, but the events taking places at them are fiction.

Cover design: Jenn Reese of Tiger Bright Studios

ISBN for Print: 978-0-9961337-5-3

ISBN for ebook: 978-0-9961337-4-6

For Colleen, who loved Charleston

CHAPTER 1

AT TWENTY-NINE YEARS OLD, Joanna Rutledge Reed staggered under the weight of her life.

If she closed her eyes, tilting her face to meet the bright October sun, she could almost make herself believe that she was happy, that moving to Rome had been a good idea.

Of course, the reality was a bit different.

Perched on the edge of the fountain in the *Campo de' Fiori*, Joanna eavesdropped on conversations from the farmers' market behind her, sifting through Italian phrases for fragments she might recognize. But their words were jumbled and broken, nothing like the calm, steady voice on the discs she'd borrowed from—and hopefully returned to—the public library back in Chicago.

Her life was supposed to be different from this.

Born into one of the oldest families in Charleston, South Carolina, Joanna's life had been laid out before her, as were her mother's and grandmother's. She was expected to marry quickly, a man from an admirable Charleston family. And she did: one month after her college graduation, she stood in the sanctuary of St. Philip's church promising to love and honor her fiancé, Russell John Reed, a man whose family ancestry dated back almost as far as her own. After the ceremony, three hundred friends and relatives gathered on the grounds of the Charleston Yacht Club, for a lavish reception to wish the couple well. She did as she was told. The rest of her life was supposed to be filled with society parties and fundraisers, cotillion and cocktails.

But somehow, she'd lost her way.

"Joanna! Ciao!"

Joanna opened her eyes to see her friend, Francesca, effortlessly beautiful in a short black dress and strappy black sandals, gliding across the square like a model on a runway. Of course, the morning shoppers parted for her, as they always did. And, as *she* always did, Francesca turned neither left nor right as she strode toward Joanna. It was an enviable talent.

She and Francesca met almost three months ago, the day Joanna moved into her new apartment. Joanna had just started unpacking kitchen boxes as her six-year-old daughter, Gracie, napped nearby. The apartment had been much smaller than it seemed from the pictures, and Joanna regretted shipping everything from her apartment in Chicago. She'd relied on a few grainy pictures from the leasing agent, a distant cousin of Nicco's, who had assured them there would be plenty of room. But as Joanna stood in the middle of her new apartment, she realized she had exactly one cabinet for dishes and one cabinet for everything else. And there were fourteen moving boxes still to unpack.

Joanna remembered the knock on the door, and Francesca's warm smile as she offered Joanna her first cup of real Italian cappuccino. Francesca had glanced at the chaos in the tiny apartment and dug in right away. They had worked, unpacking and sorting dishes and table linens until Gracie woke. Then Francesca shepherded them both downstairs to her apartment where she made lunch, something delicious and simple, and made the preparation look effortless. Afterward, Francesca took them to the *gelateria* on the corner, then a tour of the neighborhood. In the weeks that followed, Nicco retreated to his mother's house and Francesca became Joanna's lifeline. She showed Joanna how to navigate the streets and alleys of Rome and how to barter in the markets.

Now, glancing at the market bag at Joanna's feet, Francesca pouted. "You started without me?"

The genuine look of shock on Francesca's face made Joanna laugh. "You're late," Joanna teased, but she didn't really mind. She'd gotten used to Francesca's idea of time. Francesca thought being punctual meant arriving within an hour of the scheduled meeting time. "I had almost given up."

"You Americans are obsessed with time." Francesca gave the tiniest of shrugs and leaned in to brush Joanna's cheeks with a double kiss.

"I only have a few things left to buy." Joanna reached into her pocket and removed the recipe Francesca had given her. "I'll have you know that I've become an expert haggler. You're going to be very impressed." As Francesca looked on, Joanna ticked off each item with her finger. "Eggplant, from the man by the gelato place, onion, garlic, and carrots from the woman under the blue awning. I still need tomatoes, though. You told me to buy those last."

"*Certo*," Francesca confirmed. "Always, you buy tomatoes last and only from Tomas, my friend by the fountain. His tomatoes are the ripest but if you buy them first, they will bruise in your bag." Francesca hooked the top of her sunglasses with a perfectly manicured fingernail and slid them down the bridge of her nose. Peering over them, she frowned. "Bella, this recipe is not simple. I have told you that my Nona has spent her whole day just simmering the sauce and you have more than just sauce." She frowned. "If you must do this, I will help you. But maybe you have changed your mind?" she added, hopefully.

"Nope." Joanna shook her head as she moved the heavy bag from her lap. "Nicco's finally invited his friends to watch a soccer game this afternoon—the first time he's invited *anyone* to our apartment since we arrived. Gracie and I spent the day making chocolate chip cookies yesterday, and anyone can make a salad. All that's left to do is make this eggplant—" She gestured toward her bag with more confidence than she felt. "—thing. I'll be fine." She took a breath and widened her fake smile. "It'll be great."

But Francesca looked dubious. "Nona's recipe has many steps; some are not translated in the directions. This will not be easy. Have you practiced?"

Joanna glanced at her hands in her lap. The truth was that she'd imagined cooking enormous Italian meals for Nicco, his friends, and his family. They'd all sit down to Sunday dinner and she would get to know his sisters and his mother. Gracie would have cousins to play with, and they would be happy. But Nicco hadn't been home as often as she'd hoped and she had yet to meet any of his family, so there hadn't been anyone to cook for.

"There are other ways to get ready for a party, you know." Francesca flicked a strand of glossy black hair over her shoulder. "Let his mama do the cooking; that's what mamas are for. You are too young to spend the day in that hot kitchen. We will go shopping for something beautiful to wear to the party." Her gaze swept over Joanna's denim capris and old college t-shirt and she frowned. "We find you a new dress, shoes, too. And you will have a pedicure."

"Money's a little tight right now," Joanna began.

Francesca interrupted with an impatient wave of her fingers. "Surely, Nicco will not mind his fiancée and her daughter buying themselves pretty things? You are in Italy now, and that is what women do. He must expect this."

Joanna would have loved to go shopping with her friend. The truth was, she had money put aside to buy a few things for herself and Gracie, but the prices were higher than she'd expected and the sizing wasn't as generous. Worse, neither she nor Nicco had found a job yet. Shortly after they arrived, Nicco had changed his mind about working for his cousin, declaring it had always been his dream to play for the *Roma* football team. He wanted to spend his time getting in shape and practicing his skills, instead of looking for a job. But tryouts were five months away and that was a long time to live off her savings.

Joanna's own job search had turned out to be more complicated than she anticipated. Nicco had suggested that her Art History degree, and his connections in museums, would allow her to arrive in Italy and find a job in a museum. Her own job search turned out to be more complicated than she'd imagined, a tangle of work visas and language barriers. As much as she'd wished things were different, the fact was that they couldn't afford anything but the bare essentials at the moment.

Francesca sighed, resigned. "How many of his friends has he invited to this party?"

"Sixteen—no, nineteen, including Gracie, Nicco, and me."

"In that tiny apartment?" Francesca gaped. "How will you fit all these people?"

"It will be fun." Joanna brightened her smile to show that she could be spontaneous and cheerful, despite what Nicco seemed to think lately. "I'll finally get to meet all of Nicco's friends. They're coming to watch the game anyway, so I won't have to actually *talk* to any of them, just cook for them—"

"And serve." Francesca finished for her. "You should know that you will never cook as well as his mama, no matter how hard you try. She knows his favorites, and she is wound around his heart." Francesca twirled an invisible string around her finger, to demonstrate. "He is a *mammone*, and he will not change."

"*Mammone*?" Joanna repeated blankly.

"Yes, yes." Francesca swished her fingers through the air as she searched for the translation. "A Peter. A man who stays a boy."

"Do you mean 'Peter Pan'?" Joanna blinked. The man she had agreed to marry was not a Peter Pan. He was different. They'd made plans together, plans to share a life in Rome with her daughter Gracie. During the entire year they'd dated, she'd been captivated by stories of his family—his mother, his sisters and their children. Gracie would have cousins to play with, and Joanna would be welcomed in to his family. The picture Nicco painted of their life together in Rome was magical, and the vision of it sustained her during a difficult move. "Nicco's not like that."

But Francesca would not be swayed. "He is not worth your trouble, *amica*. I have watched him. He does as he pleases, like a boy."

Joanna rose from her place on the fountain and faced her friend. "Well, that's all going to change," she protested. "He'll see that I'm learning to cook. I'll get to know his friends. I'll charm his mother. We were so *happy* in Chicago, Francesca. He brought me flowers and toys for Gracie. This is just a bump."

Doubt tugged at her, but Joanna pushed it away. She refused to fail at another relationship.

She'd been married before, to Gracie's father, Russell James Reed of the Charleston, South Carolina, Reeds. She and Russell had met in college; he was a business major and she studied art history. They had a whirlwind courtship, dating only a few months before marrying just after graduation. They had planned to settle and raise a family in Charleston, but Russell believed that his career prospects were better in Chicago, so they had moved away shortly after the wedding. That move had been an adjustment, too, for Joanna. She had traded her hometown, a place where families could expect to be intertwined for generations, for a city where no one seemed to know, or care, who she was. They started a family right away, and Joanna had channeled all her energy into outfitting the nursery. Gracie was a perfect baby and Joanna had fun making their city apartment into a home.

One day, while Gracie was napping and Joanna was chopping vegetables for a pot roast, she got a text from Russell. He felt constrained, he'd said, having to provide for a wife and a baby. He made a mistake, he'd said, but he was young enough to start over. She could have the savings account and his divorce lawyer would contact her.

Joanna never heard from him again.

"*Va bene.*" Francesca's eyes were kind, and she changed the subject with a lift of her shoulder. "I will help you shop for *pomodori*. Let me see these things you have bought."

"Everything on your list." Joanna slid the bag onto her lap, and opened it. "Everything except—"

"What is *this*?" Horrified, Francesca pinched a wilted bundle of basil leaves between her fingers and lifted it from the bag.

"Basil," Joanna pointed to a table under a yellow awning. "From over there." The basil didn't look like that when she bought it. On the vendor's table, fat bunches of deep green basil leaves were tied with twine and placed in mason jars filled with water. But the clump Francesca held was droopy and brown, nothing like the displays on the table. "I don't understand," Joanna said.

Francesca glared at the vendor's table. "That *imbroglione* —does he think you are a *turista*? He will not treat you in this way."

Joanna followed her friend to the vendor's table and watched as Francesca's indignation erupted in sweeping hand gestures and accusations in rapid-fire Italian. The vendor surrendered almost immediately, holding both hands in the air, palms out, before reaching beneath the table and producing a healthy basil plant in a terracotta pot.

Francesca accepted her win graciously, with a regal nod of her head. Turning to Joanna, she said, "*Amica*, you must have potted basil growing in the windowsill, always. The cut basil, that is for tourists, and he should know better than to sell it to you."

Joanna accepted the pot and placed it carefully in her bag, wedging it between a deep-purple eggplant and eight fat tomatoes that even Francesca would approve of. "Thanks, Francesca."

"*Prego*." With the world righted, Francesca's mood lifted. "Come. It's not too late for espresso. We can even sit at the table, and you can tell me all about these wedding plans of yours." Francesca slipped her sunglasses on, gold aviators that glinted in the morning sunlight, matching the stack of bracelets on her wrist and the layer of necklaces at her throat.

Joanna laughed. "Oh, sure, you pick the one day I don't have time for coffee." Francesca had been trying to get Joanna to use counter service, like true Romans, since the day they met, but Joanna had held firm. When she imagined her life in Rome, she had been relaxing at an outdoor café enjoying impossibly small cups of espresso as she people-watched. She had flatly refused to be lined up along a crowded counter with everyone else, with no room to breathe.

Francesca waved her hand in half-hearted surrender. "Instead, I will walk you to the corner and listen to this party, all you have planned for Nicco and his friends."

They crossed to a narrow street at the end of the market. At the corner, Francesca slowed, contrite. "I'm sure your eggplant will be delicious, and the party will be spectacles."

"Spectacles?" Joanna snorted. "I think you mean 'spectacular' and thank you, it will be. I'll finally meet Nicco's friends." Ignoring Francesca's doubtful expression, Joanna continued, "I wish you could come, but I know you've got plans tonight. Come up and visit when you get home—if it's not too late—and I'll tell you how 'spectacles' the party was."

Francesca peered at Joanna over the top of her sunglasses and frowned. "You are welcome to come with me today, you and little Gracie. Leave Nicco to his friends."

Joanna shook her head. "Maybe next time. This party is important to me. It could be the start of something good and —I guess I just want it to be perfect."

"Then it will be." Francesca brushed Joanna's cheek with a kiss and turned to leave. "I will leave you to your cooking. Ciao, *amica*." Francesca crossed the street with a walk that said she knew, absolutely, all eyes were on her.

Turning into the alley of her apartment, Joanna unlocked the front door of the building. Three flights of narrow stairs led to her apartment; she ascended them with a light step. She could do this—it was only cooking, after all, and she was in Rome. Hooking the bag over her other shoulder, she unlocked her apartment door and entered the kitchen.

The shriek of a referee whistle came from the den, and Joanna hesitated. She didn't remember leaving the television on when she left, and certainly not tuned to a soccer game. Had she mistaken the time of the party? Were Nicco's friends here already?

She stopped to listen for voices.

As she stood, Nicco's growl of outrage exploded in the tiny apartment. The sound jolted through her, raising goosebumps to her skin. Joanna rushed inside, her heart thumping in her chest, jumping to one conclusion and praying she was wrong.

The scene before her unfolded in slow motion, in snapshots that didn't seem real.

The thud of Nicco's fist as it connected with Gracie's body. The contorted rage on Nicco's face. The sight of her daughter's body crumpled on the floor. The sound of her baby's voice, broken and terrified, as she whimpered for her mother.

He promised.

"Get away from her." Fury exploded inside Joanna's chest as she shoved Nicco away, but his body was solid and not easily moved. She ripped the bag from her shoulder and hurled it at Nicco, anything to put distance between them. Her throw was clumsy, and the bag hit the wall instead. Tomatoes from the market bag exploded against the white plaster. The pot of basil shattered against the tile floor, sending shards of clay skittering across the floor. The scent of bruised basil leaves filled the room. Lifting Gracie from the floor, Joanna cradled her daughter to her heart.

Nicco brushed his bangs across his forehead with his fingers in a casual gesture of impatience that Joanna used to find so captivating. Now, it turned her stomach. He glanced at the television, and shrugged. "She was in my way."

It took less than a second for Joanna to decide the course of her life.

Cradling her daughter, Joanna snatched her bag from the floor, scattering the contents. She moved toward the bedroom, pulling passports and cash from the dresser, not stopping to pack clothes. On the way out, she took Gracie's favorite toy, a blue hippopotamus named Lendard from her bed and stuffed it into the bag.

Joanna felt Gracie tremble as they emerged from the relative safety of the bedroom.

"Shhh." Joanna attempted to soothe her daughter with a confidence she did not feel herself. "You'll be okay. Everything will be okay."

Nicco stood with his hip leaning against the back of a chair, just steps from her exit. His attention seemed to be on the game, but Joanna couldn't be sure it would remain there. Pressing her lips against her daughter's ear, Joanna whispered, "Where are your shoes, little Goose?"

Hiccupping, Gracie pointed to a tiny pair of yellow sneakers in the corner. Joanna grabbed them and slipped them into the bag.

"Be very quiet, Gracie," Joanna whispered.

As Joanna moved toward the door, Nicco's gaze flicked from the television.

To her.

"Are you going somewhere?" His voice was soft, like the slither of a snake. It sent chills up her spine.

Joanna forced a lightness into her tone. "To the kitchen to get ice for Gracie's bruise."

"For this, you need your bag?" Nicco stood.

Joanna didn't reply, and Nicco approached them. Joanna listened to his footsteps across the tile floor and felt her body tense as he drew closer. Gracie drew a ragged breath, and strangely, Joanna drew strength from it. She straightened her shoulders and met his eye, unflinching.

Abruptly, his tone softened, became almost intimate, as if he hadn't just punched a six-year-old girl. "She will barely remember this, Joanna. All children are spanked here if they misbehave. She will think nothing of it by tomorrow."

Joanna had believed him once before. The night they'd arrived in Rome exhausted, hungry, and disoriented. The apartment had been different from the pictures they'd seen before she bought it. It was smaller, filthy, and without electricity or a working kitchen. Nicco's reaction then had been mercurial, his rage sudden, and blinding. When it was over, Joanna had scrambled behind a chair, cowering. Her lip split and bloody, her eye swollen shut. The only thing that gave her the strength to move from the safety of her corner was the thought that Nicco might go after Gracie. She rose, trembling, from the floor and went into the bathroom, locking the door behind her. She took a moment to breathe and to splash cool water on her face. Then she went into her daughter's room and drew her little girl close to her body. She fell into a restless half-sleep, dreaming of what had happened and planning her escape.

The morning after, Nicco had returned with cappuccino and pastry from the café downstairs, contrite and shy. He begged her for another chance, swearing it would never happen again and Joanna had been stupid enough to believe him.

But she wouldn't make that mistake again. Not ever again.

Nicco glanced at the bag on her shoulder and approached, his mouth twisted into a sneer. "Where will you go, Joanna?" he taunted. "You don't speak Italian, and you are too stupid to navigate the streets of Rome without your beautiful friend Francesca."

Joanna reached for the keys she'd left on the counter and positioned them between her fingers. If he attempted to stop them, Joanna would stab him.

From the living room, the crowd erupted in cheers as the television announcer shouted, "Goooooal!"

Nicco turned to look, and that was all the opportunity Joanna needed. Bracing Gracie against her body, Joanna raced across the kitchen and out of the apartment. Joanna's last memory of her fiancé, of her dream life in Rome, was the sound of the stadium cheering as she closed the door behind her.

Racing down the stairs, she flagged a taxi on the street and used the phrase Francesca had taught her, as a joke, when she was homesick. It wasn't a joke now.

"Portarci verso l'aeroporto, fretta!"

Take us to the airport, hurry!

As the driver navigated the traffic, Joanna turned her attention to her daughter. She smoothed her daughter's blonde curls away from her face. How could she possibly make this better? What kind of mother lets this happen? "Gracie, honey. I'm so sorry."

But Gracie pressed her face against Joanna's neck, refusing to be comforted.

As they pulled up to the curb, Joanna thrust the fare at the taxi driver, and gathered Gracie to her. Inside the terminal, she scanned the departure board for the next flight out of Rome. She didn't care where it was going. All she wanted was to leave.

The next flight left in twelve minutes, bound for Frankfurt.

Joanna approached the ticket counter. She shifted Gracie to her other hip and felt a rivulet of sweat trickle down her back. She managed to smile at the clerk, as if she and Gracie were starting a vacation. She didn't have time to be detained. Didn't have time for questions. "Two tickets to Frankfurt."

The man took her passport and tapped his keyboard. "How many bags?"

"None."

The man glanced up, his eyes sharp. He assessed Joanna, with her smudged capris and her dingy T-shirt. "No luggage?" he repeated.

"No." Joanna pushed a wad of bills from her bag across the counter.

The agent looked at Joanna, then flicked his gaze at Gracie. "This *bambina*, she is yours?"

"Yes." Joanna pointed to the passports as verification. "This is my daughter, Gracie." Joanna's heart pounded but she couldn't draw a deep breath. We're in a hurry. Please." She glanced at the clock on the wall behind the agent.

The agent frowned as he considered.

Finally, he pulled the money toward him and handed Joanna a pair of printed tickets. "Gate four."

Joanna and Gracie boarded the plane just as the doors

were closing and they left Rome without a backward glance. It was only when Joanna felt the plane lift from the runway that Joanna felt herself exhale. She tucked an airline blanket around Gracie and pulled her close. She would need the two-hour flight to plan, because the facts were pretty grim. Francesca could have been a refuge for them, but the refuge would have been temporary. She'd already wasted three months trying to be what Nicco wanted her to be, and she barely recognized herself. There was nothing left for her in Rome, and nothing to return to in Chicago—she'd sold her apartment and everything inside it to pay for their move to Rome. Most of her friends in Chicago had scattered since the divorce, and she wouldn't impose on the few she had left.

As the plane began its descent into Frankfurt, Joanna realized she had only one option left.

In the terminal, Joanna guided her daughter to a hard, plastic chair in an alcove near the gate. The other passengers, in their hurry to get home, shouldered past them. A bubble of doubt filled her chest, but Joanna pushed it back.

"Where are we?" Gracie's voice was thick with exhaustion.

"We're safe, Gracie,"

They sat in the chairs while Joanna considered their next move. An hour passed, then two. Gracie dozed fitfully on Joanna's lap. Joanna reached for her cell phone and scrolled through her contacts list, already knowing there was no one to call.

Gracie stirred, and Joanna's decision was made. Brushing a lock of hair from her daughter's cheek, she chose a number she hadn't used in a long time and she listened to it ring.

"Hello?"

"Gram, it's me. I'm in trouble."

CHAPTER 2

MARCY ELIZABETH RUTLEDGE dreamed she was a passenger on the *Titanic* and the ship was going down. The ship's alarm blared, as the white-capped waves slammed against the railing. And, in a way that only makes sense in dreams, the ship sailed in Charleston Harbor, just beyond the yacht club. The shoreline was so close to the ship that Marcy could have jumped from the deck and landed in the grass, had she chosen to. Friends that had escaped to safety called to her from the shore, telling her to save herself, pleading with her to jump. But Marcy hesitated. She had obligations and she couldn't abandon them. Her hold on the railing slipped as a sheet of icy rain slammed against the hull of the ship, pushing it away from the shore. The ship's alarm grew more frantic. The wind howled as the ship listed and the shore disappeared, and Marcy's opportunity was lost.

She jolted awake with her heart thudding in her chest and the ship's alarm still ringing in her ear. Her fingers scrabbled for a handhold until her eyes adjusted to the light. When she recognized that she was not in fact, on the *Titanic*, she slapped her alarm clock off and flopped back against the pillows. She was home, in Charleston, in the house that had been in her family for six generations.

It was just a dream, a nightmare. Another in a long line of nightmares that had been haunting her since she agreed to purchase and develop a parcel of land in North Charleston for her family's company.

Pushing her hair from her face, she watched the curtains flutter as a breeze from Charleston Harbor pushed past them into the room, bringing with it salty air and the scent of low tide. The house was shielded from East Bay by an ancient magnolia tree, but when the wind came off the water, as it did this morning, it brought with it the sound of the city. And outside, the city was coming to life. Horses' harnesses rattled, blending with the steady clop of hooves as carriages of tourists rolled along the Battery.

Marcy lifted her cellphone from its charger on the night-stand and unlocked the screen to check her messages. There were so many moving parts to this project that she could easily lose track of any one of them, and dividing her attention between them was fraying her nerves. Lately, it seemed she checked her email constantly. This morning brought email from Palmetto Trust, the bank that had agreed to finance her North Charleston project. Palmetto Trust had been their bank for years—they had always funded her grandfather's projects. Charlie Babbish, a senior vice president at the bank, had personally overseen their company's account for decades. He had been a classmate of her grandfather at The Citadel and a close family friend for as long as she could remember. In the years since her grandfather's death, Charlie had been one of the people her grandmother regularly turned to for financial advice.

Marcy skimmed the email, then sat up and read it again, not believing the words on her screen.

There had to be a mistake.

She crossed the room to her desk, dialing Charlie's direct number as she walked. As the phone rang, she flipped through the pages of the application, looking for anything that might have caused Charlie to be concerned. There had been no financial updates in the past ninety days, nothing to cause the loan to be rejected. There was no reason for that email.

"Corporate Accounts, Gary Dawson speaking."

Marcy hesitated. She must have dialed the wrong number. "I'm sorry, I was trying to reach Charlie Babbish. Would you mind connecting me? Tell him that Marcy Rutledge from Palmetto Holdings is calling about an email I just received." Marcy flipped another page as she waited for Charlie.

But the call wasn't transferred.

"Ms. Rutledge, I thought I might hear from you this morning." The man sighed. "Again, my name is Gary Dawson. As you already know, Charlie Babbish was due to retire at the end of the year."

"Yes, I know. But this is only October." Charlie's retirement is one of the reasons she'd pushed so hard for the North Charleston project. She knew she could count on Charlie's approval for the loan. "We are working together on a development project, and the closing for a key piece is at the end of the month." She shifted the phone to her other ear and picked up a pen. "How do I get in touch with him?"

"Ms. Rutledge, Charlie Babbish doesn't work here anymore. His last day was yesterday."

Marcy sank to her chair. "The email I received this morning said that your bank is reconsidering our loan."

Gary cleared his throat. "More than reconsidering, I'm afraid. We've halted funding, pending an additional review."

The room stilled.

"I can assure you that our loan doesn't need additional review." Marcy's closed her eyes, searching for the right words. "The details of our loan may be a bit unorthodox, but Palmetto Holdings has been doing business with Palmetto Trust for decades. It would seem to me, that because Mr. Babbish—a senior member of your bank—has approved the financing on behalf of your bank, you would want to honor his decision."

"Yes, I see that he has. I have the application papers in front of me," Gary said. "But the account has been reassigned —to me. It's my responsibility to see that everything is in order. There are several aspects of this application that are concerning."

This was not a conversation Marcy wanted to have over the phone. It was much too easy to give a hard 'no' over the phone. If she were to salvage this, she needed a personal meeting.

"It might be more productive if we discussed this in person." Pausing, Marcy pretended to consult her calendar, when the reality was that she would meet him whenever he wanted. This loan was too important to lose. "I'll be in your area later this morning. Are you free at ten o'clock?"

"I'm afraid that won't change the outcome." Gary paused. "After Mr. Babbish's departure, I took the liberty of researching your entire account history, to get a better financial picture of Palmetto Holdings. It seems that Mr. Babbish had been allowing Palmetto Holdings to use lines of credit for daily operating expenses, something that should not have happened and something we can't allow to continue. My email to you was a courtesy only. I'm sorry, Ms. Rutledge, but our decision is final."

"The closing for this property is already scheduled and we won't have time to find another lender if you pull funding." Marcy closed her eyes. This couldn't be happening. Not after all the work she'd done. "I'd like to appeal. Is there someone else I can speak with?"

"Mark Oliver is head of this department. I'll ask him to contact you, but I'm not optimistic about the outcome."

"I'd like to meet with him anyway."

"Okay, I'll be in touch."

After Marcy hung up, she leaned back in her chair and reviewed her options. Three years ago, when her grandmother gave her access, the first thing Marcy did was look at the financials. Marcy found a labyrinth of stacked loans and a pattern of unnecessary late payments that was damaging their credit rating, and she had been single-minded in her quest to right her grandfather's company. Acquiring the industrial complex in North Charleston would be the first step. The income from existing leases would guarantee a positive cash flow almost immediately. Later, she planned to clear an adjacent tract of land and build a strip mall, which Palmetto Holdings would manage. The income from both would give the company much needed breathing room, allowing her to focus on long term goals.

With a sigh, Marcy rose from her chair and went to start her day.

A short time later, she emerged from her room dressed in a conservative dark navy suit and a cream-colored silk blouse. She swept her dark hair off her shoulders and into a simple ponytail, securing it with a sterling clip that used to belong to her grandmother. The final touch was a simple pair of pearl studs in her ears. Bankers loved pearls; they reeked of old money. The bankers would love her, until they saw the financial statements.

Slipping her work into her bag, she made her way to the kitchen for a quick coffee before heading out the door. She walked with her phone in her hand, answering texts from her assistant, Andrea.

"Good morning, Marcy." Eudora Gadsden Rutledge, the matriarch of the Rutledge family, sat at the kitchen table with a cup of tea in her hand, already dressed for her day. Her beige tweed suit could be worn to any number of committee meetings, but she only wore the jeweled butterfly pinned to her lapel to her garden club. And Marcy had never seen her grandmother without the triple strand of Rutledge pearls around her neck.

Marcy dutifully kissed her grandmother's cheek on her way to the coffee pot. "You're up early, Gram."

"As it happens, there is something I'd like to discuss with you."

"Of course, Gram." Marcy pasted a smile on her face and reached for the coffee pot.

When Marcy's grandfather, Brock William Rutledge, was alive, he was the one who ran the family business, and he had done so with such skill that he was almost a legend in the Charleston business community. Her grandmother had been content to busy herself with garden club meetings and charity work. Now was not the time for her to show interest in the business.

Marcy snapped the lid on her travel mug with slightly more force than she'd intended. She had a million things on her mind already, not the least of which was convincing a banker to reconsider financing. She might have strategized with her grandfather but it was no use even mentioning any of it to Eudora. Her grandmother wouldn't understand. "But today is pretty full. Can it wait until I come home tonight?"

Eudora frowned as she replaced her teacup on the saucer with a soft tap. "I'm afraid tonight won't do, Marcy. Something has come up, something we need to address. I've scheduled a meeting with Mr. Kennedy at 3:00 p.m. today, and I need you to be present."

Marcy almost rolled her eyes. Daniel Kennedy had been one of the original board members of her grandfather's company, and when her grandfather died, Daniel was made trustee. Technically, Daniel had become her boss. He had final approval on every decision Marcy made and she rarely agreed with his judgment. He slowed the pace of every board meeting, questioning issues that had been addressed and resolved, and offering outdated and irrelevant suggestions. Lately, he had been injecting lengthy personal anecdotes into every conversation, leaving employees blinking in confusion. The time for him to retire was long overdue.

Brock Rutledge founded Palmetto Holdings in 1953, the same year he and Eudora were married. He listed his wife as an equal partner in the company, with shares equal to his. As the company became more successful, he set up a trust for their children. Eventually the shares were split between Marcy and her younger sister, Joanna. Each sister inherited twenty-five percent, though Marcy was the only one who had any interest in it.

Marcy opened the refrigerator and pulled out a carton of yogurt. "I'll try to come home early but I can't promise. Which reminds me: did you sign the documents I left for you? Mr. Kennedy has to sign them too, as trustee. We can't close on the property without them."

"I am quite familiar with how the business works, Marcy." Eudora's voice was sharp, and Marcy felt a sting of reproach, just as she was meant to. "Our business with Mr. Kennedy this afternoon concerns your sister, not your closing."

"If it's about Joanna's quarterly check, you don't need my permission to send it. You send it whether I agree or not." The comment was a reflex, the words escaped before Marcy could stop them. It bothered her that Eudora insisted on sending Joanna quarterly payments in amounts equal to Marcy's, even though Joanna had no interest in the family business.

"Don't be ugly, Marcy. It's not becoming."

"Gram, you know how I feel about giving Joanna money for nothing. Things are stretched right now—"

"Enough, Marcy." Eudora rested her fingertips on the base of her throat, a sign of her displeasure. "Family comes first. Always."

It didn't always. Marcy wanted to say, but the beep of an incoming text on her cellphone drew her attention. She swallowed the last sip of her coffee and set the cup in the sink. "I'll call you later from work, Gram. The agency is sending a new housekeeper today. Be nice to this one."

"I would prefer Letty." Eudora's voice cracked and Marcy turned.

Marcy softened her voice. "I miss her, too, Gram. But Letty isn't able to manage things around here the way she used to. We shouldn't ask her to. It isn't fair."

Eudora turned her gaze toward the window, indicating the conversation was over, so Marcy reached for her bag. "Please don't call Letty again, Gram. You know she'll come if you do."

∾

The moment Eudora was sure that Marcy had left for work and would not return, she rose from her chair and started her day. She filled the electric kettle with fresh water and switched it on, then moved to the pantry. On a lower shelf, in the back, was a large bag of white rice. Which she pushed aside to reveal her beloved tin of Earl Gray. Several months ago, Dr. Hadley insisted she switch to decaffeinated herbal tea, but Eudora had been drinking strong Earl Gray tea longer than Dr. Hadley had been alive and she wasn't about to stop now. But neither did she want a confrontation with her granddaughter, so every morning, she made a show of filling a tea cup with herbal tea. She let it sit, untouched in front of her, until Marcy left for work. Then Eudora threw it away and did as she pleased. She liked her routine and wasn't about to stop just because her blood pressure made some young doctor nervous.

When the water boiled, Eudora switched off the kettle and poured a bit of the water into her teapot to warm it. After a moment, she emptied the cool water from the teapot into the sink. As she spooned tea leaves into the pot, she tried to recall the previous night's conversation with her youngest grand-daughter. She couldn't remember the details, exactly. She had been asleep, after all, when Joanna called and asked for permission to come home—as if she'd needed permission. It had been far too long since Joanna was in this house, and Eudora welcomed a nice, long visit. Joanna would bring life back into this house, something that had been in short supply lately. Her quick wit and bright smile had always been a welcome contrast to her sister's more serious nature. And that boy she married—Eudora couldn't remember his name— but wouldn't it be thrilling to see him again? He was such a nice man, from such a fine family.

Carrying the tea tray to the table by the window, she settled in to wait for her granddaughter. Outside, the sky brightened, as the sun ascended the horizon on Charleston Harbor. The morning breeze would follow, as it always did. Eudora reached to open the window, enjoying the feeling of cool, salty air on her skin.

CHAPTER 3

JOANNA SHIFTED against the cracked vinyl seat of the taxi, careful not to wake Gracie. The past twenty-six hours had been grueling for both of them. Using Eudora's credit card, Joanna had cobbled together a collection of plane tickets, from Frankfurt to Berlin, to Newark, to Atlanta, and finally, to Charleston. The flights were long, the connections were longer, and she was a puddle of exhaustion and frayed nerves. All she wanted to do was go to bed and sleep forever. Resting her head against the window, she allowed the drone of the radio to lull her into a twilight half-sleep.

"You're lucky you landed when you did." The cab driver's voice woke Joanna with a start. "Traffic's lighter this early in the morning." He glanced at them through the rearview mirror, the corners of his eyes crinkled as he smiled. "So, where are you from?"

Where *was* she from? Chicago? She and Russell had moved there as newlyweds, but after he left her, she retreated into herself and it stopped feeling like home. Rome? She and Gracie had only lived there three months, barely enough to feel settled. Growing up, Joanna and her sister spent their lives in motion, a year in one place, a few months in another. Their mother Alice packed them up whenever their stepfather announced that his "golden opportunity" was somewhere else. Charleston, though, was where she had been the happiest, living in her grandmother's house on East Battery. She'd spent eight happy years there: four years in grammar school, and another four when she returned to Charleston for college.

"Hey!" The taxi swerved sharply to avoid being cut off by a bright red car packed with people and stuffed with luggage. When the car jerked, the seatbelt bit into Joanna's shoulder, and she tightened her grip on Gracie, hoping she wouldn't wake. "Tourists," the driver muttered.

"Mommy?" Gracie blinked, her eyes bleary from lack of sleep, her cheeks flushed.

"I'm right here, little Goose."

"Sorry about that." The driver's gaze flicked to the rearview mirror. "Kid okay?"

Joanna smoothed Gracie's hair. "We're fine, thank you."

The driver turned his attention back to the road, and they continued in silence. Before long, Joanna began to recognize the landmarks of her childhood. Palmetto trees and scrubby pines dotted the highway. Curtains of delicate Spanish moss dripped from the branches, with vines of soft purple-flowered wisteria threaded between.

Joanna leaned forward, suddenly anxious to see the home she'd left. "Would you drive along the water, please?"

"Sure, sure." The driver flicked on his blinker and exited the highway.

As the car slowed, Gracie stirred and pushed herself up, her child's hand splayed like a starfish across the grubby fabric of Joanna's capris. "Where are we, Mommy?"

"We're almost there."

"This is where your Gram lives?" Gracie's eyes widened as she looked through the window.

"Yes. She's my grandmother, but she's your great-grandmother—I suppose you can call her 'Great-Gram'? I know she's looking forward to meeting you." The lie slipped easily from Joanna's lips, but the truth was that she didn't know what kind of reception awaited them. Things had been strained between them since Joanna moved away.

As they drove along the Battery, Joanna rolled down the window to breathe the Charleston air: a heavy mix of humidity and salt, with a sharp thread of sulfur from the sticky mud on the salt flats and marshes at low tide. Pluff mud, Joanna remembered. She closed her eyes and wrapped herself in the familiar scent.

"What is that smell, Mommy?" Gracie's voice muffled as she pressed Lendard against her nose.

Joanna smiled as she realized what Gracie meant. "It must be low tide, sweet pea. That's the smell of pluff mud."

Just beyond the seawall lay Charleston Harbor, with sailboats skimming along sparkling water in the crisp October morning. As Joanna watched as the crew on one of the bigger boats navigated the deck, uncoiling lines and raising the mainsail, she remembered seeing Charleston Harbor for the first time. She had been six years old, and it was her first visit to Charleston. Early one morning, her grandfather had announced that they were going to the Yacht Club, declaring it shameful that neither of his granddaughters knew how to sail. From the moment she boarded the boat, Joanna had been captivated. Sailing, to Joanna, was like orchestrating magic: trimming the sails to catch even the slightest breeze, and listening for the centerboard hum as the boat found the perfect tack.

The taxi slowed, pulling her from her memories.

"Nice place." The driver gaped over the steering wheel at her grandmother's house.

Joanna paid the fare with the last of her cash and as the car drove off, she reached for Gracie's hand.

"Is this a castle?" Gracie's voice was a whisper.

"I thought so, too, the first time I saw it," Joanna answered.

Her grandmother's house was listed in the National Register of Historic Places—one of the very first, as Eudora liked to say. A classic three-story Georgian, with a wide piazza that ran the entire length of the house on all three floors. The windows on the piazza were tall and narrow, stretching from the floor to the ceiling. And each window was flanked with dark green hurricane shutters, a dramatic contrast against the pale-yellow house. The widest part of the house overlooked Eudora's garden, always cool and verdant, even in the depths of a Charleston summer. The side of the house faced the harbor and was designed to funnel even the faintest breeze into the house. It had always been a favorite stop on tours of historic homes, but to Joanna it felt like home. When she younger, she would sit cross-legged under the shade of a hanging fern, drawing pictures of garden fairies and waiting for the fireflies to come out at dusk. On warm summer nights, when nothing else was stirring, Joanna would find her way to a quiet corner on the third floor and listen to the sounds coming from the harbor.

"Just like my story, Mommy." Gracie's voice pulled Joanna from her thoughts. She tugged on Joanna's hand, her eyes bright with excitement.

"*The Secret Garden*? I guess it does, doesn't it?"

Together they opened the wrought iron gate and entered. A graveled path led visitors to a boxwood maze. At the center was blue reflecting ball resting on a carved wooden tripod. Joanna remembered playing in the maze with her sister when they were children. When they got home from school, the first thing they did was race to the center, just to make faces on the ball's surface and laugh at their distorted reflections.

In the far corner of Eudora's garden was a flowering cherry tree, known in the family as *The Proposal Tree*. It was the place where her grandfather proposed, and it provided a canopy for a spring wedding. Joanna used to sit underneath the tree when the flowers were in bloom, and shake the branches, just to feel the soft, pink petals fall against her skin.

Joanna felt Gracie stumble along the path. The night's travel had caught up to her and she needed to be tucked into bed. "Almost there, Goose."

As they climbed the garden steps to the house, Joanna skimmed the braided iron railing with her fingertips, coming to rest on the pineapple finial on the top. She automatically tapped it twice for luck, something she'd done ever since she could remember.

"You and Lendard can have a nice nap when we get inside."

"But I'm not tired, Mommy." Gracie hadn't taken a proper nap in years, but her little face was creased with exhaustion. Once settled, she'd be asleep in no time.

An early morning breeze from the harbor ruffled the fronds of the hanging ferns. Joanna paused to breathe in the humid, salty air and felt her muscles uncoil. There was a moment when she wasn't sure her grandmother would allow her to come back, much less welcome her. She and Gracie would be safe here.

Tucked into a corner of the piazza, was a pair of white wicker chairs beside a glass-topped table. On top of the table was a magnificent purple orchid in a shiny white pot, where Eudora said she would leave a key to the door. Joanna found it, fit it neatly into the lock and entered the kitchen with a sigh.

They had finally arrived.

CHAPTER 4

EUDORA HEARD the twist of the key in the lock before she was ready. Rising from her chair, she clasped her hands together to keep them from shaking. Joanna reminded Eudora so much of Eudora's daughter, Alice. Joanna and her mother shared the same easy laugh, the same optimistic outlook, the same joy of life. Joanna's presence would lift the mood of the house, as it always did. And Eudora hoped that Joanna's husband would allow her to stay for a nice, long visit.

"Hi, Gram." Her granddaughter's voice was strained, tentative. She looked as if she were being held together by determination alone. Her lips were white and drawn. Her eyes were hollowed with exhaustion, the smudges underneath so dark they looked like bruises.

She looked like a stranger.

Eudora squeezed her hands together until she felt her wedding ring dig into her palm. Something had happened to her granddaughter. Something terrible, and Eudora didn't know what to do.

But Eudora's skill was presenting a cheerful optimism, despite adversity, and she drew on that now. "Welcome home, my dear. I'm so glad to see you." She drew Joanna into a light embrace. "Leave your luggage outside, we'll deal with it later."

Joanna's chin trembled and Eudora's confidence faltered. Had she said something wrong already? Letty would know what to do. For the hundredth time this morning, she wished her friend was here.

A flicker of movement caught Eudora's attention. A little girl hiding behind Joanna's legs and Eudora heard herself gasp.

Guiding the child forward, Joanna introduced them. "Gram, this is Gracie Elizabeth Reed, your great-granddaughter." Joanna cupped her palm over the girl's blonde head. "Say hello to your great-grandmother, Gracie."

"Hello." The child's voice was a whisper, barely audible even in the quiet house.

Joanna smoothed a curl from the girl's cheek. "Gracie is a little tired. We both are. It's been a long trip."

"Of course." Eudora's reply was directed at Joanna but her gaze locked onto the little girl as if pulled there by a magnet. With blonde curls and a porcelain complexion, the child looked exactly as Alice did when she was a little girl. Eudora could almost believe that she had another chance, that her own little girl was here. How different things would be if Eudora had another chance. She reached to smooth the girl's cheek, but the child flinched and retreated behind her mother. And the spell was broken.

"She looks just like your mother," Eudora managed to say.

"I know."

"What is her name?" Eudora couldn't remember.

"Gracie."

Eighty-three years ago, Eudora had been christened

Eudora Grace Gadsden. When she married, she had replaced her middle name with her maiden name, as was the custom. She didn't think that anyone but Letty had ever known Eudora's full name, the one her mother had given her. "After —" Eudora's voice faded, so she cleared her throat and tried again. "After me?"

"Mommy, I'm sleepy." The child rubbed her eyes the same way Alice used to.

"Okay, honey." Joanna turned to Eudora, exhausted. "We've been traveling for a long time, Gram. I hope you don't mind if I put Gracie to bed."

"No, of course not." Eudora gestured to the hallway beyond the kitchen. "Your old room is ready. I'm sure you remember the way."

"I do, thank you." Joanna lifted her daughter to her hip and headed for the stairs.

As Eudora watched them leave, a prickle of warning touched her skin, an unwelcome memory. When Joanna and her sister were small, they arrive on Eudora's doorstep in much the same condition as Joanna did now, travel-worn and scared. Alice had been running from her husband then, after some disagreement. They stayed so long that Eudora was forced to remind her daughter that her place was with her husband, and that her only job was to make a home for her family. If Alice wasn't happy, Eudora had told her, it was because Alice had been neglecting her job. In her own defense, Eudora had been annoyed with Alice's behavior. She was newly divorced and had remarried far too quickly; there had been raised eyebrows. Sending Alice back to her husband was the right thing to do. There was no way to predict what happened.

Eudora twisted her fingers together. Letty would know

what to do. She always knew what to do. She would be in the sunroom, as was her custom, in the arm chair by the window, with an open dictionary on her lap, cheating on the morning crossword puzzle.

Eudora rose from her chair and went down the hall to find her friend.

At the threshold, she stopped, uncertain how to proceed. The room wasn't as she expected it to be. The window shades were still drawn from the night before, and Letty's chair was vacant. The light inside the room was dim and the surfaces were dusty.

Then Eudora remembered and the realization almost brought her to her knees. Letty had been driven from her home. If Eudora wanted to speak to her friend, she would have to use the telephone.

In the kitchen, Eudora lifted the telephone receiver from the cradle and stared at the rows of numbers as if she had never seen them before. Tears of frustration pricked her eyelids and Eudora scrubbed them away.

She couldn't remember Letty's telephone number.

CHAPTER 5

MARCY PARKED her car in front of the historic building that had housed her family's business since its founding and gathered her things to go inside. The story of the company her grandfather started had been retold so many times that it had become a legend in the local business community and Marcy was proud to be a part of it. After graduating with high honors from The Citadel, her grandfather rejected a promising career in the military, deciding instead to make his home in Charleston, a city he'd lived in all his life. His talent was a supernatural instinct for real estate—he would know in his bones what it would take to bring a neglected building back to life. He traded his life savings for an option on a building near King Street, after negotiating an exceptional price from the owners. Then he set to work bringing it back to life with a hand-picked staff of superb craftsmen. The profits from the sale of that building funded down payments for two more, both of which he kept and rented out, always with retail space on the first floor and offices on the second. And finally, as a finishing touch, he planted a palmetto tree by the entrance of every building he restored, as a tribute to the state he loved.

As she'd done every day since her first day, working part-time for her grandfather during college, Marcy brushed her fingertips across the bark of the palmetto tree on her way into the building. It was a silly ritual, and she'd never admit it to anyone, but as she grazed the tree, she hoped some of her grandfather's gift for real estate would rub off on her. Maybe then she wouldn't feel so overwhelmed.

Inside the building, tall windows flooded the lobby with natural light. Her favorite part of the room was the heart pine floors and the exposed brick wall on the far side, because both were original to the building. A single line of framed photographs stretched the entire length of the wall, from the front door to the reception desk at the far end, before and after pictures of all the buildings in the company's portfolio. The photographs were gifts from the historic society, presented with appreciation for the care the company's craftsmen showed in restoring the buildings. The before pictures showed buildings in terrible states of neglect, usually abandoned, always heartbreaking. The after pictures were silver-framed, representing the best architectural styles Charleston had to offer: Colonial, Federal, Victorian, and her favorite, Italianate.

The North Charleston property would be a departure from her grandfather's philosophy of restoring historic build-ings to their original beauty. Although the lease income would go a long way toward fixing the company's finances, Marcy wouldn't allow pictures of the concrete strip mall displayed on the lobby walls.

"Good morning, Ms. Rutledge." Marcy stifled a groan. Another new receptionist, one of a revolving group of office staff that Andrea managed. Cheerful and eager, they were part of a work-study program from a local college. Pleasant enough, though they didn't seem to do well with detailed direction; Andrea was working on it.

"Good morning." Marcy answered, as she accepted her messages. "I have an appointment with Bruce Calhoun later this morning. The moment he enters the building, I need you to call Andrea to escort him to my office. If you don't, he'll show himself upstairs, and I don't want him wandering the halls."

Bruce Calhoun was a contracted worker, hired to help organize the industrial project. He'd had success with similar projects in other regions, Savannah and Raleigh. His résumé was impressive and his skill-set was just what Marcy needed. However, there was something about him that nagged at her, something she didn't completely trust, but she couldn't quite put her finger on it.

"Of course, Ms. Rutledge," the receptionist assured her. "I'll make sure he's escorted."

Upstairs, Marcy settled into her office and spent the morning focused on contracts and spreadsheets, and waiting to hear from Gary Dawson. Just after ten o'clock, Bruce Calhoun sauntered upstairs, unescorted. To judge the man by his appearance would be tempting, but it would be a mistake. Short and squatty, he looked alarmingly similar to the troll dolls Marcy had collected when she was twelve. The hair was the same, wild and sticking up at all angles, and he favored brightly patterned, short-sleeved shirts paired with worn cargo shorts. Marcy had never seen him in anything else, even at the black-tie holiday party the year before.

Bruce opened Marcy's office door and poked his head inside. He never knocked. "Marcy, you got a minute?"

"If it's about the warehouse property, I do." Marcy closed her laptop and turned her attention to Bruce. "There are a few things we need to go over."

Bruce sank into a chair with a deep groan and fished the slim notepad from his shirt pocket. He withdrew a stubby golf pencil from the pad's spiral top, licked the point, and nodded. "Shoot."

"You first." Marcy reached for her tablet and unlocked the screen. "I'll take notes."

"Alrighty." Bruce drew a deep breath. "I didn't want to start with this, but it seems there are two more competing offers for the warehouse property. That makes four that we know of."

"I thought that might happen." She made a note, though she wasn't overly concerned. "That property is undervalued. Now that other people know about it, backup offers are to be expected."

"But not this close to settlement," Bruce countered. "They're like sharks. They can sense when something is off, it's like blood in the water." Bruce lowered his pad and fixed his gaze on Marcy. "This is a clean closing, right? No funny business?"

Marcy nodded. "Of course."

"Well, I think we should exercise the early-close option anyway. The one you added to the contract. Once we have possession of the property, we can start contacting retailers. Maybe offer special financing up front or offer custom building. Either of those things would make my job easier."

Marcy shook her head. She was in charge of the project, not Bruce. She was glad to have his expertise, but Marcy recognized a mercenary when she saw one. His loyalty was to the project and the commission it would bring him, not to her or Palmetto Holdings. "I know the owners, and they're honest people. They've accepted our offer, and I can't see them forcing us into a bidding war. As long as we close on time, we'll be fine."

Bruce scoffed. "I never seen so many competing offers for a property that ain't been listed. And there's not an agent in all of Charleston County who don't know about this closing. Makes me nervous, is all." Shifting in his chair, he crossed his leg, resting his ankle on the opposite knee, exposing a white athletic sock.

Marcy looked away, hoping he was right.

After a moment, Bruce continued. "There's something else —the title company they're using is smaller than what I expected for a property this size. And the way your family's company is structured—with the trust and all—well, that makes the closing a little tricky. The title company needs to know what's what." He shrugged and pushed himself to his feet. "It's not a straightforward closing, but I guess we'll be fine. We just need to make sure we got all our ducks in a row." Brushing the wrinkles from his shorts, he regarded Marcy with a crooked smile. "You done alright, Ms. Rutledge. You recognized the potential in those warehouses when the current owners did not, and your business plan to develop it is a thing of beauty." Flicking his hand in the air, he dismissed his previous concerns. "Ah, it's probably just my nerves. The days before any closing are always an anxious time."

Andrea appeared at the door with a lunch menu and an order form. "I'm starting a lunch order. Tradd Street Grille. Interested?"

Marcy accepted the menu from Andrea and offered it to Bruce. "Why don't you stay for lunch, Bruce?"

Bruce brightened. "Well, now, I don't mind if I do. Thank

you kindly." Fishing his reading glasses from his front pocket, he winked. "I'll just leave you girls alone while I peruse my options." He took the menu to the hall window, where the light was better.

As they watched him leave, Marcy thought she saw Andrea shudder. Andrea had never liked Bruce, which was one of the reasons Marcy had insisted on contracting him instead of hiring him. Andrea's sense of character was razor-sharp and Marcy had come to rely on it.

Andrea set a stack of phone messages on the desk. "You might want to see these," she said.

"I just picked up a bunch of messages from downstairs. Where did these come from?" Marcy picked up the pages and sifted through them.

"They're all from Eudora," Andrea answered. "She wants you to come home. Right away."

Marcy closed her eyes and pressed her fingertips into her forehead to release the headache she knew would come. "She fired another housekeeper, didn't she? I knew she would."

"I think we would have heard if she had," Andrea guessed.

"I guess I'll go find out." Marcy sighed. "Do I have any meetings scheduled for the next thirty minutes or so?"

"Nope."

"Well, I guess I'll go home and see what Eudora wants." Marcy forced a tight smile.

"Do you want me to call her and tell her you're on your way?" Andrea offered.

"No." Marcy stood. Her tone softened. It wasn't Eudora's fault that Marcy was so busy. "I'm sure she's fine. The days are getting shorter, and the change of season always unnerves her." Marcy reached for the envelope of papers that needed

Eudora's signature and slid them into her bag. "At least I can remind her that I still need her signature on this power of attorney"

"Doesn't she like the new home health care aide?" Andrea asked.

"Connie?" Marcy shrugged. "I don't know. Eudora hasn't mentioned her."

"Not Connie—Eudora fired her weeks ago. After that was...let's see..." Andrea began counting off on her fingers. "Shaundra lasted the longest, the entire month of June. After that, there was Gretchen, Missy, and—" Andrea snapped her fingers. "I can't remember. Her name began with a P or a B. Anyway, I don't understand why you don't come right out and tell Eudora who these women really are. She might understand."

"Oh, *of course* she will." Marcy snorted. "You want me to tell her that I've hired a professional nurse to babysit her while I'm at work? Someone to prepare only meals that her doctors allow, and to supervise her medication, to make sure she takes it? No, ma'am. Eudora still blames me for 'firing' Letty."

"Letty was not your fault," Andrea countered. "Letty is almost as old as Eudora, isn't she? Letty's own doctors told her to cut back on her work—to rest more—but she wouldn't. Letting her go wasn't your decision in the end."

Marcy drew a deep breath. "All I need to do is get through this month. After the closing, things will slow down, and I'll be able to delegate most of this project. Things will go back to normal."

Andrea's brows knit together. "That's not what Bruce thinks."

"Bruce? Has he told you something different?"

But Andrea didn't get a chance to reply. Bruce returned from his place at the window with a satisfied grin and a lengthy lunch order. Andrea scribbled it down as Marcy turned to leave.

"Marcy, wait!" Andrea called her back. She pulled a short stack of messages from underneath the menu. "You have messages: Mark Oliver won't see you; he said that Gary Dawson's decision is final." She looked up, a quizzical expression on her face. "Does that make sense?"

Marcy nodded as her heart thumped in her chest.

Andrea flipped the page over. "Someone from LowCountry Trust called." She glanced up and rolled her eyes. "Apparently, he's our 'new account manager' and he wants to set up a meeting to get to know you better." She crumpled the page in her hand. "I'll just put this where it belongs."

But Marcy stopped her. "I'll take that." Bruce scowled. "What do you want with LowCountry? You said the financing was secured."

Marcy waved him off. "Yes, of course it is. I'm just trying to negotiate better terms."

"Well, you won't get better terms from that place." Bruce frowned. "I have yet to hear one good thing about them. Their rates are high, and their fees are higher. Besides, it's never a good idea to change financing this close to closing, especially if other brokers are circling the water with competing offers."

"Everything is fine," Marcy assured him. The lie was remarkably easy to tell and it seemed to appease him, because he allowed Andrea to escort him to the lunchroom to wait for delivery.

When Andrea returned, Marcy had a plan for her day and

a list of instructions. She rattled them off. "I need you to call Eudora after all. Tell her something's come up and I can't come home right away."

"Okaaaay." Andrea drew out the word, then waited, expectantly.

There was no point in hiding the truth. Andrea wasn't a gossip and she'd rather chew tin foil than tell Bruce anything about the project. Plus, she'd find out anyway. "I need to go to LowCountry to convince them to lend us money. The financing at Palmetto fell through—"

"I knew it." Andrea gasped. "We don't have financing."

"Andrea, not now," Marcy warned.

"But the psychic was *right*," Andrea insisted. "I *knew* it! She said—"

Marcy held her hand up. There was nothing Andrea loved more than a thorough reading but Marcy didn't have time to indulge her right now. "I wish your psychic had given us a heads-up about financing in the first place. That would have saved me a lot of time."

CHAPTER 6

MARCY DRUMMED her thumb impatiently against her car's steering wheel as she waited for the gates at her grandmother's house to open. Her appointment with LowCountry went well, but it lasted much longer than she had expected, and it was mid-afternoon before she could leave. As she sat in her car, Marcy wondered, for the briefest of moments, what it would be like to realistically describe her afternoon to her grandmother. How she had met with the officers of the new bank and had fought for decent—not great—terms, despite the company's sagging financials. How they expected the deed to Eudora's house as collateral for the business loan, but Marcy refused to endanger her grandmother's house. In the end, LowCountry conceded, as she knew they would. The interest rate made the loan very profitable for them. Her grandfather would have understood the battle—might have even congratulated her—but Eudora wouldn't. Her grandmother didn't understand what Marcy did all day, or how hard she worked.

The only thing Eudora would see was that Marcy was late coming home.

As predicted, Eudora met her at the door with a frown of disappointment on her face. "Marcy. You're late." She'd changed her suit from that morning's soft tweed, used for social events, to the dark navy reserved for board meetings. "Mr. Kennedy has been here for quite some time, waiting for you."

Marcy followed her grandmother to her grandfather's office, dropping her keys and her trench coat on the foyer table as she passed. "Why is Mr. Kennedy here, Gram? Is there something you need? I can help, you know."

"I believe Mr. Kennedy can answer your questions."

Marcy had never like Daniel Kennedy. After her grandfather died, he came to the house more often than Marcy thought necessary, and he wielded too much influence over Eudora's personal affairs. It was always best to keep him at arm's length.

Daniel Kennedy rose from his position behind Marcy's grandfather's desk, a place that was rightfully hers. His stiff white shirt fairly crackled as he offered his hand. "Marcy, I'm glad you could make it."

Marcy bristled at his presumption, summoning her to a meeting in her own grandfather's office. She offered her hand anyway, because he was a guest and Marcy was obligated to be polite. "Daniel, it's nice to see you again."

He returned to her grandfather's desk. "Marcy, we have concluded our meeting, unfortunately. I can stay a minute more to explain the details. You'll want to know them because they affect you." He smoothed his ugly Clemson tie as he settled in.

Marcy set her bag on the floor and sat stiffly on the edge of a guest chair beside the desk. Eudora sat next to Marcy as if she were a client of Daniel's instead of the chairman of the board. Shifting uneasily in her seat, Marcy waited.

Daniel tapped the leather folder on the desk with his fat, pretentious pen. "When your grandmother called me this morning with the news, I was so pleased. Of course, there were details we needed to attend to, but everything is taken care of now."

Marcy blinked. They'd "taken care of" what, exactly? Did he mean financing? Other than Andrea, no one at Palmetto Holdings knew that she had secured new financing, and Andrea would not have told Eudora. As Daniel opened the folder, Marcy allowed herself a glimmer of hope that Eudora had recognized Marcy's efforts and would be proud of her.

Daniel ran his finger down the page before continuing. "The good news is that your sister has returned to Charleston and plans to make her home here. Eudora wants to ensure that she feels welcome."

"Sister? Do you mean Joanna?" The question hung stupidly in the air. Of course, he meant Joanna. Marcy had only one sister, five years younger and the only family, besides Eudora, that Marcy had left.

"Yes, Marcy. Mr. Kennedy is referring to Joanna." The light in Eudora's eye made Marcy wince. Joanna had always been her favorite. "She arrived from Frankfurt early this morning, but you'd left for work already. She and Gracie are upstairs, asleep at the moment."

"Frankfurt? What was she doing in Frankfurt?"

Eudora frowned, her lips a tight line of disapproval. Apparently, Joanna's waywardness wasn't a topic for discussion in front of Daniel Kennedy.

Marcy returned her attention to Daniel. "Please continue," she said.

"Yes, well." Resting his elbows on the desktop, Daniel templed his fingers. "As you know, Palmetto Holdings is held in trust for both you and you sister. It was always your grandfather's intention to keep the business in the family, and your grandmother feels this is an excellent time to include Joanna."

Marcy stiffened. She glanced at Eudora. "Really? Doing what, exactly?"

Eudora's fingertips rested on her pearl necklace, but this time, Marcy ignored it. "Gram, what do you propose Joanna do?" she repeated. "Joanna's Art History degree doesn't exactly qualify her to buy or manage any of our real estate. In fact, I don't think she's held a job since she graduated college."

"Marcy." Her grandmother's voice was tinged with disapproval. "I don't need to remind you that your grandfather didn't have any formal training in real estate when he started the business, and he was very successful. Your sister is artistic," Eudora said, as if that one trait forgave all others. "Surely, you can use her talents with your restoration work?"

Palmetto Holdings may be a family company, but it was Marcy who held it together and there was no way she'd allow her sister to interfere. "We hire specialists for everything, Gram. Architects, historians, craftsmen—Grandpa always insisted on specialists."

Marcy wondered again why she didn't just walk away from Palmetto Holdings and find another job. The offers she'd had since earning her MBA three years before were impressive, and she'd been tempted. But in the end, Marcy realized what she wanted to do was follow in her grandfather's footsteps, buying and restoring Charleston's oldest buildings. Eudora, however, had been reluctant to release her share of the trust, ensuring Marcy remain an employee instead of an owner, as her grandfather had intended.

After shuffling the papers in his folder, Daniel Kennedy cleared his throat. "Perhaps we can discuss the business details another time, when you're more receptive." He ran his finger down the length of the page. "Eudora and I have been discussing other ways to make your sister's transition to Charleston easier. We took the liberty of enrolling the child in Santee Academy, the same school you and your sister attended, I believe. Her first day is Monday."

"There is a waiting list for Santee," Marcy pointed out. "One of our project managers has been on that list for two years. How is it that Gracie can be admitted so quickly, without an application or an interview?"

Daniel glanced at Eudora for permission to continue. When she nodded, he did. "The acceptance was simply a formality, of course." Leaning back in her grandfather's chair, Daniel tapped his pen against the wooden arm. "The Rutledge name, as you are aware, carries considerable weight in Charleston."

Of course, Marcy knew that. She had always known that the Rutledge family was one of the oldest in Charleston. The name would open doors and create opportunities that might not exist otherwise. But Eudora had always insisted that it be used with discretion, when all other avenues had been exhausted.

Marcy turned in her chair until she faced Eudora. "Gram, does Joanna know you've enrolled Gracie in school?"

Eudora frowned. "I am sure your sister is aware that Gracie must attend school. That being the case, Rutledges have attended Santee Academy for more than a hundred years, and we will continue to do so." Inclining her head toward Daniel, Eudora added, "Now, if Mr. Kennedy may be allowed to finish?"

Marcy fumed at the reproach, but said nothing, as usual.

Daniel glanced at his papers before him. "We offered to make a generous contribution to the school, to facilitate enrollment this far into the term. I'm sure you understand."

"How much of a contribution? And from which account—personal or business?" Marcy straightened. Any significant withdrawals, especially before closing, would affect the financing.

Daniel's face reddened as he closed the folder. Apparently, he didn't like to be questioned, either.

Eudora frowned. "We needn't get into specifics right now, Marcy. Let Mr. Kennedy speak, please."

Marcy turned, giving Eudora her full attention and blocking Daniel completely. "Gram, I'm sorry, but we actually *do* need to get into specifics. Most of the company's cash reserves are being held in escrow for the closing on the North Charleston project. We need what's left for operating expenses. As soon as the leases are transferred, we'll be fine, but right now, our reserves are tight."

Eudora looked over Marcy's shoulder to Mr. Kennedy, though he knew nothing about the project. "Will the contribution be a problem, Daniel?"

But Marcy interrupted before he could answer, knowing that Eudora would always defer to the man in the room, no matter his qualifications. It was something Marcy had learned to expect and had come to live with, but not this time. This time, it was too important. Equally important, however, was to let her grandmother continue to live under the illusion that the Rutledge family was as powerful and as wealthy as it has always been.

"Never mind. I'll take care of it, Gram. Just give me the papers for Santee." Payment for whatever amount they had promised could be deferred or renegotiated until after the closing. Surely that wouldn't be a problem—didn't one of her sorority sisters sit on the board of that school? She would have Andrea check. "Now, if there's nothing else, I have papers to review." As she lifted her bag from the floor, she offered a neutral smile to Daniel. "It was nice to see you again, Daniel."

Eudora interrupted before she could stand. "Marcy, we have a few more things to cover, but I feel like I must ask about this project, the one in North Charleston? Are we buying something new?" Eudora's expression clouded with uncertainty, and Marcy bit her lip.

Don't do this now, Gram. Not in front of this man.

Marcy willed her grandmother to remember any one of the dozen conversations they'd had over the past eight months about the industrial property. Her tone softened. "Bruce Calhoun and I have been working on buying an industrial complex in North Charleston, near the airport. The closing is at the end of the month."

"Bruce Calhoun?" Eudora repeated. "That name does not sound familiar to me."

Marcy glanced at Daniel, but his attention was focused on the papers in front of him. She lowered her voice, not wanting to embarrass Eudora. "He doesn't work for the company; he's more of a contractor."

Eudora pressed her lips together. "Well, I wish you had told me."

I have told you, Gram. I've told you over and over for months. You don't remember.

Eudora turned to Daniel for confirmation. "Did the board approve this deal, Daniel?"

We bypassed the board because we didn't want our financials made public because they're not what they used to be. They wanted your house, Gram, as collateral, but I wouldn't let them have it.

"Yes, of course. Of course, we did." Daniel leaned back in Brock's desk chair, stretching his arms behind his head. The knot of his purple-and-orange striped tie bobbled as he spoke. "Huge project. Great opportunity."

Daniel Kennedy hadn't been to a board meeting in years. It was obvious he knew nothing about the property in North Charleston, but Eudora didn't see that. The color rose in Eudora's cheeks as she spoke. "I don't remember any discussions about this. For such an important project, I should have been consulted."

Marcy reached for her grandmother's hand and fell on her sword in front of Daniel Kennedy. "It's okay, Gram. It's my fault. I should have told you."

Eudora frowned. "Your grandfather always said he wouldn't own industrial because the contracts are too unpredictable. 'Stick to retail,' he always said. And so we have."

"I know, Gram, but I have it under control." When Daniel left, Marcy would remind her grandmother of their discussions, and everything would be fine.

"Why don't you let Joanna help?" Both women turned to Daniel Kennedy. Marcy to gape, and Eudora to beam. Now that he had their attention, his chest fairly puffed with importance. "I'm sure we can all agree that Marcy has done an admirable job managing Palmetto Holdings in the last several years."

Marcy shifted in her seat. "Admirable" was not a word she would have chosen. The consultants Marcy hired to help her untangle the finances recommended she put Palmetto Holdings up for sale—let someone else figure it out. They suggested she accept a payout and start an early retirement— maybe join a country club. They all but patted her head and it made Marcy furious. She fired them and restructured the company herself, streamlining processes and questioning practices that had been part of the company for so long, that no one could remember why there were there. It had taken eighteen months, but she did it, and the North Charleston property was the last piece—the leases already in place would generate a steady income for years, shoring up the company her grandfather started.

"Now that Joanna has come home to Charleston, this might be the opportunity we've been looking for." With a magnanimous smile, Daniel continued. "It would be nice to include Joanna. Palmetto Holdings is a family business, after all, and this will give her something to do as she settles in."

Marcy couldn't keep the bitterness from her voice. "Running a company isn't exactly a hobby, Mr. Kennedy. If Joanna needs something to do, maybe she should take up gardening."

Eudora's response was cool. She turned to Marcy. "I would like your sister to be involved in this North Charleston project. Surely, there must be some way Joanna can help."

But there wasn't. The details for the project had been finalized for months. Inspections had been scheduled, surveys completed—the whiteboards in her conference room were covered with sticky notes and checklists.

Then Marcy remembered the bag at her feet. Inside were the papers she needed Eudora and Daniel to sign. She laid the envelope on her grandfather's desk. "I need you to sign these papers for the closing—"

Daniel Kennedy reached for the envelope. "As trustee of the company, I should review them, before anyone signs them."

As he glanced at the one-page document that he and Eudora had signed a hundred times before, Marcy felt a flash of anger. She didn't have time for this man. "These are the same closing documents you've both signed every time I buy property on behalf of Palmetto Holdings. The only thing that's different is the bank we're using. But if you'd like to review them, fine." She rose from her chair. "Have Joanna deliver the envelope to the address on the front. That's how she can be 'involved'."

Daniel Kennedy rested his elbows on her grandfather's desk and frowned. "I believe your grandmother had some- thing more substantial in mind than just delivering papers. Your sister, if I may remind you, is an equal partner—"

But Marcy was having none of it. "If Joanna wants more responsibility, she has to earn it. Just like I did."

Marcy rose and left the office. She reached the first traffic light before she realized she had gotten into her car. It wasn't fair. Ever since Marcy was ten years old, she'd wanted to work at Palmetto Holdings. Her grandfather had a carpenter make a tiny desk for her, and he set it in the corner of his office. She was there, after school, three times a week, until Letty found out she crossed Broad Street all by herself and put a stop to it. When her grandfather got sick, he made Marcy promise to work hard, take care of his company, and look after Eudora. Marcy had kept her promise. A small piece of her had hoped that Eudora would notice, and maybe appreciate her efforts, but she never did. Now they wanted her to make room for Joanna, who had never shown the slightest interest in the business.

It was too much to ask.

The car behind her beeped, startling her. The driver pointed to the green light, and Marcy pulled forward. Flicking on her blinker, she parked the car and reached for her phone.

It was answered on the first ring, a familiar voice that Marcy leaned into. "Oh, Marcy, doll, I'm *so* glad it's you. I haven't spoken to a living soul all day, and I'm about to go stir crazy. I told these people that if they put a gallery all the way out here it would go under in a month. But who listens to me? *Nobody.*" She heaved a long-suffering sigh through the phone.

Cecily Beaumont had been Marcy's best friend for fifteen years. They'd met their first week of college when Cecily tripped the burglar alarm climbing in the window of the sorority house after hours, with a bottle of tequila and a sack of limes. For some reason, Marcy covered for her, and they had stayed up all night, shooting tequila and laughing. They'd been best friends ever since.

"Can you meet me at the River Rock?" Marcy asked.

"Sure, but I'm not supposed to close until ten."

"Oh, right. I forgot that Tuesday is your late night. Never mind, Cee. I'll catch up with you this weekend—"

But Cecily continued as if Marcy hadn't spoken. "Let me tell you what my day's been like. It's past four o'clock now, and you are the first human contact I've had all day—have I mentioned that? So, yes, I'm really tempted to lock up. If I died out here, no one on earth would know. They wouldn't find my body for weeks. So yes, I'd be happy to close up early and meet you."

"You're going to be fired this time, for sure." Marcy laughed.

"Good," Cecily said. "This place is soul-sucking anyway." Marcy heard a door close and the lock snap shut. "I'll meet you in twenty minutes."

The River Rock Café was tucked on a quiet side street, away from the historic district and nowhere near a river. The rumor was that the owner chose the name to confuse the tourists, ensuring their customers would always be local. With fourteen brands of beer on tap and a wide outdoor deck that showcased local bands in the summer, it was a secret that residents embraced.

On a Tuesday night, there wasn't much of a happy-hour crowd, but the day was warm and the summer deck was still open so Marcy claimed a corner table. Shrugging off her suit jacket, she leaned back against her chair and closed her eyes.

What a day.

"I see her, over there. Thanks, doll." Flicking a mass of red hair over her shoulder, Cecily plunked an oversized purse on the table and slid into her seat. She studied Marcy with a single-minded concentration, like a general studying a battle-field. Finally, with a tilt of her chin, she asked, "Why aren't you at work?"

Marcy reached for her water glass. "I could ask you the same question. I thought you liked that gallery."

Cecily snorted. "Oh, *please*." She raised her hand and counted off on her fingers, her gold rings glittering in the afternoon sun. "Number one: a real art gallery doesn't sell painted seashells. Number two: location matters, that's all I'm saying. And number three: the pay is crap."

"Then why did you take it?"

Cecily shrugged. "I thought it would be fun."

"At least it's better than the gallery in Brooklyn," Marcy pointed out.

"Ugh," Cecily groaned. "Don't remind me. That place should have been condemned."

Several years ago, Cecily had gotten an offer to manage a small art gallery in Brooklyn, which she had accepted without hesitation. Less than a year later, she had returned to Charleston, refusing to dress in any color but black. "Real" art was dead up north, Cecily said, and she would mourn its passing. Yankees appreciated nothing except money and themselves, and she wanted no part of them.

Cecily draped her wrap over the back of the chair and fixed Marcy with a gimlet eye. "Now, tell me why you're not at work. It's only four-thirty, and I know for a fact that you don't leave work before nine o'clock. You're like a vampire that way." A thought occurred to her and she brightened. "Wait a minute, did your property close early? Are we celebrating?"

"We're not celebrating." Marcy pulled the paper off a plastic straw and twisted it between her fingers. "Just the opposite, actually: Joanna's back."

Cecily's eyes widened. She turned and flagged down the server.

Because they were his only table, he arrived almost immediately. "Are you ready to order? Can I get you something from the bar?"

"Not from the bar, thanks." Cecily returned the bar menu to him. "What we *do* need is a dessert menu." She waved her hands in the air to correct her last sentence. "Never mind—no menu. This is serious. Just bring us chocolate. Dark preferably, and a lot of it."

"Well," he tapped his pencil against his pad as he thought. "We have a warm turtle brownie, with cinnamon whipped cream on the side." He frowned as a thought occurred to him.

"It's kind of big. I'll bring extra plates and forks so you can share."

It was the offer to bring extra forks that made Cecily twitch. Marcy knew what was coming, she'd seen this scenario play out many times before, and she hid her smile behind her napkin. How she loved her friend.

"Do you have a dessert menu?" Cecily asked, again.

"Of course." He brightened. "Let me get you one."

But Cecily held up her hand to stop him. "I don't need to read it. I just wanted to know if you offer enough to fill a separate menu, and I'm *delighted* to hear that you do. Just bring us one of everything. Everything you have that is made with—or from—chocolate."

The waiter's gaze cut to Marcy. She shrugged. He returned his attention to Cecily. "Can I bring you anything to drink?"

Cecily nodded. "Tea, please. Unsweetened."

When the waiter left, Marcy rolled her eyes. "You can never let that go, can you?"

Cecily gave her standard answer. "When *men* order dessert, they're not expected to share. They're never offered extra forks. I fight my battles, you fight yours." Reaching for her napkin, she smoothed it on her lap and changed the subject. "So, tell me. Why is your sister back?"

"I don't know why she came back. Why does Joanna do anything? Eudora wants to find a place for her in the company." Marcy busied herself with her water glass, tracing lines in the condensation with her finger. Finally, she blurted out what had been bothering her since the meeting. "That company should be mine, Cee. Am I an awful person for wanting it all to myself?"

A breeze ruffled Cecily's wrap, and she pulled it over her

shoulders. She didn't answer the question right away, which made Marcy nervous.

"Just tell me, Cee," Marcy urged.

Cecily pulled three packets of sweetener from the tray and tapped the edges on the table as she thought. Finally, she shrugged. "Okay, I will. The Trust makes you and your sister equal partners, so you've known for a long time that you'd either have to work with her at some point, or you'd have to buy her interest. And your preference is to buy her out, isn't it? You've been saving for years to do just that. Am I right?"

Marcy nodded.

"But your grandmother has to agree, and she won't. For some reason, she wants you girls to work together, even though Joanna doesn't seem to care about the company at all. But the part that *really* gets you is that Eudora won't sign that magic paper to make you the boss of everyone."

"There is no magic paper, Cee. The trust is actually more complicated than that," Marcy began.

But Cecily waved her hand in the air to indicate she didn't care about the details. Cecily was never about the details, but she could read someone's intentions faster than anyone Marcy had ever met, sorting the good from the bad in a wink of an eye, and Marcy valued her judgment.

"In the meantime," Cecily continued, "Eudora is the one who really runs the show, even though you've got the fancy title." She leaned back in her chair and reached up to twist her earring, something she did when she was deep in thought. So, Marcy waited.

Finally, Cecily continued. "What I can't seem to understand, Marcy, is why you don't leave, find another company to run. You've got the credentials, and you've had offers, good ones—though my rule still stands: you're not allowed to move farther away than Atlanta, or I'll never see you." She paused as the waiter delivered their drinks. When he left, she continued. "My point is that Eudora will never change. She wants you and Joanna to be the best of friends, but you won't be. You're too different."

"You know why I can't leave." Marcy slipped the straw into her glass of tea.

"I know why you don't *want* to leave. That's not the same thing as *can't*." Cecily ripped open three more packets of sweetener and dumped them in her tea. "And it's not a bad thing, wanting to continue what your grandfather started. It's not your fault the finances tanked and you can't afford to restore pretty buildings anymore."

"I hate that North Charleston property." Marcy's voice was barely a whisper. She hadn't been able to admit that to anyone, not even Andrea. The warehouses on that property were ugly—cold and soul-less. And the strip mall she'd planned to develop beside them was equally ugly. But Palmetto Holdings needed the lease income if they were to continue to expand. Her grandfather would have expected her to expand.

"I know you do." Cecily stirred her tea. "But you're doing it to help your family's company, and that's not a bad thing. The heck of it is that your family will never know."

The patio doors opened, and the waiter emerged carrying a tray as big as a truck tire. After distributing nine chocolate desserts across the tabletop, he slipped a lighter from his apron pocket, snapped it, and lit the candle in the center of the table. The light flickered across their own personal buffet.

"Can I bring you anything else?" The waiter smirked in good humor but managed to keep a straight face.

To Cecily's credit, she did, too. She tapped her glass with her fingertip. "A refill, please. Unsweetened."

As Marcy dug her fork into a hunk of walnut-caramel brownie, she asked, "Does your gallery *really* sell painted seashells?"

Cecily rolled her eyes as she skimmed the frosting from the corner of a fudge cake. "It's not my gallery, but yes. Yes, they do."

Marcy reached for her tea. "I still can't believe she's back. You know, she hasn't spoken to me in five years?"

"Five years?" Cecily blinked. "Has it really been that long?"

"Yes." Marcy shrugged, as if it didn't matter. But it did. "I've gotten a couple of short texts, which I ignored, and last year Joanna sent me an e-card a week after my birthday."

Cecily grimaced. "That animated computer thing? I hate those."

Marcy set her glass down and wiped the condensation from her fingers on her napkin. "About a year after she and Russell moved to Chicago, Joanna stopped calling. I called her cell number a couple of times, just to make sure it still worked. It rolled to voice mail every time, and she never called me back." Marcy twisted the corner of her napkin, a little harder than she needed to. "You should have seen what Joanna's disappearance did to Eudora."

Cecily dipped her spoon into a ramekin of mousse and dragged it through a mountain of whipped cream. "Eudora must be happy now, at least. How long does Joanna plan to stay this time? Is it a visit, or is it permanent?"

Marcy shrugged. "I don't know. Gracie is with her, but I don't think Russell is. And it gets worse: Eudora had a meeting with Daniel Kennedy."

"That little toad from the board?" Cecily spoke with her mouth full.

"The very same." Marcy swept her fork through a river of caramel. "They want Joanna to be more involved with the company."

"More involved in what way?" Cecily sipped her tea. "She doesn't *want* the company, does she?" She set her drink back on the table with a thud. "Oh, my word—is this a take-over?"

Marcy shook her head, though the thought had occurred to her. "I don't think so. She's never expressed any interest in the company before. I think this directive is coming from Eudora; she's always wanted us to share the company equally."

"So, why is Joanna here, did she tell you?"

"I don't *care* why she's here, Cee." Marcy's fork landed on the plate with a sharp clink. "I haven't spoken to her yet, and I don't plan to. If the past is any indication, she'll be gone soon anyway. Then it will be another decade before she shows up again." As she listened to her words, Marcy felt her face flush. She sounded like a petulant child, and she hoped Cecily hadn't noticed.

But she had. Cecily narrowed her eyes. "You're still mad at her for leaving, aren't you?"

"I guess I am." Marcy said, simply. "Joanna promised Eudora that she would always live in Charleston, because she knew it was important to Gram. Then she and Russell decided to leave, and I can still hear Joanna say the words: 'I'll call you every Sunday, Gram, no matter what.'" Marcy shook her head. "I *knew* she wouldn't Cee. I knew it the minute she spoke. Joanna's always been flaky, and I learned a long time ago not to believe anything she says." Marcy swallowed. It felt good to finally be completely honest about her feelings for her sister. "It's like she found a better life some-where else and now she doesn't want us anymore." Marcy's voice hardened. "She followed that snake to Chicago, and dropped off the face of the earth."

"Maybe something happened?" Cecily offered. Cecily always had a soft spot for Joanna and Marcy could never understand why.

Marcy pushed away the half-eaten brownie. "Nothing bad ever happens to Joanna; she's like a cat. She's got nine lives, and every one of them is charmed."

Cecily's voice lowered. "Did you ever tell her that Russell made a pass at you that one time?"

Marcy shook her head. "What good would it have done for Joanna to find out the worm she'd insisted on marrying not only had another woman on the side, but that he had also propositioned me during his own engagement party? Joanna wouldn't have believed me."

"Maybe not." Cecily signaled the waiter. "But, I still think you should have told her."

When the waiter came, Cecily offered her brightest smile. "Would you box this up for us?"

The waiter's glance swept across their private dessert buffet. "All of it?"

"Yes."

He left the check, and Marcy reached for it, despite Ceci-ly's protests. "It's my turn. Plus, that gallery pays nothing."

"It pays commission," Cecily countered.

"Which you will never get because they will be bankrupt by the end of the year." Marcy plunked down her credit card without looking at the total. Whatever it cost, it was worth every penny to spend time with her friend. "I'm telling you, Cee: it's time for you to open your own gallery."

It had been a much-discussed topic, and Cecily didn't respond, so Marcy changed the subject. "Eudora told me that Joanna called in the middle of the night. From Frankfurt," Marcy said after the waiter collected the check.

That got Cecily's attention. "Are you kidding me? What was she doing there?"

Marcy shrugged. "I have no idea."

CHAPTER 7

IN THE DISTANCE, Nicco laughed, low and foreboding. Joanna woke with a start, her heart pounding in her chest.

He had followed them.

Joanna ripped the blanket from her body and dropped to the floor, her eyes searching the dimly lit room.

Gracie—where was Gracie?

As she listened for him, her eyes adjusted to the light and she recognized the bed and the vanity by the piazza window. Her pulse slowed as she recognized her daughter, sleeping peacefully under a tangled sheet.

It was only a dream. She was in Charleston, and they were safe.

She climbed back into bed, reached for her daughter, and heard herself exhale. She didn't realize she had been holding her breath.

Leaning her head against the pillows, Joanna closed her eyes and allowed herself to imagine what her life would be like if she had stayed in this house with her sister and grandmother. How different her life would be. She and Marcy might be friends again, instead of circling each other like feral cats. Joanna would have spent more time with Letty before she retired. Maybe Letty would finally have taught her to cook, and Eudora would have taught her the proper way manage a formal garden.

Both of those things would have been wonderful, and she wrapped herself in the possibility.

Joanna must have drifted back to sleep because when she opened her eyes again, the room was considerably brighter. With her hand resting lightly on her daughter, Joanna woke slowly, looking at the room she'd chosen, automatically the night before. It was the room she and Marcy had shared when they were younger, and it hadn't changed at all. The same light blue walls and glossy white trim. The white desk in the corner belonged to Marcy. In fifth grade, she'd insisted on a proper place to do her homework. At the time Joanna was too young to need one, and she was content to spread out on the floor with her crayons and markers, coloring pictures as Marcy studied. When they were kids, Joanna was always happy to have her sister nearby.

They were supposed to share the vanity near the piazza window, but it became a dumping-ground for Marcy's make-up and the surface was usually a jumble of tubes, compacts, and lotions. One rainy afternoon, Marcy decided to teach Joanna the correct way to apply lip gloss. It was unusual to have Marcy all to herself, and Joanna committed every detail to memory—the scratchy feeling of the wand on her lips and the closeness of Marcy's breath on her skin as she explained how to apply the color.

As she thought about it now, Joanna realized how much she had missed her sister.

"Mommy?" Gracie stirred, her little voice soft in the quiet of the room.

"I'm here, sweetie." Joanna drew Gracie close.

"Where are we?" Gracie squirmed from her mother's embrace and sat up. "Are we still in the castle?"

"We're still in Charleston, so I guess the answer's yes."

"Nicco?" Gracie's voice was soft, barely a whisper. As if she was afraid to say his name.

"No." Joanna was emphatic. "We won't see him again, not ever."

"I don't like him," Gracie ventured.

"I don't like him either. He shouldn't have hit you, Gracie. I'm so very sorry that I couldn't stop him in time." Joanna had hoped for forgiveness, but Gracie was silent.

In the distance, Joanna heard the thrum of a humming-bird's wings, and she turned toward the sound. On the piazza, a tiny, iridescent bird darted among the red blossoms of a hanging geranium.

Joanna whispered. "Goose, look outside. There's a hummingbird having his breakfast. If you're very quiet, you can watch him."

Gracie's head swiveled as she searched the piazza for the bird. Joanna pointed toward the hanging plant. "See? Over there by the red flowers."

Joanna remembered how she and Marcy used to wait for the hummingbirds to come to her grandmother's garden when they were young. In the late afternoon, just before dinner, the birds flew into the garden, darting around the flowers and the glass feeder. Letty had told them it was good luck to see one, that it meant a change was coming. Joanna hoped Letty was right, especially now.

"I'm hungry, Mommy."

"We can fix that." Scooping the twist of clothes they'd tossed on the floor the night before, Joanna said, "I know these are awful, but they're all we have at the moment. We'll find something else after breakfast."

Ignoring the disgust on her daughter's face, Joanna stuffed herself into the same clothes she'd been wearing for three days. The fabric practically stuck to her skin.

Venturing downstairs to the kitchen, Gracie stopped to admire the grandfather clock that had graced the front entry of her grandmother's house for decades. A gift from the Historical Society in recognition of her great-grandfather's restoration work around the city, it was enormous, standing almost as tall as the front door it stood beside, with a pendulum as big as a dinner plate and counterweights as heavy as an August afternoon.

"See this clock, Gracie? Aunt Marcy and I used to sit right here in front of it when we were little and wait for it to gong, on the hour."

"Can I do that, too?" A spark of interest lit in Gracie's eyes, the first Joanna had seen since they left.

"Absolutely."

But first, they needed to eat. Joanna steered her daughter toward the kitchen. "Let's get some breakfast first, something better than stale airport cookies."

Joanna pulled a carton of eggs from the refrigerator and set it on the counter. Eggs were a good start, but it would take a while longer to find pans and plates. Someone had rearranged the kitchen while Joanna was away. She had just closed the last cabinet when she heard someone climbing the stairs from the back garden. Eudora's home had two entrances. The front of the house was the formal entrance, for visitors. The family entrance led directly to the kitchen, through Eudora's garden. So, whoever was climbing the stairs was family. Joanna turned toward the door, expecting her grandmother or her sister.

Instead, it was Letty, a woman Joanna hadn't seen in far too long.

"Letty!" Joanna rushed toward the woman who had been the heart of the Rutledge family ever since she could remember. She wrapped her arms around Letty and held tight.

"Now, now—first things first. You gots to let a person breathe, Miss Joanna." Letty untangled herself and pointed to the grocery bags outside. "G'won and get the rest of those bags for me. I'm too old to be dragging them things into the house."

Joanna did as she was told, simply because it was Letty who spoke. Letty Montgomery had been with the Rutledge family longer than Joanna had been alive. A force of nature, she wielded undisputed authority, probably because she knew more about the Rutledge family than anyone, but more importantly, because she held those secrets close. When the girls had trouble adjusting to a new school, it was Letty who greeted them with warm gingerbread and a sympathetic ear. On the days that Alice refused to leave her room, it was Letty who served the girls a hot supper and saw that they finished their homework. And when their stepfather returned after four years away to claim his family, it was Letty who saw them off. She told them to be strong, that she would see them again. And she did, years later when first Marcy, and then Joanna returned to Charleston to attend college. They may have lived in their grandmother's house, but it was Letty who made it feel like home.

After Joanna set the last bag of groceries on the counter, she asked, "Where is everybody?"

Letty snorted. "When you sleep this late, missy, you're

gonna miss some things." She chuckled and held out her arms. "We'll worry about everyone later. Now c'mere and lemme finish hugging your neck."

As Joanna stepped into Letty's embrace, she breathed in the familiar scent of talcum powder and yellow jasmine. It was the smell of home, and she melted into it. "I'm so happy to see you, Letty."

"Well, you'd best be happy, all the trouble I took, going to —" Letty fell silent.

Joanna followed Letty's gaze and smiled. "Miss Letty, this is my daughter, Gracie. Gracie, this is Miss Letty."

Letty's face shone with happiness. "Miss Gracie, I been looking forward to meeting you since the day you was born."

Gracie glanced at her mother, unsure of what to do.

"It's okay, Gracie," Joanna encouraged. "Take Miss Letty's hand and tell her you are happy to meet her."

Gracie's voice was soft, barely audible. "Happy to meet…M…Letty."

Letty snorted. "You gots to speak up, child, if you want to be heard in this house." Seeing Gracie's face cloud, Letty softened. "Well, we'll just have to work on that later. Right now, let's get you some food. You gots to be hungry. Your mama loved my praline pancakes. You want to try some and decide for yourself?"

Gracie looked up. "What's a praline?"

"Lord, child," Letty gasped, then glared at Joanna. " 'What's a praline?' "

Joanna had the good sense to look away.

Turning her attention back to Gracie, Letty decided. "We don't have a minute to waste. You look like a smart girl, like you might know your way around the kitchen. If that's so, then I surely could use your help." Letty's look turned serious as she asked, "Can you measure?"

Gracie nodded solemnly. "Measuring was my best thing in Miss Jeffrie's class before we moved away. And I didn't forget how."

"That's good because I need an expert." Pointing to the hallway, Letty continued. "There is a little blue bathroom right down there. Go in and scrub your hands good, with soap. Then come back and we'll make us a mess 'a praline pancakes."

As Gracie skipped down the hallway, Joanna pulled a carton of milk from the bag and slipped it into the refrigerator. "I've missed your cooking, Letty."

Letty didn't answer right away, so Joanna lifted a box of animal crackers from the bag and carried it to the pantry. Letty rose stiffly to her feet, using the countertop for balance. Joanna rushed to help, but Letty shooed her away with a glare. "Why am I just now meeting this baby?"

Joanna felt herself blush. She didn't have a good answer.

Letty pursed her lips, a signal she was displeased. She slipped off her cardigan and draped it over the back of the barstool. Then she turned to Joanna. "How old is that child?"

"She's six—almost seven." Joanna slid onto a barstool, determined to get back into Letty's good graces. "She's so smart, Letty."

"Uh-huh." Letty pulled a red apron from the pantry and quickly tied it. Pulling an armful of ingredients from the pantry, she set them on the countertop. "Little Bitty looks just like you did at her age." After a pause, she added, "It's a shame none of us has laid eyes on her before now."

Joanna felt the sting of the reproach, as she was meant to.

"I'm sorry, Letty. Things got complicated." It was a weak explanation, and her embarrassment flamed her cheeks.

"Life is as complicated as you let it be," Letty muttered. Returning to the counter, she folded the paper bag, smoothing away the wrinkles before slipping it into a lower cabinet. "How long has it been since you came home, Miss Jo? At least as long as that baby's been alive because I don't recall getting an invitation to visit."

Automatically, Joanna shook her head. "It couldn't have been that long." Then she calculated, counting on her fingers. "Russell and I moved to Chicago right after graduation, then Gracie was born the next year—"

"And how old did you say that baby is?"

Then Joanna understood. It had been more than seven years since she'd been home. She glanced at Letty, not knowing what to say.

Gracie skipped into the kitchen with a smile on her face and her hands dripping a trail of water on the hardwood floor. "Mommy, there are little flower soaps in there. I used two. Can I show them to Lendard?"

Gracie wrapped her arms around her blue stuffed hippopotamus. She must have found it on the chair where Joanna had put it the night before.

Joanna grimaced as she reached for Gracie's toy. "Later, you can, Goose. Lendard is filthy. I know he'll feel better when he's washed."

Letty slid a dish towel from the waist of her apron and deposited it into Gracie's wet hands. "Dry your hands real good, little missy. You don't want no flour sticking to them." Then she crossed to the kitchen pantry and pulled out a long yellow apron. "I hope you like yellow."

Gracie nodded, her attention focused on her task.

"Well, that's good because this yellow apron is my favorite and I only lend it to my special helpers." Returning with the apron, Letty offered it to Gracie. "This loop goes over your head and then it ties in the back. I can help you, if you like."

"I can do it," Gracie insisted.

"You are going to love praline pancakes, Gracie." Joanna reached for three plates from the cabinet and set them on the table. "Best thing you've ever tasted. I can't wait." She smelled the butter sizzling and her stomach growled.

As Letty untangled Gracie's apron ties, she glanced at Joanna. "Your grandmother will expect afternoon tea in the garden today. My guess is she's upstairs getting ready right now, so you best be getting ready, too."

For anyone visiting the Rutledge house, afternoon tea was more than a tradition, it was a requirement. It was served in the rose garden, and everyone dressed in their best, which Joanna didn't have.

Joanna blushed as she assessed the condition of her travel-stained clothes. "I can't have tea with Gram looking like this."

With a quick glance at Joanna, Letty nodded. "No, you surely can't."

Joanna continued. "We don't have any other clothes."

Letty finished the bow and drew up a step stool beside her for Gracie. "No clothes? Didn't you bring no luggage?"

"We left—" The words stuck, so Joanna cleared her throat and tried again. "We left in kind of a hurry."

Instead of responding, Letty turned her attention to Gracie. "Looks like we might have a bit of a problem, Miss Gracie. I see that you missed a spot when you was washing your hands and we need to be extra clean when we make pralines. Do you think you can try washing them again?"

Gracie's voice was hopeful. "Can I use the flowered soaps again?"

"You surely can. Now get a move on, we got work to do."

Joanna heard Gracie jump off the step stool and felt Letty move around the counter to her side.

"No luggage, and no word that you coming." Letty's voice trailed off, expectantly.

But Joanna didn't have an easy answer, so Letty heaved a sigh, the weight of the Rutledge family on her shoulders. "We'll talk about this another day. For now, know that you can't meet your grandmother dressed as you are." The sound of the butter sizzling brought Letty back to the stove. As she swirled the pan, she offered an alternative. "You might could borrow one of your sister's tea dresses."

Joanna groaned. "You know nothing in her closet will come close to fitting me."

Where Marcy was tall and willowy, like their mother, Joanna was "sturdy," like their father—at least Joanna assumed she was built like her father. She didn't know for sure. Her parents had divorced when Joanna was three, and her father had disappeared entirely less than a year later. She'd found some pictures once, hidden in a drawer. He looked like a nice man, despite what Alice said.

"Can't we have tea tomorrow?" Joanna offered. "I can go out and shop today. We need clothes, shoes, and shampoo. I'm sure Gram will understand, just this one time."

Letty pursed her lips as she removed a carton of cream from the refrigerator. Setting it down, she placed both hands on the countertop. "Let me see do I have this straight: you and baby girl were stuck at the airport, no one to call, nowhere to go—'cept for your Gram. Your Gram is the one you called from the airport when you had no one else, that about right?"

Joanna nodded.

"She welcome you home? Bought the tickets you needed?"

Joanna swallowed and nodded again, this time staring at the floor. She knew where this conversation was going

"Do you know who Miss Eudora called right after she talked to you? First phone call?" Letty turned to address Gracie, who had returned from washing her hands. "Can you measure two cups of this sugar for me?"

With Gracie occupied, Letty finished her thought. "That phone call was to me, missy. And I will never forget what she said. She said, 'My grandbaby is finally coming home,' and then she asked me to come, to make it nice for you. So, I don't much care that you're nervous. You will go upstairs and you will dress for tea in a way that pleases your grandmother."

"Is this right, Miss Letty?" Gracie's face was a study in concentration, her thoughts focused on her task. The thick ceramic bowl was dusted with white sugar, as was the counter and her apron but Letty rewarded her with a smile.

"That looks exactly right, Gracie. We'll make a proper Southern lady out of you yet."

"Is Marcy's room still upstairs?" Joanna kept her voice light but could see that it didn't fool Letty.

Letty's lips pursed in disapproval. "Seems like you should know where your sister lives. She's had the same room since college." Letty slid a bag of brown sugar and a clean measuring cup in front of Gracie. "We're going to need a full cup of this brown sugar." She leaned in and whispered to Gracie. "The brown sugar is what makes it taste good."

Gracie reached into the bag with her chubby fingers and

scooped out a few lumps of brown sugar. Cupping them in her palm, she dropped them one by one into the measuring cup and tamped them down, flat.

"That's good, baby," Letty crooned. "I can see you're a careful worker. After this, we add the pecans, then we can make pancakes. When we're finished, we can get started on cucumber sandwiches for tea."

Joanna loathed cucumber sandwiches.

With her voice deliberately casual, Joanna addressed Letty. "Is Marcy at work today?"

Letty snorted as she spread a sheet of parchment on the counter and began scraping a stick of frozen butter against a box grater. "If she's breathing, your sister is working, weekday or no."

Joanna watched tiny curls of butter dropping onto the parchment, remembering when it had been Marcy's job to grate and Joanna's job to measure. With a start, she realized she didn't even know where her sister worked. So, she asked. "Does Marcy work at Palmetto Holdings?"

"Where else?" Sliding a jar of molasses closer to Gracie, Letty instructed her. "We need a full tablespoon of this. The recipe says a teaspoon, but they's mistaken."

They both watched Gracie fumble with the measuring spoons for a moment before Letty said, gently, "It's the big one, baby. The tablespoon is the biggest one in the bunch."

Then, as Gracie measured, Letty turned her attention to Joanna, the disappointment clear in her expression. "You girls used to be so close. Those years you all came to live here when your stepfather worked in Tiberia—"

"Singapore."

"Wherever." With a flick of her fingers, Letty showed the name of the country didn't matter to her in the least. She had never been a fan of their stepfather. "The point is, for the four years you all lived here, you spent every summer day in each other's back pockets." With a quick glance at Gracie, she continued. "Didn't you both take some kind of lessons at your grandfather's club? You two used to be gone all day. Left here with a sack of biscuits and honey butter in the morning, didn't see you 'til supper, sunburned and happy."

"Swimming lessons and sailing, both." Joanna remembered the very first sail on her grandfather's boat, just two days after arriving in Charleston with their mother. From the moment she boarded, she was hooked. Even the short sail in the harbor was exciting, the sounds and the smells unlike anything she'd known before. The *thwap* of the halyard on the mainsail, the *whoosh* of the spinnaker as it was launched from the shoot, and the *snap* as it caught the wind and unfurled— she loved it all.

Letty's voice broke into Joanna's thoughts. "Time for you to get moving, Miss Jo. The afternoon won't wait for you. The way I see it, you have two choices: you can risk your sister's wrath by borrowing a dress from her closet, or you can insult your grandmother by showing up in that." Letty wrinkled her nose. "Either way, you need to fix yourself up because you can't stay in my kitchen the way you are. I'm sorry to be the one to tell you, but you smell."

Gracie giggled from her place at the counter, and Letty turned to her with a smile. "What'choo giggling about, little missy? You're a close second." Turning back to Joanna, Letty continued, pointing at her with a wooden spoon before handing it to Gracie. "G'won now."

There was no point in stalling. "Fine, I'll go, but it would have been nice to at least have a cup of coffee first."

Letty gestured toward the pot. "Take one cup and be on your way."

After filling up the biggest cup she could find and adding a generous amount of cream, Joanna dropped a kiss on the top of her daughter's head and turned to leave the kitchen. On her way out, she gave Letty one last hug. "Thank you, Letty."

Letty returned Joanna's hug with a squeeze. "You be strong now, Miss Jo. Tea with your Gram won't be as painful as you think." She added, "'though maybe it should be."

Joanna trudged upstairs into her bathroom and eyed the soaking tub with longing, but she didn't have the time. Instead, she reached into the shower and turned the knob to scalding. Twenty minutes later, pink-skinned and freshly scrubbed, she stood in the doorway of her sister's room, wrapped in a towel and afraid to enter.

Marcy's room looked like something pulled from an architectural magazine, beautifully curated but bare, as if all traces of her sister had been erased. On her way to the closet, she brushed Marcy's bedspread with her fingertips. Smoky gray, pulled taut across the king-sized bed, so different from the sister she'd known. A monogrammed coverlet lay at the foot of the bed, and at the top, two rows of lush pillows.

When they were kids, they were constantly in trouble for jumping on their beds, for dropping clothes in heaps on the floor, for leaving dishes on the nightstand. It seemed that her sister had changed while Joanna was away.

Joanna continued to her sister's closet and snapped on the light.

"Wow," Joanna whispered.

Her sister's closet was cavernous, as big as Joanna's entire bedroom in her Chicago apartment, and it smelled heavenly, like cedar and new clothes. Joanna decided that if she had kept every item of clothing she'd owned in her entire life, it still wouldn't be enough to fill this closet. Business suits and dresses hung from padded hangers, some with price tags still attached. On the far side, a wall of little cubbyholes held shoes, some wrapped in tissue, some still boxed. Joanna thought of the shoes she owned, twisted and forgotten under her bed in Rome. She felt like a little kid playing dress up. She would never be stylish, like Marcy, so why was she trying?

Joanna ventured inside, feeling a bit like Indiana Jones on a quest for lost treasure. She flipped through the dresses, noting that Marcy seemed to have lost weight since college, while Joanna had definitely gained some—there wasn't much in this closet that would fit her comfortably. Finally, stuffed in the back of the closet was a beige linen dress with a square neck, with the price tag still attached. Shapeless and ugly, the number on the tag was off by at least two sizes, but maybe the cut was generous.

Joanna lifted the hanger from the rod. "Come with me, ugly dress. We have a command performance in the garden."

On her way out, Joanna grabbed a pair of strappy green sandals from one of the cubbies. At least they shared the same shoe size.

CHAPTER 8

WHEN HER HUSBAND WAS ALIVE, the master bedroom had been furnished in a heavy masculine style, Brock's preference, not hers. It had been the way of things then, to defer to your husband's wishes, so Eudora had remained silent, but in the years following his death, Eudora began to think about redecorating. First she repainted the walls a soft powder blue, then replaced the dark furniture she had never cared for with lighter pieces. Bedding came next, linens and pillows, in shades of cream and white, and oversized down comforters that chased away the deepest cold. Brock cared for none of those things, but Eudora did, and now she couldn't imagine this room any other way.

Eudora lifted a pearl earring from the velvet-lined box on her vanity table and clipped it on. Had she been truthful, Eudora might have admitted that she didn't care for this set. The earrings were heavy and they pinched. The ostentatious matching necklace was not her style at all. Brock's mother had presented them Eudora on her wedding day, with the expectation that the Rutledge Pearls would take the place of the set given to her by her mother. Eudora had married a

Rutledge, after all, she should expect their history would become her history.

Eudora rose from her vanity and crossed her room, to the tall windows that opened onto the piazza. This had always been her favorite part of the house, and she was proud of its history. Only a handful of the historic homes in Charleston could showcase a piazza that wrapped the length of the house on two floors. In the spring and fall, Eudora opened the Rutledge home to the public, for tours to benefit the Historic Society. Visitors loved the history, and stories of the family who lived there.

The home Captain Rutledge commissioned was intended to be a modest home, a place for him to conduct business in town—until his wife took over the planning. While he was at sea, she met with the architect and changed the designs, adding two additional floors, with a ballroom, guest suites, and a nursery with adjoining rooms for a governess and a night nurse. Eliza Rutledge was the one who insisted the windows to the piazza be low enough for a lady to comfortably step across and wide enough to allow a hoop skirt to pass though, without touching the fabric. The house was already framed and bricked when Captain Rutledge returned.

Eudora's favorite place on the piazza was outside her bedroom, overlooking her garden. In the course of her marriage, there were many nights spent on the wicker settee, waiting for the gates to open and Brock's car to enter the courtyard. He was sure she didn't know the reason for his late nights, but she did. And in that, too, she'd deferred to his wishes.

A dash of movement from the garden below caught Eudora's attention, and she moved toward the railing. Her children, William and Alice, raced around the boxwood maze searching for Easter eggs and squealing in delight when they found one. Alice wore the yellow dress that Letty had carefully starched and ironed that morning because Eudora's mother-in-law insisted her grandchildren be presented in a certain way. William had shed his suit jacket, tossing it carelessly by the front of the maze. Alice's Easter hat lay beside it, the pale yellow ribbons ground into the dirt. Eudora's grip on the railing tightened as she realized the punishment awaiting her children if Brock saw the way they'd treated their things. So little could set him off these days.

Eudora drew a breath to summon the nanny, and the garden below blurred, the edges curled as if she were watching a photograph melt. The daffodils that had swayed a moment before receded into shadow. Eudora pressed against the railing and brought her fingertips to her forehead.

It happened again.

As she closed her eyes, wondering what to do, a soft thump of the closing kitchen door on the floor below brought her attention back to the present. She watched her youngest granddaughter navigate the garden path and Eudora frowned. Generations of Rutledge women had been instructed to walk gracefully, but Joanna tromped across the ground as if she were a farmer in a cow field. Both of her granddaughters had attended classes, in preparation for their debut, though Marcy had been the only one formally presented. Marcy's walk and her curtsey were flawless, unlike her sister, who tugged at the hem of a dress that didn't fit and walked with her arms folded in front of her as if she wanted to disappear.

"Oh, my dear girl," Eudora whispered, "we have work ahead of us."

CHAPTER 9

"Marcy, do you have a minute?" Andrea poked her head into Marcy's office.

Truthfully, she didn't, and Andrea knew that better than anyone. But if Andrea was asking, it must be important.

"What's up?" Turning from the spreadsheet on her computer monitor, she gave her assistant her full attention. "Please, tell me—this *one* time—that it's something that can be solved quickly."

Andrea closed the door behind her, and Marcy's heart sank. This wasn't going to be a quick-fix problem. "The health care agency called. Eudora's fired another aide this morning, and they won't send a replacement until they talk to you."

Marcy's eye twitched and she pressed her fingertip to her brow. "When?"

"They said the aide showed up at eleven o'clock, as planned, but Eudora wouldn't let her in. She told the woman that she—" Andrea consulted her notes, "was 'fine and didn't need any help—today, or ever again.' I tried calling Eudora, but she didn't answer the phone, and the agency refuses to talk to anyone but you."

"Of course, they won't." Marcy sighed. She never had these problems when Letty was around. "Can you get them on the phone? I'll talk to them now."

"I tried. They've gone to lunch, and the office is closed."

Marcy looked up. "Seriously? Who closes a business for lunch?"

"Can't Joanna help?" Andrea asked.

The only one Joanna has ever helped is herself. The comment was on the tip of her tongue, but Marcy held it back. Instead, she said, "Joanna won't know that Eudora's medications are timed and which ones she has to take with food. The morning meds are the most important; they're for her blood pressure. Marcy glanced at her watch. "She's probably missed them by now."

"Do you want me to call Joanna? I can give her instructions."

"No, it's easier for me to go than to try to explain what to do." Marcy glanced at her afternoon schedule. "I need you to cancel my one o'clock with Skip."

Andrea groaned. "Can we reschedule instead of cancel? Skip's been waiting all week to see you. He's got pictures for you to see."

Skip Peterson was an enthusiastic junior project manager, hired fresh out of college. He had potential and Marcy had intended to mentor him, using the Meeting Street project as an example. The property had been far enough from the historic district that it might not matter what mistakes Skip made and when they were finished, they could sell the property and still make a profit. But things didn't work out as she'd planned. The North Charleston project had ballooned from something manageable into something massive, demanding every minute of her time. As a result, Marcy had essentially dumped Meeting Street on Skip's lap and had left him to sink or swim. She wasn't eager to see what he'd done to it.

"I'm sure the pictures are great, but, as you can see, my afternoon is pretty full." Marcy grabbed her keys and headed out.

When Marcy pulled her car into the courtyard, she noticed Letty's old yellow hatchback parked near the garden. She tightened her grip on the steering wheel. Of course, Letty came, the Princess Joanna was home. Everything stops for Joanna.

Dropping her keys onto the pedestal table in the foyer, Marcy strode toward the kitchen. On the day Letty left, Marcy insisted she keep her house keys, explaining that she was welcome to visit anytime she wanted, as family, not staff. But Letty wasn't the kind of woman to lounge, and old habits were hard to erase. There didn't seem to be a solution.

Marcy approached the kitchen, she noticed the smell of something baking and it stopped her in her tracks. Letty was baking ginger scones.

Marcy closed her eyes and breathed in the scent of ginger and lemon, imagining Letty in the house again. She could almost make herself believe that the last few years had never happened. That Letty still anchored the Rutledge household from the kitchen, that Eudora's health had never faltered, and that Joanna had never left.

The thud of the oven door closing ended the dream. The facts were that Letty *was* gone, that Eudora's health *was* failing, and that Marcy had been left to deal with all of it by herself. She rounded the corner and entered the kitchen. "Letty, please tell me you're here as a guest, that you're not baking anything."

"You can see that I am." Letty wiped her hands on her apron. "And that's a fine greeting, I must say."

"Gram called you."

"You know she did."

Marcy slid her hand into an oven mitt and took the tray. "You can't come running every time she calls." After setting the tray on the counter, she guided Letty to a chair. "The doctor said you're supposed to rest."

Letty had been the heartbeat of the Rutledge home, since before her mother was born. Asking Letty to leave was the hardest thing Marcy had ever done and she resented having to do it alone. But years of caring for Marcy's family had taken a toll on Letty's diabetes and, eventually, her doctor insisted that she retire because she refused to slow down. As matriarch, Eudora should have been the one to explain things to Letty, but she refused, taking to her room in a fit of despair at the very thought of her friend leaving. Letty's coming back added another worry to Marcy's growing list. At some point, Marcy would have to address this too, but not today. She didn't have time today.

Opening the refrigerator, Marcy scanned its contents. "Is this tea unsweetened?"

Letty scoffed. "Not in this house."

Neither Eudora nor Letty were allowed sweet tea, so Marcy pushed aside the jug of tea and chose a pitcher of lemon water instead. She poured it into a glass and added ice. "Letty, please, sit down and drink this. I can finish the baking. You should rest."

Letty's tone was unexpectedly sharp. "I ain't dead yet, missy. And all your fussing won't put the years back on me."

"That's not what I meant at all." Marcy winced. But that was exactly what she wanted to do. For years, she'd been trying to hold back time for both Eudora and Letty, through sheer determination. "I'm just trying to follow your doctor's instructions. Why do you and Gram both make everything so difficult?"

"Because we don't like being treated like children." Letty's tone softened as she reached for Marcy's hand. Her grip was strong and warm, reassuring. Letty always made her feel safe. Marcy felt tears prick behind her eyelids. "Your grandma and I have been through a lifetime together, so when she calls me and tells me her youngest grandbaby in trouble and could I come and help, don't you know that I will."

Joanna again.

Marcy rose from her place and went to the stove. Picking up a spatula, she lifted the scones from the baking tray and transferred them to a wire rack to cool. "I'm sure she's fine. Joanna is *always* fine."

Her voice was sharper than she had intended because she was annoyed at herself for not realizing this was all for her sister. Of course, Gram had called Letty because the entire world stops when Joanna comes home. The last few months had been critical for Marcy, too. She'd been working long hours to pull together a project that she didn't even like, working with a man she didn't entirely trust, but Letty didn't come to comfort *her* or bake *her* scones.

"You girls need to get right with each other."

"Some sisters don't get along." Marcy reached into a drawer for a linen napkin. "It's just the way things are."

Letty allowed the comment to pass, unchallenged. "Then let's talk about you, missy. What's taking up your time now?"

"Work, mostly. And Gram's doctors," Marcy replied, as she laid the napkin in the silver basket Eudora had always used for her teas. "Tell me, Letty. Why does Gram keep firing the housekeepers I hire?"

"Eudora knows those women ain't housekeepers." Letty rose from her chair and filled the kettle with water.

Marcy blinked. She'd left detailed instructions for the agency. They promised that Eudora would never figure it out. "How long has she known?"

"That you're passing off health care workers as house-keepers?" Letty chortled. "Oh, honey, your grandmother has been surrounded by staff her whole life. She can tell a fake from the real thing."

Marcy flinched at the admonishment. "It's not like this is *fun* for me, Letty. Do you know how long it took to find that agency? The background checks I did? The aides who come here are supposed to be retired nurses because I need someone who can manage Gram's medication and make sure she eats what she's supposed to. I can't do *everything* myself."

Letty patted Marcy's arm. "I know you trying your best."

But that only made it worse. It had taken weeks to find a qualified agency, and Eudora fired them on a whim.

Marcy's phone dinged with a text from Andrea. *Bruce Calhoun needs thirty minutes today. What do I say?*

Marcy tapped a quick reply. *Tell him yes. I'm on my way back.*

Letty set the teapot on the tray and fixed Marcy with a pointed gaze. "Ain't you staying for tea?"

Marcy didn't meet her eye. "I wasn't invited." She knew she sounded like a child, but she couldn't seem to stop herself.

"Bitterness is not an attractive quality, missy," Letty admonished. "There might be more to this homecoming than you know. Why don't you ask?"

"Because I don't care." Marcy's answer was unintentionally sharp. "All I care about is how long Joanna's staying and how she treats Gram while she's here."

"You hold on to too much, baby girl." Letty wrapped her thin arms around Marcy. "Your Gram loves you both, you know."

Marcy closed her eyes and leaned into Letty's hug. She breathed in the scent of the jasmine-scented powder that Letty had worn for decades, and she felt herself relax for the first time in months. Letty had the power to do that. Letty had known how to distract two scared girls in the kitchen as their mother unraveled in her bedroom, and she knew how to pull the pieces of a fragmented life together now. But she had come for Joanna, not Marcy.

Too soon, Letty released her and moved toward the counter. "Made you something." She removed a brown lunch bag from the refrigerator and offered it to Marcy.

The bag crinkled as Marcy opened it and looked inside. There, at the bottom, was a bright green Granny Smith apple and a triangle neatly wrapped in foil.

"You made me lunch?" Marcy asked. She felt herself smile.

Letty offered a slow smile. "Yes, ma'am, I did. Peanut butter and honey."

"You haven't made peanut butter and honey since I was twelve."

"Haven't needed it since you was twelve." Letty folded a warm scone into a cloth napkin and tucked it into the bag. "You need to be patient with your Gram, honey. She's made mistakes you don't even know about and she's trying her best to right them."

"Mistakes? With Joanna? I don't think so. Joanna has

always been her favorite." Marcy scoffed as her phone beeped with another text from Andrea.

Bruce is here. Wants to wait in your office.

Rising from the barstool, Marcy grabbed her bag. "I have to go. Can you please make sure Gram takes her medicine? The one in the morning is the most—"

"The most important." Letty finished for her. "Do you think this is my first day? I already checked. She took everything she supposed to."

"Thank you, Letty."

"You're welcome, sugar."

Marcy hesitated before leaving. "I don't suppose it would do any good to ask you to rest while they have tea outside?"

Letty's answering smile was wide. "For you, honey, I will."

On her way toward the front door, Marcy glanced out the window to the garden, but couldn't see the table they would use for tea. That meant the table was set on the slate patio beneath the magnolia tree, a place reserved for special occasions. That knowledge felt physical, like a punch in the stomach, but she let it go. Like she always did.

Marcy continued down the hallway to the front door and let herself out.

CHAPTER 10

JOANNA HATED WEARING her sister's ugly beige dress. It was too tight, for one thing. The price tag she had hidden under her arm poked her skin, and the waistband dug into her stomach. Even so, she remained seated because to leave before her grandmother's arrival would be unthinkable. Joanna had already begun to perspire in the humid afternoon; she felt trails of it dripping down the small of her back. Marcy's dress would be ruined, and Joanna would have to replace it.

Her stomach growled. That and the humidity were making her irritable, and that wasn't the way to greet her grandmother. She was grateful that Eudora had welcomed them back. Without her, she and Gracie might still be in the Frankfurt airport.

To distract herself from the heat, Joanna turned her attention to the table, admiring the Rutledge tea service in the center. It was said to have been imported from France, years before Paul Revere had given a thought to crafting anything in silver. The Rutledge teapot was sterling silver, with a bone handle, and an etching of magnolia blossoms and jasmine vines circling the base. One day, when the girls were younger, Eudora removed the teapot from its cabinet and explained its history. The chip in the handle was from the shovel that buried it near the spring house as they prepared for Sherman's army to plunder the city. The scratch along the side had come from a rock in a hastily dug hole—there hadn't been time to wrap anything before they buried it. The people of Charleston matched wits with the Yankees, hiding their valuables and their jewelry in the ground, in the spring house, and underneath loose flagstones. When the Yankees came, expecting plunder, they would find nothing.

And Charleston won.

"In the end, Sherman didn't come," Eudora had told them. The gleam in her eye suggested that, had she been there, she would have stopped the general herself. "Not even *he* dared to destroy our beloved Charleston. It was Columbia he wanted, anyway. Stupid man."

In the center of the table, next to a tall crystal vase filled with her grandmother's roses, was a three-tiered silver platter stacked with sandwiches, scones, and tarts. A silver bowl of red grapes was placed close enough to Joanna that she could see the sugar coating on each grape. She reached toward the bowl but dropped her hand back into her lap when she heard the back door close. Shading her eyes, Joanna watched her grandmother descend the stairs. As Eudora drew closer, Joanna noticed details she had been too tired to see the morning they had arrived: The shuffle in her step, the way her cardigan hung loosely from her shoulders, how thin she'd become. She hadn't expected her grandmother to change.

Joanna rose from her chair and greeted her grandmother with a kiss on her cheek. "The table looks beautiful."

"You're welcome, my dear." Eudora settled into her chair

and smoothed her napkin across her lap. "I'm glad you've come home, Joanna, and I am delighted to finally meet Gracie. Though I must say, I've been wondering how you all managed to end up in Germany. Were you and Russell vacationing?"

Joanna blinked, surely her grandmother remembered their phone conversation, from the airport, not two days before. Joanna had told her everything. But maybe she hadn't. Maybe Joanna had been so tired that she just thought she did. She explained again. "Russell and I aren't together anymore, Gram. We divorced six years ago."

"I see." Eudora lifted the teapot from the silver tray and poured for them both. "Had you mentioned that before and I'd forgotten? It seems like something I'd remember."

"I may have left out some details." Joanna shifted her weight to cross her legs. The seams on Marcy's dress stretched along Joanna's thigh, so she shifted back. Pasting a smile on her face, she searched for a neutral topic. "Your rose garden is beautiful, Gram. You seem to have more roses than I remember."

"Do you think so?" Eudora returned the pot to the serving tray, turning it so the family crest was visible. "You know, Mr. Mason, my gardener, retired last year. Your sister hired some sort of landscaping company to replace him, but I find them lacking. They don't have quite the talent with roses that Mr. Mason did. I've had to demonstrate the proper way to mulch roses and prune wisteria." Reaching for the sugar bowl, she asked, "Do you still take sugar?"

"Lemon—" Joanna's voice came out a croak, and she cleared her throat. "Lemon, please."

Eudora offered the plate of lemon slices. "I remember you being quite fond of the sugar tongs when you were younger."

Joanna smiled as she remembered. "I used to trace the scroll-work with my fingers. I was fascinated by it." Joanna returned the lemon plate to its place in the center of the table. "You once told me the tongs were meant to transfer a single sugar cube, so one afternoon, I used them to transfer every single sugar cube from the bowl to my cup. By the time you poured, I had at least a dozen cubes hidden in the bottom of my cup."

Eudora chuckled. "That must have been awfully sweet, Joanna. Did you drink it?"

"I don't remember, Gram." But she did remember. Marcy had been at the tea, seated next to her grandmother, and Joanna hadn't wanted her sister to see her mistake. So, Joanna drank the whole cup.

Eudora stirred milk into her tea, then rested the spoon on the saucer. "There are things we should talk about, Joanna, and I would encourage you to tell me everything. I was delighted to get your telephone call, of course, but the circumstances are troubling. Keep in mind that any problem can be solved, as long as we begin with the truth, don't you agree? One can move forward from a place of truth."

"Yes, the truth is a good place to start." A prickle of warning touched the back of Joanna's neck. Her grandmother was very traditional. She valued marriage and commitment above all else, and Joanna wasn't sure how much she could reveal.

"Good. You can start by telling me what brought you home after so many years away."

Joanna watched Eudora remove a cucumber sandwich from the tray and suppressed a shudder. Cucumber sandwiches had been a staple at every tea Eudora had ever hosted, but Marcy was the only one who seemed to like them.

Joanna lifted one from the tray and added it to her plate, simply because that's what she'd always done. "Where would you like me to start, Gram?"

"We lost track of you and Russell after you moved to Chicago. You may start there." Eudora sipped her tea.

Joanna drew a nervous breath. "There's not much to tell, Gram. It just didn't work out. I haven't seen Russell in years." She let her voice trail away, watching for her grandmother's reaction.

After a moment, Eudora asked, "Does he support you and Gracie, financially?"

Joanna focused her concentration on dotting jam onto a scone, so she wouldn't have to look at her grandmother. She had learned Eudora's opinion about divorce when she was a little girl. Joanna had been a flower girl at her mother's second wedding, completely captivated by the fancy dress she got to wear. She'd found a mirror behind a dressing screen and was twirling in front of it, watching the skirt flare, and had only noticed the adults in the room when she heard her mother cry. "I don't want to do this," Alice had said. Joanna had taken a step toward her mother but stopped when she heard the sharp tone of her grandmother's voice. "You brought this upon yourself, my girl," Eudora had said. "Now dry your eyes and be thankful you found a man willing to marry a woman with two children."

"Joanna?" Eudora's voice broke through Joanna's memory. "I'm speaking to you. I asked if Russell supports you and Gracie."

"No, Gram. He doesn't. Gracie and I have been on our own since he left."

"Then you must persuade him to return," Eudora

decided. "Men don't always know what they want, Joanna. It's up to women to guide them."

Joanna blinked, not entirely sure she'd heard correctly. "He left us, Gram. He texted me from work, saying he didn't want to be married anymore, and he didn't come home. I haven't seen him in years, and I don't want him back."

"I'm not sure you're thinking clearly." Eudora's voice was firm. "A woman with a young child to care for requires the support of her husband. We can discuss this in more detail later when you've had a chance to consider your position."

Joanna squeezed her hands together in her lap. "Thank you, Gram, but I am absolutely sure that I don't want him back. Russell was never the prince you thought he was."

Eudora frowned as she reached for her tea. "There's no need to be ugly, Joanna. This situation is surely a tempest, and I'm sure we can sort it out." Eudora set her teacup down with a soft tap. "In the meantime, I am looking forward to getting to know my great-granddaughter. What are your plans for her school?"

"I hadn't thought that far ahead, to be honest. I'd like to keep her close to me for a while. But when she's ready, maybe after Christmas, we can think about school. She's only in first grade. I think she'll be able to catch up." Joanna smiled, hoping Eudora would share the joke, but she didn't.

Instead, Eudora lifted her napkin from her lap to the corners of her mouth. "I have taken the liberty of enrolling Gracie in Santee Academy. She starts Monday."

"Santee Academy?" Joanna swallowed her tea too quickly, and it burned her throat. There was no way Joanna could afford private school tuition. "I don't think that's an option right now. We haven't applied, and school is already—"

"Nonsense." Eudora replaced her napkin on her lap. "Rutledges have always attended Santee. You may consider this matter settled, and we can move on to other things." Joanna opened her mouth, but her grandmother had decided. "Gracie's first day will be Monday."

Joanna shifted in her chair, ignoring the pull of Marcy's dress across her hips. "Gram," she began, but Eudora stopped her.

"It's all taken care of. Tuition has been paid, and you may shop for uniforms and pencils tomorrow after you meet Gracie's teachers."

Joanna blinked. At some point, she'd have to consider school for Gracie, but they'd only just arrived. "Tomorrow is Saturday, Gram. There's no school on Saturday."

"Nevertheless, the teachers will be prepared to meet you and Gracie at ten o'clock." Eudora refilled Joanna's teacup and then her own. After replacing the pot on the tray, Eudora folded her hands in her lap and met Joanna's gaze. "Now, on to the question of your employment. As you are aware, Palmetto Holdings has been held in trust for you and your sister since your grandfather's passing. It has always been my intention to turn it over to both of you when I believe the time is right."

When it was clear that Eudora would offer no other details, Joanna asked. "You want me to work at Palmetto?"

"Yes."

"With Marcy?"

"Of course."

"Does Marcy know about this?"

"Your sister understands that Palmetto Holdings is a family company and that I am the majority shareholder. She will do as I ask."

Joanna imagined herself venturing into the lion's den. Her

sister had always been protective of the company their grand-father had started. Joanna would not be welcomed, no matter what Eudora said. "Gram, I'd rather not."

Eudora scoffed. "Nonsense."

"Gram—"

"We can discuss the details later. I'm afraid the sun and the humidity have given me a bit of a headache." Eudora folded her napkin and tucked it under her plate. She rose unsteadily from her chair. "I'd like to rest."

"Do you need help?"

Joanna moved to her grandmother's side, but Eudora brushed her away. "I'm fine, dear. It's nothing." Her grand-mother straightened. "I will have Letty telephone Santee to confirm your appointment tomorrow morning at ten."

"Gram, I really don't think—" Joanna tried again.

Eudora continued as if Joanna hadn't spoken. "In the meantime, you might want to put that dress back before Marcy notices it's missing. It's not flattering on you, my dear."

Joanna flushed, smoothing the puckered seams of Marcy's dress. "We didn't bring anything with us."

"In that case, you will need to use the house account with Chastains' on King Street. Call them now and ask that they deliver what you need immediately. In the morning, I will give you my charge cards, and you can shop after you meet Gracie's teachers. Feel free to buy whatever you need."

The humiliation of Joanna still needing her grandmother's credit card to buy clothes and school supplies stole the breath from her chest, but Joanna managed a smile. "Thank you, Gram."

At least they had a place to stay, and that was a start.

CHAPTER 11

MARCY SAT in her car in the courtyard of her grandmother's house, listening to the crickets and drumming her fingers on the steering wheel.

Joanna had waited up. The lights in the kitchen were on, and Marcy could see her sister perched at the table near the door.

So Marcy sat in her car, feeling like a teenager breaking curfew instead of a grown woman with a career. As she sat, deciding whether to continue into the house and greet her sister, or drive back to work and spend the night staring at spreadsheets, she wondered what it was, exactly, about Joanna that annoyed her.

It was because life had always been easy for Joanna. People always paved the way for her. Eudora had hosted an afternoon tea for Joanna, the first one in years. Marcy couldn't remember the last time she and Eudora had a conversation that didn't include scheduling. Daniel Kennedy bribed Santee Academy to admit Joanna's daughter, with a donation they couldn't afford. Marcy suspected the tuition would be taken care of too, so Joanna wouldn't have to worry. But the thing that hurt the most was that Letty had returned to the kitchen for Joanna. Marcy was the one who made her leave and Joanna is the one who brought her back.

After their mother died, Joanna was removed from high school for an entire year, and spent her days at home, with Letty, while Marcy continued with college, finishing the year with honors. Marcy did what was expected and it was hard; Joanna always took the easy way out and it never seemed to matter. People were always there to prop her up, take care of things for her. Now, Joanna was back and was the center of attention again, but Marcy just wasn't in the mood to cater to her sister.

She had just slid the car into reverse when she saw the curtains part in the den. Marcy pushed the gear back into park and turned off the motor, disgusted with herself. She wasn't going to run. Joanna would leave when she got what she wanted, just as she always had. In the meantime, Marcy would remind her sister that this was *not* her home.

Marcy fitted her key into the front door, and Joanna met her at the door.

"Marcy—finally. I'm so glad to see you." Joanna's hug was unexpected. They had never been a hugging family.

"Hello, Joanna." Marcy untangled herself and continued into the kitchen.

Joanna followed. "I've been waiting for you." Pinching the seersucker fabric of her bathrobe, she pulled it away from her body. "Do you like my new bathrobe? Gram had it delivered from Chastains', but what's really amazing is that no one had snapped it up before now." Joanna pointed to the repeating images of cardinals and goldfinches perched on magnolia branches. "The choice of pattern is particularly lovely, don't you think? And look at this—" she lifted the zipper at her throat and slid it up and down along the track, "—an old-lady zipper. What's not to like?"

"Interesting choice." Marcy brushed past her to fill a glass with ice. Of course, Eudora would have had clothes delivered; everything stopped when Joanna came home.

Joanna leaned against the countertop with a dramatic sigh. "I had to have afternoon tea with Gram. You should have been there. I'm pretty sure the grapes had been individually glazed with sugar."

Marcy selected a lemon from the basket. "Gram put a lot of effort into that tea; she always does. It's a special occasion for her and you should appreciate it."

Joanna fell silent and bit her thumbnail. Biting her nails was a disgusting habit she had developed when she was little; it was worse when she was nervous. Marcy glanced at Joanna's fingers; the cuticles on two fingers were bloody.

Joanna pushed her hand in her bathrobe pocket and offered a weak smile. "Well, you were always better at that stuff than I was. Remember the prep classes Gram made us go to? She wanted us to debut so badly."

There didn't seem to be anything to add, so Marcy set the lemon on the cutting board, and selected a knife from the block.

Joanna tried again. "I saw Letty today."

"Gram asked her to come to the house to make scones for your tea." She added, "But she shouldn't have. Letty doesn't work here anymore."

Joanna pulled the pitcher of iced tea from the refrigerator. "Why not?"

Drawing her knife across the lemon, Marcy sliced a little harder than she needed to. The lemon split into two and rolled off the board. "Complications from her diabetes. Her doctor wants her to rest."

Joanna froze, the pitcher of tea in her hand "Why didn't you tell me?"

The accusation echoed in the quiet kitchen.

"What do you *mean* why didn't I tell you? When have you shown any interest in what goes on around here?"

"You could have called me, Marcy."

"I didn't know where you were."

"You know my cell number. I've had the same phone for years."

"Then why didn't you use it to call Gram once in a while, like you promised?"

"That's what I've been trying to explain, Marcy." Joanna began, but Marcy stopped her. It was late, and she was too tired to fight.

"Why are you here, Joanna?"

"I've come home." Joanna blinked. "I brought Gracie."

"I can see that. The question is why now? What do you want?"

"What do I want?" Joanna repeated. "I want my family. Something happened, and I don't know how to fix it—"

"Stop." Marcy held up her palm, and Joanna fell silent. "Something is always 'happening' to you. You attract chaos, Joanna, you always have. But guess what? I don't care. You have Gram and Letty to make you feel better. Letty doesn't rush over to bake *me* scones when I've had a tough day. Eudora doesn't invite *me* to the garden for tea. It's just you, Joanna. The world stops *for you*." Fury sizzled in her chest. "It always has."

"That's not what it is at all." Joanna reached for her sister, but Marcy shrugged her off. Joanna continued anyway.

"Something happened, in Rome. Something bad. Gram doesn't understand, and I didn't have a chance to talk to Letty. I need to talk to you."

"No." Marcy's voice was ice.

"What?"

"Do you know you're still listed as a trustee at Palmetto Holdings? Apparently, it's not enough that we send you quarterly checks for doing nothing. Now, Gram wants you to be a part of the company, the same as me, even though you've never worked there a day in your life."

"Fine. I'll work." Joanna almost shouted. "I'd *love* to work, in fact. I'd be happy—"

But Marcy whirled on her, hissing like an angry cat. "Don't you *dare*. You have everything else—Gram, Letty, and a grand welcome home. But don't you dare interfere with Grandpa's company. Palmetto Holdings is *mine*."

Without another word, Marcy walked the steps to her room, and closed the door.

CHAPTER 12

JOANNA PULLED herself from a restless sleep. She pushed the blanket aside and swung her feet onto the floor, careful not to wake Gracie. Slipping on her robe as she left the room, she closed the door softly behind her and padded down the stairs toward the kitchen. Her cell phone was still in the charger. She unplugged the cord, unlocked the screen, and called the number before she could talk herself out of it.

Francesca answered, her voice rumbly with sleep. "Prego."

"Francesca, it's me."

Instantly alert, Francesca's voice was razor sharp. "Joanna, amica, where are you?"

"I went home, Francesca. Gracie and I are home and we're safe. I just wanted you to know in case you were worried."

"Of *course* I worry. Joey on the corner saw you both getting into a taxi. He also said to me that he heard shouting." The sound muffled as Francesca changed her position. "But I'm glad you went to your family. They will help you." She paused. "What happened?"

Joanna squeezed her eyes shut to keep the image away. Her voice was ragged. "He did it again, Francesca."

Francesca sucked in a breath. "Bastardo! He will regret—"

But Joanna cut her off, surprised at how defeated she sounded. "Don't, Francesca. Just leave it."

"I will *not*."

"I'm not coming back. Not this time."

"You must promise me." Francesca insisted. "You must swear to me so I believe you this time."

Joanna cupped her forehead with the palm of her hand. Her face felt hot and her stomach rolled, as if her body forbade her to speak the words out loud. But beyond the shame was a tiny kernel of strength, a memory of the kind of woman she used to be, and she drew on that. "I am not coming back, Francesca, because this time," Joanna swallowed and forced the words out. "This time, Nicco hit Gracie."

The words hung in the air as Joanna felt the room spin around her.

But she hung on, and she felt the kernel stir.

"What are you going to do now?" Francesca's words were soft.

"I don't know."

"You'll figure it out, bella. You will call me if you need me, just not this early."

A shock ran through Joanna at the mention of the time. She glanced at the clock and heard herself laugh. It felt strange, but good. She hadn't laughed in a long time. "I'll do my best not to bother you before 10:00 o'clock."

"Grazie."

After she hung up, Joanna found a tin of black tea in the pantry and filled the kettle. While she waited for the water to boil, she wandered toward Eudora's sitting room, studying the framed pictures that lined the hallway. Eudora's pictures spanned decades and were mostly candid shots of family—Joanna's mother, Alice, and Alice's little brother, William, as children at the yacht club, securing lines from a tiny sailboat to the dock at the yacht club. A silver-framed picture of Alice on her wedding day, dressed in a soft white gown with a long lace train, looking hopeful and happy. Next to that, a picture of William at The Citadel, impressive in the gray jacket and sharp white pants of his graduation uniform. Further down, were pictures of Joanna and Marcy as children and then again in college. No matter her age, Marcy looked straight at the camera in each picture, completely aware of her surroundings and claiming her right to be there. The pictures of Joanna were more dream-like, as if she didn't know where she was, and she didn't care. So long as Joanna had her art books and her pencils, the world could explode, and she would never know it.

Joanna moved closer to the last picture on the wall, taken in college, before Russell, before Gracie, and before Nicco, when her life was her own. She had just come from the art studio, and her arms were filled with papers and books, but it was the smile on her face that drew Joanna closer. Her lips were parted, as if she were about to laugh and her eyes sparkle with joy. Joanna had no memory of that picture, of that life, and it made her sad now.

When was the last time she was that happy?

In the kitchen, the tea kettle whistled, and Joanna turned toward it. Things would be different now, because she wanted them to be. It wouldn't be easy, but she would do it.

And she would start with her sister.

CHAPTER 13

No one liked the Saturday status meetings, but it was the best way to track the company's projects, so for the past few months Marcy had insisted on them. Everyone—work crews, leasing agents, and office staff—was required to attend and they weren't happy about it. But after the North Charleston closing, things would return to normal.

Marcy entered the conference room and took her place at the head of the table. "I'll make this meeting as short as I can. I know we all have other places to be." She glanced at the first item on the agenda and turned her attention to her senior crew chief. "Pete, how long until Meeting Street is ready for occupancy?"

Pete Blankenship was the best construction manager at Palmetto Holdings. Burly, with tattoos running the length of his arms and across his fingers, he rode a vintage Harley to job sites and worked at least as hard as the crew he managed. He had volunteered to work on the Meeting Street restoration, pulling some of his best crew to work with him, which was surprising because the scope of it was relatively small. At least, it was supposed to be. The building had been condemned, and Marcy bought it for next to nothing, as a way to keep her crews occupied until the industrial property was ready. She planned to transfer everyone to North Charleston as soon as it closed. Skip could keep a skeleton crew on the Meeting Street project, and they'd sell it as soon as it was finished.

"The problem we're facing right now is electrical." Pete ran his knuckles across his stubbly beard. "It's an old building with old wiring. Most of it needs to be replaced."

Marcy ran her finger down the list of expenses. "Did you include the cost of new wiring in your projections?"

"We thought we could salvage what was there."

"And you can't?"

Pete sighed. "If we had to, we could, but it would take time to sort through it all. It's safer to replace it."

"If it's safer to replace it, we should." Marcy made a note of the additional cost, then turned her attention to Skip. "Skip, do you have an estimate for the overrun?"

"I didn't get a chance to include the electrical overrun because I wasn't sure if you'd want to salvage the old wires."

"If it's a question of safety, we're rewiring. Meeting Street may be a small property, but it needs to be done right."

Skip nodded as he flipped the pages in front of him. "I'll have updated numbers by the end of the day."

"What do we have in the way of tenant interest?" Marcy continued.

Skip's straightened in his chair, a broad smile spread across his face. "It's good news—unexpected, actually. The Meeting Street space is unique. And with the renovation, I'm not sure our rent projections are accurate."

"Really? Do you have comps? I'd like to see them."

"Well, that's just it." Skip's smile widened. "There are none. Most of that area is zoned residential."

One of the painters shifted in his seat, hiding a yawn behind his hand. Across the table, a broker pulled out her phone and scrolled through her messages. People were clearly losing interest; Marcy would have to speak to Skip privately.

"Skip, let's —"

"Hello? Is anyone here?" A voice called, loudly, from the lobby.

Decorators with samples and messengers with updated plans were the only people who came by the office on Saturdays, but Marcy couldn't remember a scheduled delivery. She glanced at Andrea, who shrugged and rose to investigate.

With Andrea gone, Marcy tried to continue the meeting. "Skip, we should follow up later—"

The conference room doors swung open, and Joanna entered, her arms overflowing with plastic restaurant bags. "Good morning, everyone." Joanna slid everything onto the middle of the conference table. "I thought you all might be hungry, but you have to help set up first. Can someone find forks and napkins? I forgot to ask for those."

The yawning painter suddenly came to life, jumping from his seat. "I'll get them."

One of the electricians followed him out the door. "I'll help."

"We need plates, too," Joanna called after them.

As Joanna unpacked bags, the rest of the conference room erupted into chaos as everyone stood at once to help.

Joanna's smirk was quick. It disappeared in a flash, but it reminded her of when they were kids, how Letty always gave Joanna special attention. And how Joanna wallowed in it.

"Would you like some breakfast, Marcy? I've brought plenty, as you can see."

Several of the employees glanced at Joanna and smiled. Most of them would remember her, and all of them looked grateful.

Marcy felt her fingers tighten around her pen. "Joanna, can I see you in the hallway, please?"

"Sure, Marcy. Whatever you want." She removed the lid from a tray of cinnamon rolls and called to the room, "There's plenty to eat, and I don't want leftovers, so dig in everyone."

The moment the conference room door shut behind them, Marcy whirled on her sister, hissing like an alley cat. "What are you doing here?"

Joanna met Marcy's fury with ice. "I've been told that I'm part owner of this company, with shares equal to your own. So, I've come to work."

"You don't care about this company."

To Marcy's surprise, Joanna shook her head. "No, I don't." Then her eyes narrowed. "But I do care about being bullied." She straightened her shoulders. "So, I'm going to need my own office. It doesn't have to be next to yours, but it *does* have to be as big."

"This may be a game to you, Joanna, but this company *is my life*."

Andrea chose that moment to emerge from the conference room, her good humor restored with a plate of hot food. "What a great idea it was to bring breakfast to this meeting. Everyone seems much happier. In fact, a few of the painters are actually talking to the sheetrock guys. That never happens." She looked at Marcy, then at Joanna, then back to Marcy. "Did I interrupt something?"

"Of course not." Joanna slipped her arms into one of the ugliest cardigans Marcy had ever seen. "I was just leaving."

"You should stay, Joanna." Andrea urged. "Most of the staff remembers you and they'd want to say hello. I can introduce you to the others."

But Joanna shook her head. "I can't today. Gracie's waiting and we have errands to run." She gave Marcy a pointed look. "But I'll be back on Monday."

Marcy watched her sister leave. Something was different about her sister, but Marcy couldn't put her finger on it. It didn't matter though because there was no way she would let go of this company.

Inside the conference room, the mood had lifted considerably. They'd set up a makeshift buffet, and employees were gathered in small groups, chatting. Betsy Tripe, a broker from Sullivan's Island, chatted with Skip and two of the electricians from Pete's crew. Betsy has always complained about Saturday morning meetings, but she looked almost happy now, with a mug of steaming coffee in her hand and a plate of hot food on the table beside her. On the far side of the room, near the basket of muffins, Pete had finally caught up with Carl from accounting. They seemed to be getting along, which was surprising because Marcy had been called on to settle arguments between them several times. Carl was a stickler for accuracy, and Pete's receipts tended to be nothing more than wadded balls of paper. Maybe catering this meeting wasn't a bad idea after all—it lightened the mood, at least.

Marcy headed to the coffee table and pulled a mug from the stack. "'Morning, Ben."

Ben Appleby was a senior stone mason, an expert at his craft and a generous mentor to the apprentices. Short and wiry, with a full beard and a bald head, he'd been with Palmetto Holdings as long as she could remember. Long enough that he didn't feel the need to hide how much he loathed Saturday work meetings. He reminded her of her grandfather, and his opinion had always meant a lot to her.

He tapped a packet of sugar into his cup. "I see your sister's back."

Marcy nodded as she poured herself a cup of coffee. "For now."

Ben reached for a spoon and stirred. "That's good. You've been taking on too much and if you're not careful, this place will take over your whole life. I've seen it happen."

"I'll be fine. Things are a little busy right now, with the transition, but when Grandpa was here, he worked at least as hard as I am."

"He wasn't by himself," Ben countered. "There was a team behind him, and the projects we took on were smaller than what you got yourself into." He reached for a green apple from the bowl and polished it against his shirt. "This was a good idea, having breakfast delivered. Something your grandmother might do."

"Grandmother? Don't you mean 'grandfather'?"

"No, I absolutely did not." Ben smiled as he slipped the apple into his shirt pocket. Now, let's wrap this thing up. We're burning daylight, just sitting here jawing." Ben snapped a lid on his cup, and went to rejoin his crew, leaving Marcy without any time to ask what he meant by his remark.

In any event, there wasn't much point in continuing the meeting, so she ended early.

The conference room cleared quickly, but Skip stayed behind. He approached Marcy with a binder filled with papers. "I've got the latest pictures of Meeting Street. I had the original molding removed before the electrical work started, and we can reuse most of it. That should save us some money."

His smile was hopeful, and Marcy knew what he wanted. Meeting Street was his first project and it was normal for him to want to hold on to it. Marcy had wanted to keep her first renovation, too, but the fact was that Marcy just couldn't make the numbers work. The company needed to use the proceeds to fund the early stages of development in North Charleston. "Thank you, Skip. I'll take a look, but I'm not sure it will change anything."

"Selling this building would be a big mistake." Skip's abrupt tone startled her; it was just a building, after all, and a minor one at that. Skip blushed at the look Marcy gave him, but his gaze didn't waver. "This is a good property. It has potential."

Marcy suppressed a sigh. If she had mentored him more closely, she could have taught him not to become attached. She softened the blow. "They're all good buildings, Skip, that's why we chose them."

She turned to leave but he stopped her.

"There's something else I want to talk to you about. I came across another property—a plat of three, actually. They all need work, but the owners might be willing to—"

Marcy shook her head. The budget for the rest of the year was razor-thin. "Skip, I appreciate your initiative, but we're shifting our focus to other projects. Everything in the Historic District has already been restored. There's not much left."

"But these aren't in the Historic District, not exactly."

"That doesn't make it better—in fact, that's actually worse."

Marcy's phone beeped with an incoming text from Andrea

and Marcy tapped a quick reply. When she returned to her conversation with Skip, she saw that his expression crumbled, so she softened her tone. "Do you have the listing?"

"No," he stammered. "It's not actually on the market yet."

"Send Andrea what you've got, and I'll look it over if I get a chance."

"I can walk you through it if you want." He offered. "You may not be able to read my notes."

"Now, son, you might want to be content with what you've got." Bruce Calhoun's rich baritone came from the hallway as he leaned against the doorframe of Marcy's office. "Never walk anyone through a presentation. Always let your research speak for itself."

A flash of annoyance crossed Skip's face, and Marcy was surprised. She knew Andrea didn't care for Bruce, but she didn't know anyone else felt the same way. Skip quickly gathered his things and left the room.

Bruce called down the hallway after him, "Give her a few days to look over your proposal, son, then follow up."

After Skip left, Marcy asked, "Have you seen Skip's proposal?"

Bruce shrugged, completely unconcerned. "Nah, no idea what he's working on. The boy could do with a little encouragement, is all."

"Where have you been?" Marcy asked as she watched Bruce scrape up the last of the eggs and load his plate.

"Oh, here and there." He stacked three biscuits and a slab of ham on top of the eggs and slid into a chair. After smoothing a paper napkin across his chest, he looked up, his face pasted with a satisfied smile. "While you all were in here, doing whatever it is that you do, I was out conducting business." Picking up his fork, he pointed it at Marcy. "And what was I doing, you might ask? Well, I'll tell you: I was out getting our first tenant for North Charleston."

"That's sounds like good news, Bruce, but the warehouses are occupied for the next four years. I've read the leases." Marcy refilled her coffee and joined him at the table.

Bruce jabbed a biscuit with a plastic knife and split it open. A tendril of steam rose from the middle. "I'm not talking about a tenant for the warehouses. I'm talking about a tenant for the strip mall you want to build on the adjacent land."

Marcy set her cup on the table. "We don't have any space to offer a new tenant. We don't have a structure, or permitting to build one. We don't even own the property yet, Bruce."

Bruce scooped a knob of butter from the tub and spread it across the surface of his biscuit. "Sometimes, the first tenant can grease the wheels a little with the city. Especially if you have the right tenant. Which we do."

"How can you offer a legal contract on property we don't own?" Marcy persisted.

Bruce shrugged as he reached for a fork. "Well, it's not exactly a *formal* contract, just a handshake agreement between fishing buddies, you might say. I offered terms that he couldn't pass up. In return, he's going to help us get permitting."

Goosebumps rose on Marcy's arm. Her plan for that project was very clear: build the structure first, gather the tenants second. Bruce knew that. His actions, in speaking for the company, had opened it up to tremendous liability if they couldn't deliver

Marcy leaned forward. "You don't speak for this company, Bruce. I do. You will tell that to your 'fishing buddy' and next time you will check with me before offering terms to anyone."

Bruce glanced up, his eyes sharp. "I had an opportunity, and I took it. The anchor tenants set the tone for the development, everyone knows that. And the first tenant to sign gets special allowances. Everyone knows that, too."

But Marcy wouldn't budge. The reputation of her grandfather's company was at stake. "That's not the way we do things."

Bruce's expression hardened. "Look. You hired me to do a job, and you need to let me do it."

The air in the room crackled with tension as they stared at each other. She should have fired him on the spot for going behind her back, but the property was set to close in less than a week, and it was too late to hire another consultant.

She shook her head, refusing to compromise her principles. "We don't do business that way. All contracts go *through* me and all offers are approved *by* me. Before they are offered. Tell your 'fishing buddy' that we don't have a deal."

Bruce's fingers tightened around his plastic fork, though his tone was even. "You're the boss."

Marcy returned to her office, leaving Bruce to finish his breakfast in the conference room. He'd told her what he did this time; next time, he might not. And if this was the way he did business, she would need to watch him more closely, and let him go as soon as the property was theirs.

CHAPTER 14

"IT SHOULDN'T BE TOO MUCH LONGER, Mrs. Reed." The receptionist cradled the phone against her shoulder, raising her voice over the din of children in the play corner. "Dr. Morrison is running late—again." Turning her attention back to her work, she finished a call just as another rang through.

Dr. Morrison had been their pediatrician when Joanna and her sister were younger. He seemed old then and to be honest, Joanna was surprised he was still practicing. But the school required a complete checkup before they allowed Gracie into the classroom, and there wasn't time to find another doctor before Monday. Eudora suggested Dr. Morrison, and luckily, they had an opening. Closing the cover of a rumpled parenting magazine, Joanna tossed it back onto the table with the others. She glanced at Gracie, who had made friends with another little girl in the toy corner and it made Joanna smile. Hopefully, moving to Charleston wouldn't be as difficult for Gracie as moving to Rome had been.

"Reed?" A harried woman in a lab coat printed with cartoon characters glanced up from a clipboard. "Gracie Reed?"

"Over here."

They were escorted to a small room, and Joanna settled into a green plastic chair as Gracie hopped onto the exam table.

The nurse recorded Gracie's temperature and blood pressure, then closed the folder and slipped it into the plastic holder on the door. "Everything looks normal, Dr. Morrison will be right in." She paused with her hand on the door and offered an apologetic smile. "It's not usually this busy."

When they were alone, Gracie rubbed her arm, her brows drawn together in a scowl. "I didn't like that squeezy machine."

"Nobody does, Goose." Joanna brushed a strand of hair from her daughter's face. "Even grown-ups don't like it."

The knock on the door was sharp, and a doctor entered, her attention on Gracie's chart. But it wasn't the elderly Dr. Morrison that Joanna expected. Instead, it was a woman about Joanna's age, her dark hair swept into a loose ponytail. Trailing from the side pocket of her lab coat was a streamer of puppy stickers.

Glancing up, she smiled at Gracie first. "Hi, Gracie, I'm Dr. Morrison. I hear you need a checkup for school."

Gracie's attention was locked onto the stickers.

Dr. Morrison followed Gracie's gaze and laughed. "Gets them every time. No one pays attention to me if there are stickers close by." Turning, she offered her hand to Joanna. "I'm Dr. Morrison."

"Courtney? Courtney Morrison?"

A shadow of confusion crossed Dr. Morrison's face as she regarded Joanna. After a moment, her expression cleared. With recognition came a smile that crinkled the corners of her eyes. "Joanna? Joanna Rutledge?"

"It's Joanna Reed now, and this is my daughter, Gracie." Joanna shook Courtney's hand.

"Your daughter? Has it been that long?" Courtney clasped her hands over her heart. "Where does the time go? It feels like we were just in sorority."

Courtney had been a senior when they met, only months from graduating and moving on to medical school when someone noticed that she was short three art credits. The only class available was an eight o'clock survey class, which Joanna loved, and Courtney loathed. With a full class load, and labs in between, Courtney was dangerously overscheduled. It was Joanna's class notes that helped Courtney pass and graduate on time.

"You became a pediatrician, just like you wanted. That's fantastic. I'm really happy for you."

Dr. Morrison offered a wry smile. "It's worse than that, actually—I own the whole place. I bought the practice from my father last year."

"Seriously? That's great news. I would love to catch up if you have the time," Joanna offered. "I can leave my phone number at the front desk. Call if you want to have coffee."

"I'd love that." Courtney crossed to the sink and turned on the faucet. She addressed Gracie with a smile. "I'm happy to meet you, Miss Gracie. Your mama and I go way back." Pulling a paper towel from the dispenser, she dried her hands and glanced at Joanna. "They said this appointment was for school, but hasn't school started already? It's almost Halloween."

"We just arrived," Joanna said. "We've moved back to Charleston."

"That's wonderful. Welcome back."

"We're going shopping after this," Gracie chimed in,

finding her voice at last. "I have to wear a dress every day. A special one."

"Uniforms," Joanna corrected. "She's enrolled at Santee."

The exam was routine, and after listening to Gracie's heartbeat, Courtney draped her stethoscope around her neck. "You seem very healthy to me, Gracie."

Thrilled that the exam was over, Gracie swung her feet over the table. "Can I have a sticker now?"

"Almost. Let me just check your spine. It won't take but a minute." Dr. Morrison rubbed her hands together to warm them. "Is it okay if I lift the back of your shirt so I can see how strong your bones are?"

Gracie stiffened.

"It's okay, Goose." Joanna laid her hand on her daughter's knee. "You can let Dr. Morrison look."

Joanna's pulse pounded in her ears as the doctor lifted Gracie's shirt because she knew what was there.

Courtney's smile faded immediately. Yellowed and splattered with purple, the bruise Nicco had inflicted on her daughter covered most of her daughter's shoulder blade. The doctor's eyes narrowed, and her gaze cut to Joanna. Joanna looked away, humiliated.

Immediately, Courtney stepped between Joanna and Gracie. "Gracie, do you mind if I take a closer look at this?"

Gracie's eyes widened, and her gaze darted to Joanna just before Courtney blocked her view.

"It's okay, Gracie. I'm right here." Joanna's heart skipped as she lost sight of her daughter.

Courtney addressed Gracie in a gentle voice. "Gracie, I need to know where this bruise came from. If you want to tell me in secret, we can go into another room."

Gracie replied, her voice halting and unsure. "Nicco was mad because I talked too much."

Joanna's hands began to tremble, so she clenched them together in her lap.

"Nicco? Who's Nicco?" Courtney asked.

Gracie's voice was inaudible, and Joanna's body tensed. They were going to take Gracie from her. Friend or not, Courtney would do her job and would notify CPS. And how would Joanna explain that bruise?

"Does he live with you?" Courtney continued.

"Not anymore. Mommy took us away."

Jagged images of that morning in Rome flashed in her mind and Joanna relived the moment again. Her baby girl sprawled on the floor, howling in terror. Nicco's hand curled into a fist, his body stiff with rage. Joanna dug her fingernails into her palms to distract herself from what was coming. She concentrated on the blood pressure machine affixed to the wall, counting the dials, noticing the nicks on the front, and the stitching on the seam on the cuff. Anything to stop the images that would come next, but they came anyway. The *thwap* of Nicco's fist punching her daughter's little body echoed in Joanna's head and her heart shattered.

"Okay, Gracie, that's enough for now." The doctor's voice was crisp, professional.

The tissue crinkled as Gracie hopped off the exam table.

"Mommy?" Gracie's voice was unsure.

But Joanna couldn't move. What had she done to her baby girl? What had she allowed to happen?

Dr. Morrison glanced at Joanna, then turned her attention back to Gracie. "There are lots of puppy stickers at the front desk, even more than what I have in my pocket Why don't you look through them while I talk to your mommy?"

As the door closed behind Gracie, Courtney turned to face Joanna, her expression guarded. "I am a mandatory reporter, Joanna, which means I am legally required to report all cases of child abuse or neglect to the state. I need you to tell me the absolute truth. How did Gracie get that bruise on her back?"

Joanna drew a breath but there wasn't enough air in the room to fill her lungs. She swallowed and forced the words out. "Four days ago, my ex-fiancé hit Gracie. We left right after it happened." Those were the barest of facts and her ears rang at the hollowness of it. She was a terrible mother.

"Where is your fiancé now?"

"We left him in Rome."

"Does he know where you are now?"

"No and I don't plan to tell him."

"Do you plan to have *any* further contact with him?"

"Absolutely not." Joanna felt her hands cramp and she realized she'd been clenching her fists.

"Has he done this before?" The question hung in the air.

"No, of course not." The reply was automatic, but the truth was that she didn't know for sure. Maybe he had, and maybe Nicco had threatened Gracie to keep her quiet. The thought was like a knife in her soul. A wave of nausea burned her throat, and Joanna dropped her gaze to her lap. Her voice was barely a whisper, a weak defense. "We left, Gracie and me. We left right away, with nothing. All of our clothes, everything we own is still in that apartment."

Joanna focused on the blood pressure machine on the wall again. The seam on the cuff was crooked and the disorder bothered her. She wanted to smooth the edges and tuck it neatly into its pouch.

"Joanna." Dr. Morrison's voice was sharp.

Startled, Joanna looked at Dr. Morrison.

"I asked: does your family know?"

Joanna shook her head. Her vision blurred as a tear fell. She scrubbed it away with the heel of her palm.

"I have to ask one last question, Joanna." Courtney's tone softened, and Joanna's heart squeezed at the unexpected kindness. She didn't deserve it. "Is Nicco Gracie's biological father?"

"No. Gracie's father left when she was a baby. I haven't seen him in years."

Courtney scribbled notes on Gracie's chart. The sound of her pen scratching the page filled the quiet room and Joanna wondered what they were going to do to her.

"You should tell your family. They can help you."

Shaking her head, Joanna replied, with absolute conviction. "They can't do anything." She'd tried to tell Marcy, but her sister wouldn't listen. And Eudora still thought that Joanna was married to Russell.

"Gracie is here for a school physical, so I'm assuming you're here to stay."

"That's right."

"Okay." Courtney closed the cover of Gracie's folder and tucked it into her pile. "This is what we're going to do. Gracie seems okay right now, but if she starts having nightmares or if her behavior seems off, I want you to contact me right away. I can recommend an excellent child therapist, if she needs one. When does she start school?"

"Monday." Joanna's voice cracked, so she cleared her throat and began again. "She starts on Monday."

Courtney nodded. "If you ever need to talk, I want you to call me. There are resources for you, too."

Joanna stood. Her knees threatened to buckle, so she

placed her palm on the exam table to steady herself. "Thank you, but I'll be okay. We'll both be okay."

In the lobby, Joanna found Gracie shifting through the stickers and bargaining with the receptionist. "Can I trade a blue puppy and this rainbow sticker for a glitter fairy?"

"Well, I don't know," the receptionist tapped her chin with her finger as she considered. "The glitter stickers are pretty special. We usually save them for kids who have gotten a shot. Did you get a shot?"

"No." Gracie shook her head, her face clouded with thought. Then she brightened. "But I start school tomorrow."

"Monday," Joanna corrected.

"Monday," Gracie agreed.

"You do? Well, that's pretty special." She pushed her chair back and opened a deep desk drawer. "In that case, you should have two. And you can take a prize bag from the treasure box, too." She pulled out another box, this one decorated with plastic jewels and glitter.

Gracie gasped.

In the end, they left the office with three prize bags and a fistful of fairy stickers.

"You're quite the negotiator, Gracie," Joanna commented.

Gracie nodded absently, her attention on her stickers. "We need a kitten, Mommy. A real one."

CHAPTER 15

EUDORA'S HOME was in the oldest part of Charleston where tourists wandered cobblestoned alleys and peeped through vine-covered gates into private gardens, hoping to glimpse the fairy tale inside. Old Charleston lived in this neighborhood, and Eudora had no wish to ever live anywhere else.

When she married Brock, she married his family. Their history became her history, and she became its curator, whether she wanted to be or not. Those first years of marriage were difficult, and Eudora had shuttered the memory of it years ago. Brock's mother was a horrible woman, conniving and cruel and Eudora had been too naïve to fight back. Until she met Letty; Letty had always been her truest friend.

At the time of her marriage, it had been customary for a new bride to incorporate a few personal touches to the garden—a preference for color in seasonal flowers, or perhaps a favorite rose, but Eudora had done more than that. When her mother-in-law died, Eudora wasted no time hiring a team of gardeners to transform the tangled garden into something else. When they were finished, the garden was her own, filled with roses, vining wisteria, spring bulbs and summer flowers.

She had claimed the garden in a way she couldn't claim the house. Her garden had become her haven, a place to rest when she was tired, a place to think, a place to visit with friends. It hadn't gotten much use lately, but everything would change now that her girls were home again, where they belonged.

Eudora unwrapped the cashmere blanket from her legs and tossed it to the side. She needed to think, and she couldn't do that bundled up like an old woman. She had thought to be outside no more than an hour, but her apprehension had grown as the morning waned.

Perhaps directing Joanna to bring food to Marcy's meeting this morning had been a mistake. Palmetto Holdings had been under Marcy's care since Brock's death, and it consumed her as it did him. Eudora had hoped that Joanna's arrival would relieve Marcy of some of the burden she placed upon herself. If only she could get the girls to talk to each other, but they'd barely spoken since Joanna's arrival. Eudora had hoped the food she insisted Joanna take to the meeting would be the gesture they needed to help things along.

The thump of a car door in the courtyard drew Eudora from her thoughts. Marcy emerged from her car frowning, her face set in hard lines. So that was the way of it then. With a deep sigh, Eudora gathered her strength as Marcy pounded across the garden path, the gravel crunching under her heels.

By the time Marcy joined Eudora on the piazza, her face was flushed, and her eyes snapped with fury. "Gram, did you send Joanna to interrupt my meeting this morning? She wouldn't have thought of something like that on her own."

So, it was to be a battle then.

Eudora tapped the seat cushion beside her. "Sit. You should join me for tea. The pot has grown cold, but I believe your newest pretend-housekeeper is still here. I could ask her to bring a fresh pot."

"'Pretend housekeeper'" Marcy echoed. "You knew?"

"Of course I knew."

"You know it wasn't my decision to let her go." At least Marcy had the decency to look embarrassed. The key to keeping her oldest granddaughter cowed was appealing to her distorted sense of responsibility.

"Why did you do it, Gram? Why did you send Joanna to the status meeting? I've told you how pressed for time we are. She sent everything into chaos, like she always does." Marcy sagged with fatigue and Eudora's heart went out to her. Marcy looked like her grandfather, if only he'd had her work ethic. "I know you wanted me to include Joanna in the business, but she doesn't fit in anywhere."

"Palmetto Holdings is a family business, and your sister is family. I suggest you *find* a place for her, just as your grandfather did for you." Eudora's words were sharp, and Marcy flinched, as she was meant to. Eudora would not allow the sisters to be divided.

Marcy looked away, so Eudora softened her tone. "You remind me of your grandfather, you know." Marcy worshiped that man, though, Heaven knows, he didn't deserve it. "It's true," Eudora continued. "Every Saturday morning, you met him at the bottom of the stairs, ready to follow him wherever he went: to the golf course, to the yacht club, to the office on Saturday mornings. Since you were ten years old, you've known what you wanted to do with your life, and that knowledge makes your whole life easier."

Marcy scoffed, but softly enough that Eudora could overlook it.

"It's true, my dear. Life is so much harder for those who

wander. Your sister reminds me of your mother, always restless, always searching for something but not finding it. That's a difficult way to live." Eudora laid a hand on Marcy's arm to still the response she knew was coming. "I know you believe your sister to be scattered and maybe a bit selfish, but things are never what they seem, dear girl."

A memory of her husband presented itself, and Eudora watched, unable to stop it. The yacht club swimming pool where her son William had been forced to take a swim test before he began sailing lessons. William had always been scared of the water, a trait Brock dismissed as weak and effeminate, and he assigned himself the task of toughening up his son. To her shame, Eudora had not stopped him. William's preference for books over football, caring for animals over hunting them had made him an outcast among the other boys. The sooner this could be addressed, the more normal his life would be.

Brock used his position as commodore of the yacht club to order the pool open one night, after hours, for the test. Eudora watched her husband's anger turn to rage as William cried, pleading for his father to change his mind. The fact that a few of Brock's friends had gathered beside the pool and witnessed the display only made it worse. Brock pushed William into the deep water, watching him flail, furious at his son for being imperfect. After what seemed like an eternity, someone pulled her son from the water and wrapped a towel around his heaving shoulders. William was only six years old.

Eudora touched her pulsing temple with her fingertips. Knowing that she'd do things differently now, if given the chance, was no comfort to her. William never trusted her again.

"Gram?" Marcy's voice pulled Eudora back to the present. "Why are you welcoming Joanna back, at all?"

Straightening her back, Eudora regarded her granddaughter. "Sometimes people make mistakes, and they need to be forgiven, even if they don't ask to be. I won't live forever, Marcy, and when I go, Joanna and that baby will be the only family you have left."

Marcy rolled her eyes, a childish display that suddenly irritated Eudora. Frustrated with a situation she couldn't control, Eudora used the only leverage she had. "I see that I must remind you of the terms of your grandfather's trust. You and Joanna are equal partners. Now that she has come home, I insist that you find a place for her at Palmetto Holdings. Because, as the founding member and majority owner of the company, I wish it to be so."

Marcy rose from the bench, her voice cool, the opportunity for closeness lost. "I don't need to be reminded that Palmetto Holdings doesn't belong to me. You've always made that very clear. So, I'll do what you say because I have no choice." She turned away. "If you will excuse me, I need to get back to my office."

Eudora leaned her head against the back of the chair and listened to the stones on the path crunch under Marcy's feet as she walked away. Eudora had won the battle but feared she was close to losing the war.

CHAPTER 16

"Do you want to come with us, Gram?" Joanna called down the hallway. "We're going to shop for Gracie's school uniforms."

No answer.

Joanna added a healthy pour of cream to the cup of coffee she'd just brewed and listened for her grandmother's response. Her grandmother wasn't one to shout, so Joanna didn't really expect a reply. She replaced the carton of cream in the refrigerator and closed the door with her hip.

"Mommy, can we go now?" Gracie rushed into the kitchen, clutching Lendard to her chest. "I want to show Lendard all my pretty dresses."

"Not yet, Goose." Joanna glanced at the clock. "The store isn't open yet." The only store in town that sold school uniforms closed every day for lunch. "Go outside and play—but stay in the yard. I need to check on Gram."

It was a short walk from the kitchen to her grandmother's office, and Joanna sipped her coffee as she went. "Gram?" The door was ajar, and Joanna pushed it with her elbow, speaking as it opened. "Gracie and I are—"

Instead of sitting at her desk as Joanna thought she would be, Eudora was seated in one of her guest chairs by the window, her head resting against the back, her eyes closed. Joanna was shocked at how frail she looked.

"Are you okay?"

"Yes, of course." Eudora's voice was a croak. She opened her eyes and shifted her position in the chair. "I was just resting my eyes."

But Joanna didn't believe it. Eudora's smile was brittle and her face was pale. Joanna went to her grandmother's side, resisting the urge to check her forehead for fever, as Letty would have done. "Would you like to take a nap? Or read in your room? I can open the doors to the piazza to let in the harbor breeze."

"I don't need a nap," Eudora bristled. "As it happens, I've had a very trying discussion with your sister. About you and your role in the company."

"I've been meaning to talk to you about that." Joanna dropped into the chair opposite her grandmother. She traced the edge of the cushion with her fingertip as she considered her words. "Palmetto Holdings has always been more Marcy's thing than mine and I'm not sure I want to work there. So, after Gracie is settled in school, I'll find a job outside the company. I think that would be best for everyone."

"Nonsense." Eudora's expression hardened and Joanna's hope that she would somehow make her grandmother understand dissolved. "Palmetto Holdings is a family business. It was your grandfather's wish that both of you girls share the company. Marcy understands that."

"I don't know, Gram. You didn't see Marcy's face when I

brought breakfast to the meeting this morning. She wasn't happy."

"Your sister has had a complete change of heart since our discussion." Eudora looked away, and Joanna suspected that she wasn't being entirely truthful.

Joanna shifted in her chair as she realized the implications of what her grandmother had done. If Marcy had changed her mind, it was because Eudora had forced her to. The coffee sloshed in her mug as she turned. "You didn't."

"Speak to your sister?" Eudora's eyes were sharp. "I most certainly did."

Eudora sat, stone-faced and silent, giving the impression that she believed, without question, that she had done the right thing, when she had actually made things worse.

Joanna sighed. She didn't care about her grandfather's company like Marcy did. It didn't matter in the slightest if Marcy controlled it all. Rising from the chair, she smoothed her capris. Though freshly laundered, the fabric still looked dingy, and the tear she'd sewn days before had begun to unravel.

"Joanna?"

"Yes?"

"I believe you've gotten your money's worth from those pants, dear heart. I suggest you find something else to wear."

Joanna hesitated. Surely Eudora remembered the conversation they'd had just three days ago. It was Eudora herself who had arranged the delivery of pajamas from Chastains'. "We didn't bring luggage with us. I mentioned that at afternoon tea in the garden. Do you remember?

Eudora furrowed her brow but said nothing. Her confusion was unsettling, but Joanna brushed it away.

"You know what? It doesn't matter. Gracie and I can go

uniform shopping another day. We'll stay home today and keep you company."

"Nonsense." Eudora's voice was sharp. "I don't need a babysitter, Joanna. I had hoped you, of all people, would understand that I don't wish to be coddled."

"Okay, If you're sure." Joanna bent down to kiss her grandmother's cheek. "The pretend-housekeeper should be arriving soon. We'll see you when we get back."

CHAPTER 17

"Are you still here?" Andrea poked her head inside Marcy's office. "You're going to be late to the brunch."

"I'm coming." Marcy scanned her inbox for email that needed immediate attention. "Did they deliver the gift?"

"Right here." Andrea waved a square package wrapped in blue paper. The silver ribbon trailed behind. "All you have to do is sign the card."

"Great. Thank you." Marcy scribbled her name at the bottom of the monogrammed card and handed it back. "What did we get her?"

"Something nice," Andrea assured her. "Do you want me to call for a car?"

"No, it's not far." Marcy switched off her monitor and retrieved her shoes from under her desk. "It's a beautiful day, and I'll enjoy the walk."

"It's a million degrees out there." Andrea glanced out the window, dubious. "You'll wilt before you get there."

But Marcy wouldn't be swayed. "The restaurant is only a few blocks away, and I've been looking forward to a walk down Church Street."

A walk in her favorite neighborhood was just what she needed to clear her head. She'd been jumpy and short-tempered lately, something that had become obvious at this morning's status meeting. She shouldn't have let Joanna get to her like that. And she shouldn't have rushed home to confront Eudora, either.

On her way out, Marcy hesitated at the door. Things had been crazy in the past six months, and Andrea had done more than anyone to make sure nothing was forgotten. "Things will slow down around here when North Charleston closes, and we'll be back to normal."

To her surprise, Andrea frowned. "That's not what Bruce says."

Marcy stopped, her hand on the doorknob. "What does Bruce say?"

"Oh no, not this time. Leave work behind for once." Andrea shooed her out the door. "You're going to be late and Cecily will have my head."

It was a good decision to walk. As Marcy strolled along her favorite section of Church Street, she felt the tension lift from her shoulders. Every house in this neighborhood had a window box at street level, glossy black boxes whose plantings changed with the season. Tucked behind custom iron gates, private gardens were framed with orange mums and hanging ferns. Overhead, a canopy of trees filtered the bright southern sun through a lace of Spanish moss, casting the cobblestoned street in dappled shadow. Marcy paused under the deep shadow of an oak tree, closed her eyes, and breathed in the scent of her home. The sweet scent of jasmine and the sharp tang of freshly laid pine straw, the salty air, and the mossy cobblestones. She held it all close to her heart. She knew every inch of this city and she loved every bit of it. By the time she reached the end of the street, she felt lighter. The confrontation she'd had with her sister at the morning's meeting and the disagreement she had with Eudora at noon seemed less important, less weighty

She was ready for Jenna's party.

The party was really a brunch, a going-away party for a younger sorority sister whose husband, Steven, had bought a law practice in Oregon. The rumor, direct from Cecily, was that he bought the practice without telling her. Worse, Cecily said that Jenna had flatly refused to move, threatening to live with her parents rather than "slog to some outpost in the wilderness."

"No way I'm missing *that* party," Cecily had said when they'd received the invitation. "After four attempts, Steven had finally passed the bar exam. Reason enough to celebrate —but buying a law practice on the west coast without telling Jenna? There's going to be fireworks, and I want to see them."

Marcy's phone buzzed with a text from Cecily. *Where are you??*

She typed a quick reply. *Just arriving now.*

As she entered the restaurant, an explosion of laughter erupted from a table near the back, where six of her favorite sisters crowded around a table meant for four. The table's surface was a jumble of half-filled wine glasses and plates of nibbled appetizers. Cecily caught her eye and waved. Marcy slid her present on the gift table and made her way to the back, happy to see her friends.

"Marcy!" Jenna's squeal sliced through the hum of conversation, stopping Marcy in her tracks.

Jenna Beaumont stood like a beacon in the center of the room, wearing a bright pink baby doll dress, with a paper crown on her head and a yellow feather boa draped around her shoulders. She'd been a sorority sister since sophomore year, only because—according to Cecily—Jenna was a legacy, and the chapter was forced to offer a bid. But, also according to Cecily, Jenna only accepted when her first choice rejected her. Twice.

"You're late, but I'll forgive you." After a quick air kiss, Jenna made a point to look over Marcy's shoulder. "Didn't you bring someone?" she drawled. "Marcy, the invitation said, 'plus one'."

"I did see that, Jenna. I came alone."

"Oh, my. You still don't have anyone special in your life?" Jenna placed her hand over her heart. "I only ask because I'm concerned. You don't come to our chapter meetings anymore, even the mandatory ones. We are alumni, after all, and we should set an example for the younger girls. They do rely on us, you know."

Marcy smiled and deftly changed the subject. "How exciting that Steven has his own practice. I'm sure you must be excited."

Jenna flicked a blonde curl from her shoulder. "Steven is there now, you know. He says Inlet Beach is the *cutest* little town, very up-and-coming. It was a complete surprise to me, of course, especially since Daddy had offered him a junior position in his office. Daddy's a senior partner, you know."

"You've mentioned that before," Marcy said, dryly.

But Jenna continued as if Marcy hadn't spoken, which was just as well because it took the pressure off of Marcy to keep up her end of the conversation. "Steven has the only law office in town. In fact, he's just gotten his first client. Won't tell me any details, of course—attorney-client privilege and all that." She took a deep breath and fluttered her fingers in front of her face as if the details were too overwhelming.

"We'll probably buy a house on the beach. Y'all can visit anytime you like—there'll be plenty of room."

"That's wonderful, Jenna. When are you moving?"

"Not until March." Jenna's smile faltered, ever so slightly "I'm staying at Mama and Daddy's until then."

Cecily's theory was that Jenna was hiding at her parents' house, reviewing her options, and getting legal advice from her father. She predicted that Jenna would never make the trip. "I can't see Jenna living more than ten miles from her mother," Cecily had said, and Marcy had begun to believe her. Jenna's eyes were too bright, like a trapped animal's, and her words were too rushed, as if she were trying to convince herself.

There wasn't much to say after that, so Jenna turned her attention to someone else, gushing about the gift they had laid on the growing pile. Marcy saw her opportunity, and joined her friends in the back.

At the head of the table, Cecily lounged against the back of a wrought iron chair, fanning herself with a menu. She'd dressed entirely in black, despite the temperature.

"You're late," Cecily declared. "You missed the paper crowns Jenna made us all wear. There was a ceremony and everything. *That* was fun. Apparently, we are all her loyal subjects now."

"It's a shame I missed that." Marcy dragged a chair next to her friend.

Cecily lowered her sunglasses and glared at Marcy over the frame. "You look terrible."

"You should talk. It's eighty-five degrees outside, and you look like you're going to a funeral."

"Just like Johnny Cash, baby," Cecily took off her sunglasses and raised her tea in a mock toast.

"How are you doing, Cee?" Marcy settled into her place and signaled for the server.

Cecily lifted a mass of glorious red hair off her neck. "Well, let's see. I am currently unemployed, but that's okay. I have an interview at another dinky gallery, but at least this one is a little closer to the peninsula. The pay is nothing, and I'm not even sure they have air conditioning." She interrupted herself when the waiter appeared. "Unsweetened tea, please. Extra lemon."

The waiter nodded and turned his attention to Marcy. "Tea for you as well?"

"Yes, thank you." Marcy turned her attention back to Cecily, with an offer. "Cee, another gallery like that last one will be just as bad. You'll hate working there, and the pay will be dismal —again. So, I have an idea: why don't you come work for me, at least for a little while? I can find something for you to do until you figure out what you really want to do."

Cecily stopped fanning and gave Marcy a pointed look. "You can find a job suitable for me, but not for your own sister?"

Marcy shrugged to cover her embarrassment. One of Cecily's super-powers was that she could assess and evaluate any situation. Marcy reached for her water glass. "I like you better."

But what Cecily said was true, as usual: Marcy had no intention of making things easier for her sister. If she were honest with herself, she might consider that she was still punishing Joanna for leaving, and that, at some point, she would have to stop.

The waiter came with drinks, and Cecily waited for the server to set them down before continuing. "Seriously, I don't understand all the friction between you two. Didn't you used to be closer?"

"Sure, we were, growing up." Marcy squeezed lemon into her tea, a little harder than she needed to. "But then she married an idiot, then moved away."

A bray of laughter came from across the room.

Cecily slipped her sunglasses back on. "Sally's here."

Sally Preston had been their sorority's most enthusiastic member. She distributed rule books to new pledges, sweat-shirts to new sisters, and scheduled every activity down to the minute. Her intentions were good—she'd raised money for charity and organized food drives—but her energy was exhausting. It didn't take long before even the newest members walked the other way when they heard her coming.

"Marcy Rutledge, I thought that was you," Sally made a beeline for their table.

"Oh, no, not this time." Cecily muttered as she rose to leave.

"Don't you dare," Marcy hissed through a pasted-on smile as she grabbed Cecily's arm.

As Sally approached, she adjusted her plaid headband, a nervous habit she'd had since she was a pledge. "Hey, y'all." She wedged a chair between Marcy and Cecily. "Marcy, I heard you'd been invited, but I was sure you wouldn't come. You never do." She tilted her head in mock concern. "Seems like we see you less and less, doesn't it, Cecily?"

"It does. It really does," Cecily agreed, her eyes sparked with mischief, despite Marcy's glare.

"How have you been, Sally?" Marcy reached for her glass, her fingers sliding across the condensation.

"Oh wonderful. It's all good news," she bubbled. "Where should I start?" She drew a deep breath. "Boomer's dealership is leading the Southeast region in used car sales." She tapped the tabletop with her index finger for emphasis. "That's where the real profit is, you know. Used cars, because the depreciation has already been taken. And, of course, we get to drive the very latest pre-owned models. It's one of the perks of his job."

"You don't say," Cecily said, her eyes dull.

Marcy glanced down the length of the table. "Donna!" She poked Cecily. "Why didn't you tell me Donna was here?" She turned to Sally. "Sally, Donna's here, all the way from Raleigh."

Donna Babcock, a sorority sister from Marcy's own pledge class, called down the length of the table. She pushed back her chair and came to join them. "I didn't see you down here, girls. Guess I need to pay more attention. How are y'all?"

Eight months pregnant and clearly miserable in the heat, she wore a gauzy linen dress more suited to August than October, and her face glistened with perspiration.

"I'd heard you moved." Cecily offered.

Donna nodded. "I did. Finally got my Ph.D. from Duke, thank you very much. Paul and I just moved to Raleigh this past spring."

Signaling a passing waiter, Donna palmed the last roll and offered him the empty basket. "Would you bring more bread on your way back, please?"

"Are you sure you want that bread?" Sally interrupted, with a concerned frown. "In each of my pregnancies, I didn't allow myself to gain any more than twelve pounds. It's easier to lose the weight if you don't gain it in the first place."

"Well, Sally. I'll just keep that in mind." Donna speared a knob of butter with her knife and spread it across her roll. "By the way, I just spoke with Jenna, poor thing. She's got so many questions about layettes and strollers. I can't answer because this is my first." She offered a slight shrug. "And her mama can't help her because things have changed so much since she had Jenna."

"If only someone could help her," Cecily reached for a napkin to hide her smile.

"Jenna?" Sally glanced around the room. "I spoke with her just a minute ago, and she didn't mention a thing about needing help, bless her heart. Where is she?"

"Still at the head table, I think." Donna pointed with her knife. "Look for the yellow crown and the bright pink dress. You can't miss her."

"Well, she can't navigate this pregnancy on her own, can she? I have four children myself, and each one is a tiny miracle. I feel sure I can help her out. If you'll excuse me." Sally rose from her chair and threaded her way across the room.

She had barely left the table when Donna's smile unfurled, wide across her face.

"That was so mean," Marcy laughed. "You know Jenna won't have any idea what Sally's talking about."

Donna popped a corner of bread into her mouth and chewed. "I didn't like her then, and I don't like her now. And I *certainly* don't need her dieting advice. When we all lived in the sorority house, I had the unfortunate luck to be closest to the bathroom. I've heard that girl throw up more times than I can count."

"I personally think gaining *only* twelve pounds during a pregnancy isn't nearly enough. That can't be healthy." Cecily reached for a roll when the waiter brought the basket. "I can gain that much in a weekend."

Donna nodded. "Yup, I gained ten pounds before the stick turned color—just that fast." She snapped her fingers. "Being pregnant in ninety-five degrees is miserable, and carbs are my only comfort. If this baby doesn't come soon, I'll be as fat as Clara Buix."

Cecily hooted. "Clara Buix! I haven't heard that name in forever. Remember that time she made us scrub the bathroom with a toothbrush because she found a bottle of tequila under the radiator? Whatever happened to that harpy? Does anyone know?"

"Don't remind me." Donna rolled her eyes and groaned. "I can't even *look* at tile grout anymore without getting dry heaves. Clara Buix is the reason I have a regular cleaning service."

Marcy offered a weak defense because the observation Cecily made about Marcy being purposefully hurtful to Joanna still stung. "She had a difficult job. I'm not sure any of us could do it any better."

Donna lowered her roll and stared at Marcy. "You can't be serious. That woman was as crazy as a bedbug. I can't believe the college let her continue after what she put our pledge class through."

Cecily chimed in. "Listen to Donna, Marcy. She's the one with the fancy Ph.D."

Donna raised her glass in a toast to herself. "That's right. All it took was eight years of my life and a staggering amount of student loan debt. Now, I can officially diagnose *all* the crazy."

"And what's your opinion of this group?" Marcy leaned back in her chair and surveyed Jenna's going away party. The guest of honor holding court in the center of the room, with a wilted paper crown on her head.

"Oh, honey, it's bad."

When the party had thinned out and it was clearly time to

leave, Donna leaned across the table. "Y'all know it's been far too long since we've been together. You want to go take this party to the River Rock and see who's playing? I could use a night out—a good one."

Simultaneously, Cecily said, "Absolutely!" and Marcy said, "Sorry."

Both women looked at Marcy, disappointment clear on their faces. But the closing for the North Charleston property was just days away, and Marcy couldn't shake the feeling that something was off, and this property was too important to lose. She needed to return to work to look at the closing documents one more time.

"I'm sorry," Marcy said again. "I have to take a raincheck. Some other time."

Donna dug in her purse for her wallet. "You know I'm just here until tomorrow, don't you? After that, I'm driving right back to Raleigh."

"I know. I promise I'll do my best to see you before you leave town."

Cecily dropped her credit card on the stack. "Well, I'll go with you," she declared. "I love the River Rock. Best cheeseburgers in all of Charleston. Awesome dessert menu."

Outside, Jenna and her mother loaded a minivan with Jenna's plunder. The rest of the women gathered their things and said their goodbyes, promising to keep in touch.

Marcy watched them go, then returned to her office. She had work to do—there was always work to do.

CHAPTER 18

IT WAS late afternoon when they'd finished shopping. Joanna and Gracie walked along the Battery, Gracie skipping on the slate path beside the seawall while Joanna juggled bags filled with uniforms and school supplies. The store offered to deliver everything, but Gracie wouldn't hear of it. She thought her uniform jumpers were the most beautiful things she'd ever seen and wouldn't let them out of her sight. So, Joanna had arranged to take a few jumpers with them, and have the rest delivered on Monday.

A sail snapping in the breeze caught Gracie's attention, and she climbed the metal railing to look. "Mommy, what are they doing?" Gracie pointed to a sailboat moored offshore.

They watched the crew scrambling around the deck, gathering the sails, and coiling lines.

"It looks like they're putting everything away." Joanna moved behind Gracie, so she could catch Gracie if she slipped.

Gracie watched the activity for a long time before asking, "Where did they go?"

"I don't know, Goose. Around the harbor, or maybe they

raced to Fort Sumter. We used to do that a lot when Aunt Marcy and I lived here."

"You raced boats?" Gracie turned to face her mother, her face alight with questions. "Did you go fast? Were you scared?"

"We went really fast—at least it seemed fast—but we weren't scared at all. Grandpa made sure we could swim the length of the pool at the yacht club before we even got on a sailboat."

"Where did you go?"

Joanna pointed to a wide brick building on the edge of the harbor. "Over there. We were members there, and Grandpa was even Commodore. He liked to tell us that he was in charge of everybody—and everything—in and around that building."

When Joanna and her sister were younger, summer days were spent on the water. Early in the morning, Letty would fill their breakfast plates with eggs and buttery grits. When they finished, she would send them off with instructions to have fun but to be careful. She and Marcy would spend the entire day in the sun, sailing and swimming until the afternoon light shifting from bright yellow to a softer gold signaled the end of the day's activities. Whatever Joanna was doing, she stopped and watched the sunset, captivated by the mix of colors on the horizon. As the sun dipped toward the water, the sky transformed into a canvas of purple and gray before finally surrendering to the deep blue of twilight.

After sunset, the clubhouse was transformed into something magical. Doors to the wide sun deck were slid open, and workers arranged tables for the night's dinner dance, lighting tea candles, arranging flowers, and polishing silver so it gleamed in the soft warm light. Joanna's favorite place to watch was from a branch in the magnolia tree, on the far side of the building. She had been too young to attend the dinner dances, but if she was very still, she could see the first cars arrive, men tossing the keys to an eager valet and women ascending the carpeted stairs in a cloud of tulle and glittering jewelry. The whole thing seemed like a fairy tale to her, and she could watch for hours.

Gracie tapped Joanna's arm. "Mommy, you're not listening. I said, 'Did you race to Fort Summer too?'"

"It's called Fort Sum-*ter*, Goose. And, no, I wasn't old enough yet to race there. I had sailing lessons, though. Over there." The sheltered cove on the far end of the property. "In a little yellow Sunfish."

As the sun lowered, a breeze blew in from the harbor, scattering the scent of sea salt and kelp into the air. Joanna breathed it in, remembering whole days spent on the water and how much she had loved it.

The *clop* of horseshoes on the cobblestone street diverted Gracie's attention, and she hopped off the rung to watch. Gracie waved at the carriage of tourists as they rolled by, and a few of them smiled and waved back.

"Look, Mommy. They're waving."

"I see that, Goose."

They watched until the carriage was out of sight, then Joanna reached for Gracie's hand. "We should get back home now. It's getting late."

"Okay, Mommy. Can I show Great-Gram my new backpack?"

Joanna lifted the backpack from one of the bags. "Why don't you take it now? You can practice wearing it."

Gracie slipped her new monogrammed backpack over her shoulders, and they headed home. They crossed the street and ducked into a narrow cobblestone alley, a shortcut back to Eudora's house. The alley was one of Joanna's favorites, with mossy brick walls on either side, dotted with errant ferns and laced with vining wisteria.

They arrived just as the light was beginning to change in the garden, and long shadows stretched across the floor of the piazza. Twilight had always been Joanna's favorite time of day. They climbed the steps, and Joanna unlocked the door. Inside, the house was strangely dim and filled with shadows. Joanna set her house keys on the counter and flicked on the kitchen lights. Down the hall in the sunroom, a television blared.

Joanna paused.

Eudora never watched television. She called it the "idiot box," saying it was only for the weak-minded who couldn't entertain themselves with a good book, and it wasn't likely that that she would change her mind so completely.

"Hello? Gram?" Joanna slid the packages onto the table. "We're home."

No answer.

"Mommy, where is Great-Gram?" Gracie tapped her mother's leg. "I want to show her my pretty dresses."

Joanna offered a bag to Gracie. "Why don't you go upstairs and show Lendard your new things? I bet he'd love to be the first to see your uniforms."

"Okay, Mommy." Gracie took the bag and headed for the stairs, dragging her backpack behind her.

Joanna followed the sound of the television to Eudora's den. Normally tidy and peaceful, this was Eudora's private space where Joanna would often find her with a book and a pot of tea.

Joanna rounded the corner, and froze, not understanding the picture in front of her.

The room was a wreck. Cushions from the couch were tossed onto the floor, next to the lunch tray Joanna had prepared before she and Gracie left. Most of the food had been eaten, the rest were thrown on the side table. A shriveled apple core was stuffed into Eudora's cherished Waterford goblet. A crumpled soda can had leaked, soaking the linen placemat. And finally, in a corner of the tray, under a wad of plastic wrap, were the remains of a slice of cheesecake Joanna had made especially for her grandmother.

A pudgy, greasy woman in a pilled, beige cardigan had fallen asleep, sprawled across Eudora's blue armchair, using Eudora's favorite cashmere throw as a pillow.

"What is this? Where is my grandmother?" Joanna's voice was sharp. The woman startled awake with a grunt, kicking the soda can and sending it skittering across the floor

The woman wheezed as she pushed herself to her feet, her mousy brown hair fell in a knotted mess to her shoulders. "The agency sent me." Her voice was low and gravelly as if she smoked heavily. She hooked the edge of her cardigan with her thick thumb, flashing her plastic nametag pinned as proof of her right to be there. "Name's Flora."

"Where is my grandmother?" Joanna demanded.

The woman blinked, her eyes watery and pale behind smudged eyeglasses. "Still asleep, I'm guessing." She slipped her fingers underneath her collar and popped her bra strap back into place.

"You *guess*? It's five o'clock. How long has she been sleeping?"

She sniffed and cleared the phlegm from her throat "Well, that's a question, id'nit? The old ones are like chil'ren, ya know. You don't wake 'em up if you don't have to. They're less trouble that way."

On the television, the squeal of car tires and the pop of bullets exploded in the small room as a car raced along a dark city street. Joanna snatched the remote and flicked the set off.

Flora's tiny pig eyes darted toward the set. "Hey! I was watching that."

Joanna stood over the lunch tray, shaking with anger. "Did you eat that?"

Flora met Joanna's glare with defiance. "Eugenia said she wadn't hungry. Besides, the law says I'm supposed to get a lunch break. It's my right."

"Eudora," Joanna spat out the correction, feeling the anger expand inside her chest. "My grandmother's name is Eudora, not Eugenia." She stepped into the hallway. "You need to leave this house. Right now."

"I don't see wha'cher so upset about. Her name don't really matter, does it?" Flora wiped the back of her hand across her nose as she shuffled toward the door. "They can't hear anything half the time anyway." As she stepped into the hallway, she crossed her arms tightly in front of her chest, as if a thought had just occurred to her. "Your sister hired me, and *she's* the only one what can fire me. So, I'm staying until my shift ends at seven o'clock. I'm gettin' my full day's pay."

It took Joanna less than a second to weigh the consequences of what she was about to do. Then, deciding she didn't care, she grabbed the woman with both hands and dragged her from her grandmother's house.

Flora howled in outrage as she scrabbled for a handhold, spit flying from her lips. "You can't touch me—that's assault, and I can call'a cops on you."

"You do that," Joanna growled. "I will tell them how you left an old woman alone while you ate her food."

As they crossed the kitchen, Flora managed to hook the marble corner of the breakfast island, and Joanna got a better look at the type of woman her sister had hired to care for their grandmother. Flora's hands were filthy, her fingernails stained yellow with nicotine, and dirt smears dotted the inside of her arms as if she'd never washed. Joanna recoiled at the thought of this woman ever touching her grandmother.

Joanna pushed the woman toward the front door. "Get out. You're fired."

Flora skittered down the stairs, turning only when she'd reached the sidewalk. "I only come a'cuz your sister promised extra, if I did. And I want it. You tell that sister a'yours that I still expect that money. You tell her."

Joanna closed the door and locked it behind her. If Flora was the best Marcy could do, then Joanna would take care of Eudora herself.

"What's happening?"

Startled, Joanna turned to see Eudora standing behind her, her eyes hazy with confusion. Her cheek was creased from the way she'd slept on the pillow, and her lips were pale. In all her life, Joanna had never seen her grandmother without lipstick.

"It's okay, Gram." Joanna guided her grandmother toward the kitchen. "Someone was here, but they've gone now." As they walked, Joanna straightened the twist of Eudora's collar and smoothed the wrinkles from her cardigan. "Sit here, Gram. Let me get you something to drink."

Joanna made her way to the refrigerator, eyeing the telephone on the counter. She wondered if she should call her sister, the agency, or even the police. Almost immediately, she dismissed the idea of calling her sister; Marcy would want to know what happened, and that wasn't a conversation Joanna was ready to have. Not after how she'd interrupted her sister's meeting.

She needed a minute to think, to process what happened, to make sure her grandmother was alright.

"Is sweet tea okay, Gram?" Grabbing the pitcher from the refrigerator, Joanna reached into the cabinet for a glass.

First thing in the morning—every lock in the house would need to be changed, without question. The key code for the entrance gate would need to be changed, too. Joanna didn't like the idea of that woman having a way into the house. In fact, Joanna considered filing a police report as she took a glass from the cabinet, and a lemon from the basket, ignoring the dirty dishes piled in the sink and the overflowing garbage can.

She took a deep breath and pasted an encouraging smile on her face. "We can visit while I fix dinner, Gram. I can bake you some chicken if you're hungry, and—"

"Stop *fussing*. I don't like fussing," Eudora's voice was a screech, high-pitched and jagged.

Joanna froze, still holding the lemon. She watched Eudora's eyes widen as she looked wildly around the room.

"Where is Ginger?" Eudora's voice had dropped to a whisper, desperate and childlike. "What did you do with her?"

"Who's Ginger, Gram?" Despite her thumping heart, Joanna kept her voice deliberately casual as she scanned the kitchen, tracking Eudora's gaze.

Gracie skipped down the hallway and into the kitchen, the heels of her black patent Mary Janes tapping against the wood floor. "Mommy, look at how pretty!" Pinching the hem of her pleated jumper between her fingers, she twirled. As she let go, the fabric caught the breeze, flaring to a wide arc, and Gracie giggled with delight. "I look so pretty!"

"Stop it!" Eudora jumped to her feet, the chair behind her wobbled, then slammed to the ground. "Stop all of this!" Eudora's shriek raised goosebumps on Joanna's arm. The room stilled.

"Mommy?" Gracie's voice quivered.

"It's okay, honey." Tossing the lemon on the counter, Joanna rushed toward Eudora.

"Gram, are you okay?" Joanna attempted to guide her grandmother to another chair, but Eudora shook her off. Her grandmother turned on her, teeth bared. "I *told* you not to leave the door open. *Now, look what you've done.*" Eudora pounded the tabletop with the palm of her hand. Her wedding rings cracked against the wood surface.

Joanna's gaze cut to Gracie. Her daughter stood rooted to the spot, her fingers trembled as she held the hem of her skirt. Joanna wanted to go to Gracie, to tell her that everything was okay, but she wasn't sure it was the truth.

Instead, she turned. "Gram, I don't know who Ginger is—"

Eudora lowered her head and hissed. "You've always been jealous of that cat."

Joanna struggled to keep up. Eudora's face was flushed now, the color high and red on her cheeks. Her chest rose and fell as she looked wildly about the room. Surely, Marcy would have told her about a cat if it was this important to their grandmother.

Joanna's hand trembled as she picked up the phone, her words to her grandmother were slow and reassuring, as if she were coaxing Gracie from a nightmare. "We'll find your cat, Gram. Everything will be okay, you'll see."

As Joanna dialed the only phone number she remembered, her grandmother keened. The wail cleaved the air, and Gracie screamed. Joanna reached for her daughter and pushed her behind her back.

One ring.

Two rings.

"Ginger!" Her grandmother wailed as if she'd lost a child. "Ginger!" Eudora rushed through the house, calling for the cat.

Three rings.

Joanna's heart pounded in her chest.

"Hello?" Letty's voice was friendly, almost conversational.

"Letty." Joanna's words came out all at once, and she prayed that she wouldn't have to repeat herself. "Something is wrong with Gram. She's looking for a cat named Ginger. She said I let it out somehow. If I did, I didn't know it—." Aware that Gracie was still behind her, Joanna slowed her words so as not to frighten her daughter, though her own heart pounded. "Tell me what to do."

Something in the hallway clattered to the floor. Joanna felt Gracie jump and heard her whimper.

"Oh, Lordy, not again." Letty breathed. "I'll be right there."

"What do I do until you get here?"

"I don't know, child. I don't know." The connection was muffled as Letty moved around. "I'm on my way—five minutes."

"Right." Joanna hung up and turned to Gracie. "Gracie, I want you to go to the little blue bathroom and lock the door behind you. You can play with the flower soaps —you like those soaps."

"Mommy?" Tears filled Gracie's eyes.

Joanna knelt on the floor in front of Gracie and looked into her daughter's eyes. "Gram doesn't feel well, and I need to help her. I don't know what's wrong and I don't have time to explain, so you need to do what I say right now, okay? Take Lendard and go into the bathroom. Don't come out until I come get you. Can you do that?"

Gracie nodded and moved toward the bathroom, clutching Lendard to her chest. The moment Joanna heard the bathroom door lock, she reached Eudora just as she opened the front door.

Eudora crossed the doorway onto the piazza. "Ginger! Come back. Come home."

"Gram, come inside." Joanna placed her hand on Eudora's shoulders, a little firmer than she wanted, hoping to guide her back into the house. But Eudora slapped Joanna's hands away with surprising force and moved toward the front stairs, just steps from the street.

Joanna stood with tears of frustration pricking her eyelids. She had no idea what to do until Letty arrived. She tightened her grip and pulled her from the stairs. "You can't go out there, Gram. Please, just wait a minute. Letty's coming."

Eudora shook Joanna off, turning on her with a sudden fierceness. "You've lost her, Alice. You *stupid* girl." Eudora descended the first two stairs toward the street.

On the street, a car's headlights sliced through the dark as it turned into the driveway.

"Letty's here," Joanna breathed. "Letty's come, Gram."

Letty punched the security code into the keypad, and the gates opened, slowly.

Pulling her cardigan tighter around her body, Letty marched toward the house, grumbling to herself. "...too old for this nonsense...calling an old woman from her supper table..." But as she climbed the stairs, Letty's tone softened when she addressed Eudora. "Miss Eudora, you know this ain't no place for you to go wandering. All the neighbors can see, and you're not even properly dressed."

"But I can't find Ginger." Eudora's voice was barely a whisper.

Letty slipped her arm around Eudora's shoulder and guided her back into the house. "That's because you're looking outside, and you know Ginger ain't allowed outside. Did you look inside the house real good? You know how she likes to hide up under them cellar stairs."

Letty looked at Joanna, then gestured to the front door with her chin. Joanna closed it and clicked the lock, then followed the women to the kitchen.

As Letty took charge of Eudora, Joanna rushed toward the bathroom to her daughter. She knocked softly on the door. "Gracie? Honey? It's me. You can open the door now."

From behind the door, Joanna heard a loud sniffle. Then the door opened. Gracie's face was tear-streaked and puffy. She clutched Lendard so tightly against her body that he had folded in half.

The realization came to Joanna with a crash. She knelt on the floor and wrapped her arms around her daughter. "This is not the same thing, Goose. I promise, it's not the same thing. It's not." Joanna held her daughter close to her heart and listened to her ragged breathing. She stroked Gracie's back as her daughter caught her breath. "I *promise* you, Gracie: What happened in Rome will never happen again. I won't let it."

Joanna held her daughter as she trembled, smoothing her

hair and whispering reassurances. Finally, when Gracie's breathing quieted, Joanna lifted her up and made her way up the stairs to the bedroom they shared. She tucked her into bed and sat at her daughter's bedside until she finally surrendered to sleep. Then, Joanna removed her daughter's little school shoes and covered her with a blanket.

"I promise you." Joanna whispered into the dim light of the bedroom. "It will never happen again. Never."

Joanna rose from the bed and Gracie stirred. "I'm tired, Mommy," Gracie murmured.

"I know, honey. You and Lendard sleep now, and when you wake up, I will make your favorite: grilled cheese and tomato soup."

"Lendard, too?" The words were mumbled as Gracie settled against the pillow.

"Of course, Lendard too. I know how much he likes grilled cheese." Joanna smoothed a lock of hair from Gracie's face as she watched her daughter drift back to sleep. Dropping a kiss on her daughter's cheek, Joanna closed the bedroom door behind her.

When she returned to the kitchen, Joanna joined Letty at the table. Coffee brewed on the counter behind her. The shades were drawn and every lamp in the house, flooded the first floor with bright yellow light.

Joanna squinted as she entered the room. "Where is Gram?"

Letty sighed, her body sagged with fatigue. "Finally resting. I'll go up to her directly."

Joanna fell into the chair beside Letty. "Did you find the cat? I didn't mean to let it out. I didn't even know she had one."

The coffee machine beeped, and Letty started to push

herself up from her seat, but Joanna stopped her. "Let me get that for you, Letty. Do you still take cream and sugar?"

Letty frowned. "Cream only, missy. My diabetes won't let me have the sugar. I do miss it, though, I must say."

Joanna filled a cup for Letty and one for herself. "Can I make you something to eat? I can't cook as well as you, but I'll do my best." Joanna set the cup in front of Letty and added a splash of cream.

Letty reached for the cup, then gestured at the bright lights. "Would you mind turning off those lamps now? The bright helps her in the late afternoon, but it's hard for me to think with so much of it."

Joanna turned off all but a few, and the room seemed cozier. A cool evening breeze drifted into the kitchen from the piazza, bringing with it the scent of the harbor as it fluttered the draperies. Joanna pulled a soft woolen throw from the blanket chest and draped it around Letty's shoulders.

Sliding back into her chair, Joanna reached for her own cup. "I wish someone had told me that Gram had a cat. I would have been more careful about leaving doors open."

Letty sighed as she rose from her seat. "There is no cat, missy. Not anymore, anyway. That cat that Miss Eudora was looking for has been gone now, for more than forty years."

Joanna blinked. "I don't understand. She *insisted* there was a cat. We looked for it."

"The cat ain't the problem, Miss Jo. The problem is that Miss Eudora's mind isn't what it used to be. Sometimes, she gets confused. It's worse if you try to correct her, which I suspect you did." Letty reached for Joanna's hand and she squeezed it. "Your grandfather gave Eudora a ginger kitten shortly after they got married. Something to make up for the long hours he worked, I suppose. When your Gram is especially tired or upset about something, she looks for that cat."

"How long has Gram been like this?"

Letty cracked three eggs into a mixing bowl. "It's not like that, Miss Jo. What you seen doesn't happen every day, or even every week." She pulled a whisk from the drawer and started beating the eggs. "Miss Eudora has always found comfort in her routine. All this upheaval got to be hard on her."

"So, I shouldn't have come home?"

Letty shook her head. "No, baby girl. You belong here, with your Gram and your sister. It's right that you're home. I don't know what brought you here, but I 'spect it's not good. Prob'ly a hornets' nest 'a trouble. But it's right that you're finally home."

Joanna watched as Letty settled into a rhythm, pulling ingredients from the refrigerator, and chopping vegetables. "I don't mean to toot my own horn, but I've been a part of this household for a long time. I was the first person your grand-mother hired, all on her own, to staff this house, and we have been through quite a bit, your Gram and me. More than six decades."

"I didn't know that."

"Hmmm," Letty said. "There's lots that you and your sister don't know."

"Then why is Gram upset?"

Letty shot Joanna a sharp look. "I'm getting to that, missy. You just hold your horses."

Joanna rested her chin on her palm to hide her smile. She'd forgotten how much Letty loved to tell a story.

After tossing a handful of diced ham and red peppers into the mixing bowl, Letty continued. "It was hard on your gram when I left. Harder still with all these hooligans your sister gots parading through the house, trying to take my place."

"I saw the type of person Marcy hired," Joanna scoffed. "You'd think she'd pay more attention."

Letty looked up, her eyes sharp. "Now, don't you go blaming your sister. She's doing the best with what she's been handed. It's not easy to look after your grandmother and run a company, both." As she poured the contents of the bowl into a sizzling pan, Letty offered a final observation. "Your sister might could use your help, and I've yet to hear you offer any since you got home."

"Marcy doesn't want my help."

"Have you offered any?"

Joanna stiffened at the reproach. "I know enough not to."

Letty pointed her spatula at Joanna. "I've been waiting years for y'all to act like sisters, and I'll be waiting still when the Lord comes to take me. Y'all ain't never going to get it right." The toaster popped behind her, and she pointed at it with her spatula. "Get you some toast over there. I'm too aggravated with you all to mess with it."

Joanna slid off the stool and did as she was told, without a word of comment.

"You think I don't know what goes on in this house, missy?" Letty continued. "I may not be here every day, but I still know everything that happens. That sister of yours is putting body and soul into that business, just hoping your grandmother will notice. But your Gram won't never notice because Marcy isn't a son. It ain't right, but that's how it is." Letty slid the omelet onto Joanna's plate. "You eat that now before it gets cold."

Joanna picked up her fork and took a bite. The omelet was

delicious, dripping with melted cheese and salty country ham. No one could cook like Letty. "This is delicious, Letty."

"I know it." Letty brought the pan to the sink and turned on the faucet. The water hit the hot metal with a hiss, and a cloud of steam bloomed in the air. "You and your sister still fighting?"

Joanna shrugged, wishing she didn't have to answer but knowing better than to ignore Letty's question. "It's not much of a fight. Marcy accused me of breaking my promise by moving away, and breaking Gram's heart when I stopped calling."

Letty was silent.

Joanna froze, her fork in the air. "That's not true, is it?"

"Yes." Letty's answer was firm, unexpected. "Yes, it is, and you did. All those years away without so much as a post-card? And you come home with a great-grandbaby your Gram ain't never seen? What you think that will do to a person? Strong as your Gram is, she ain't made of bricks."

The omelet turned to ashes in her mouth, and Joanna laid her fork on her plate. "There was so much going on, I didn't think."

"Oh, I *believe* you didn't think," Letty said. "Now that you know, you have a chance to start over. There are bridges to mend, missy, with your sister and with your Gram. More than you think, I imagine. You can start with your sister because that will be the hardest fence to mend. Sisters are complicated—no one on this earth loves you more than a sister, and nobody can aggravate you more, besides. I should know—I have five of them myself."

Letty moved toward the refrigerator, then hesitated. "Do you think that baby upstairs will want an omelet, too? Won't take nothing to make another one, fresh."

"Thank you, but she doesn't like ham." Joanna glanced at the clock and rose from her chair. "I promised her grilled cheese. I'll go wake her up." After bringing her dishes to the sink, she turned to Letty. "Thank you, Letty. I don't know what I would have done if you hadn't come tonight."

Letty's voice was unexpectedly gentle. "It's hard seeing Miss Eudora like that, I know. It was hard for me the first time she didn't know where she was." Letty frowned as she glanced out the window. "Your Gram asks for that cat when she's fretting about something. I don't know what has her so worried, but if I were you, I'd find out."

Joanna leaned against the counter, folding her arms across her body. A shiver brought goosebumps to her arms as she remembered what her grandmother had said.

"She called me Alice, Letty. Gram called me by my mother's name."

Letty nodded. "I expect she would."

"But why?"

Letty sighed as she turned from the window. "She's always blamed your mother for letting that cat out." Letty untied her apron and hung it in the pantry. "Your mama was just a slip of a thing back then, younger than little bitty upstairs. She didn't deserve that much anger, especially from her mama. We had harsh words about that, your Gram and me, worst disagreement we ever had. I don't believe in hitting children. They's a gift and should be treated as one. Your Gram thought otherwise"

Letty crossed her arms and held Joanna's gaze. "I don't know exactly what brought you back here, Miss Jo, but I'm glad you're here. There's work to do, so you'd best settle in." Lifting her cardigan from the back of the chair, she pushed her arms into the sleeves. "I'd start by canceling those nasty health workers, and you take care of Miss Eudora yourself. Family does for family, and it's time you start learning that."

Joanna opened her mouth to reply, but Letty steadied her with a look. "And don't blame your sister. That agency was the only solution she had, but you can help set things right now. Your sister sees spreadsheets and numbers; you sees people, so it falls to you."

"Letty—" Joanna began but stopped. What would she say? That she didn't have time to care for her grandmother? Or that she couldn't take care of her grandmother because Joanna couldn't seem to take care of herself?

"You'll be fine, child. Call me if you need me, but don't tell your sister if you do. You two got enough trouble between you."

Joanna watched as Letty got into her car and drove away. When the car's taillights were nothing but a memory, she shut the door and sagged against it, as the weight of what happened settled on her. Her grandmother was the strongest woman Joanna had ever known and it was hard to understand how a woman like that could fold so quickly.

Marcy might know, but the sisters were barely speaking. It was a mistake to go to Marcy's office, that morning. She'd embarrassed her sister in front of her employees and she might never be forgiven for that. Maybe she could make Marcy understand that she had no interest in Palmetto Holdings. Maybe that would set things right.

Joanna took a deep breath and went to wake Gracie and Lendard for dinner.

CHAPTER 19

I<small>T WAS LATE</small> when Marcy arrived home, too late to meet the new health aide. She'd returned to work after Jenna's party and lost track of time. This new agency had assured her that Eudora would be well taken care of, that Flora was one of their best, and that seemed to be true this time—the dishes were done, and the kitchen was in order. Maybe this one would work out.

Marcy gathered her things from the passenger seat of her car and headed for the front door. Except for the light in the kitchen window, the house was dark. Not a good sign; that meant Eudora had gone to bed early again and that was never good.

Slipping the key in the lock, she entered the house and kicked off her shoes, her mind still on her work. She wasn't able to find anything obviously wrong with the closing documents so maybe she was just being overly cautious. Maybe she could have joined Cecily and Donna at the River Rock after all. It had been so long since she'd been anywhere but work or home.

"Long day?"

Startled, Marcy turned toward the voice. Joanna sat at the kitchen table, her expression unreadable.

"Not at all. I'm fine." Dropping her keys into the ceramic bowl on the table, Marcy moved past Joanna, too exhausted to argue. She pulled a container of peach yogurt from the refrigerator and a spoon from the drawer.

"We need to talk about Eudora."

"What about her?" Marcy peeled the foil top from the yogurt container.

"What kind of people did you hire to watch Gram?"

"They don't exactly *watch* her, Joanna—they're not babysitters. They're certified."

"Have you ever met one of them? One of the aides the agency sends?"

Marcy gaped at her sister. "Of *course*, I've met them—"

"The one who was here today, for instance," Joanna continued as if Marcy hadn't spoken, and it was irritating. "Have you met Flora?"

Marcy bristled. "If you have something to say, Joanna, just say it. I'm too tired for games."

In the beginning, Marcy had made a point to interview every aide before they entered the house. But Eudora had never been more than distantly polite to any of them, so it didn't seem to matter who the agency sent. Eventually, Marcy had stopped trying so hard to replace Letty and had turned her focus back to work, to problems that were solvable.

"Where is Gram now? Asleep?" Marcy hated having to ask; hated that Joanna knew something that Marcy didn't.

"Yes."

"It's a little early for that." Unless she fired another health worker and had gone to her room in protest. She'd done that before. Marcy turned her attention to an incoming text. She'd left Pete and Skip at the office, working on updated numbers for the Meeting Street property, but they should have left just after she did. If they were still there, something was wrong.

"We had a rough afternoon. Gram was upset—" Joanna began.

Marcy heard only a little of what her sister was saying. Instead, she punched in the password for her phone and pulled up Pete's text: *The estimate for new wiring for QS is finished. You want to see it now?*

Marcy typed a quick reply: *Yes. Send me everything you have, then you should go home.*

New wiring would put them over budget, but they might be able to make up the cost by—

"Marcy." Joanna's voice was sharp, unexpected. "Put that phone down—*now*." Joanna's face was creased with anger; she looked like a toddler about to have a tantrum.

Curious, Marcy lowered her phone. "What do you want, Joanna?"

Joanna leaned forward. "We need to talk about Gram."

"What about her?"

Joanna drew a deep breath, and Marcy groaned. She didn't have time for one of her sister's stories. "Something happened today, and I think you should—"

Marcy interrupted, her patience spent. "Is Gram hurt?"

Joanna blinked. "No."

"Is she ill? Is she in danger?" The questions came rapid fire, and Joanna flinched after each one, but Marcy didn't care.

"No."

"Then I'm sure everything will be fine. I'll take care of it." Marcy threw her uneaten yogurt in the garbage and her spoon in the sink. Then she gathered her things and headed for the stairs.

"Everything is *not* fine." Joanna blocked her exit. "You're not *listening* to me."

"Fine—I'll listen, but I don't have time for a long story." And, of course, Joanna's story was long. She began by describing uniform shopping with Gracie, so Marcy let her talk while she turned her attention to the plat for the North Charleston property, imagining different configurations for the strip mall she'd planned.

"I don't think Gram knew where she was. Letty told me it's happened before."

"Letty was here?" Marcy worked to pick up the thread of the conversation.

"Yes, but that's not the point." Joanna blinked, incredulous. "This is important, Marcy. Don't you *care* what happens to Gram?"

"Don't I care?" Marcy rolled her eyes, unable to look at her sister a minute longer. Joanna was nothing but drama, always had been. "You've been here less than a week, and all of a sudden you're an expert on Gram?

"I didn't say I was an expert. Just that—"

"You come here without an invitation—"

"An invitation?" Joanna's eyes sparked with fury as she rose from her seat. I don't need an *invitation* to come here. This is Eudora's house, not yours." The color rose in her cheeks as she paced the floor. "And you have *no idea* why I came here, so don't pretend to know. You haven't said two civil words to me since I arrived."

"That's because I don't *care* why you're here, Joanna." Marcy's voice was like ice, and it stopped Joanna in her tracks. "and I wouldn't believe you if you told me. But we can talk about Gram if you want to, sure. Let's start with you moving to Chicago even though you promised her you wouldn't leave. In all the time that you and Russell lived up there, you never once invited Gram to visit, even though you said you would. 'I'll call as soon as we get settled, Gram. We'll have a room ready for you, Gram.'" Marcy mocked, and Joanna flinched. It felt good to hurt Joanna as much as she'd hurt them. Marcy's anger fed on the memories—every time Joanna promised to call and didn't, or promised to call, but texted instead— and Marcy's anger grew stronger. "Did you know Gram wouldn't leave the house? She spent *fourteen days* in the house, refusing to leave because she thought she'd miss your call if she did. I bought her a cellphone and showed her how to use it, just so she could go to garden club meetings, and or visit her friends." Marcy spit out the last words as if they were poison. "But you don't care, do you? All you care about is yourself."

"How about when Gracie was born?" Marcy continued, unable to stop. All of the anger and frustration that Marcy felt about being left behind while her sister lived her own life erupted. "It's a three-hour flight from Chicago to Charleston —I looked it up one day. I was going to surprise Gram and Letty with tickets to visit you and Gracie, but they weren't able to travel that far."

Marcy's hands shook, she was so furious. She balled them into fists by her side. Eudora and Letty spent weeks planning a surprise baby shower for Joanna, so convinced were they that Joanna would come home. But she never did and the disappointment they felt was heartbreaking to watch. Marcy would never forgive her sister for what she put those women through though. "So, don't tell me how *concerned* you are now because I don't believe it. Where was your concern before today?"

"You make me sound horrible." Joanna's voice cracked. "I sent pictures when Gracie was born. I did."

"Ah, the pictures. I remember them: grainy and out of focus. Sent from your phone." Marcy nodded sagely. "Well, I'm sure that was good enough, wasn't it? That makes everything better."

"You have no idea what my life was like," Joanna began.

"I don't *care* what your life was like, Joanna. Look around you." She swept her hand across the room. "I take care of *everything* here. Every doctor appointment gets scheduled because *I do it*. Every bill gets paid because *I pay it*. I have more than enough here to keep me busy without worrying if my sister is having a nice time *living in Rome!*"

Lowering her voice to a furious whisper, Marcy lobbed her final shot. "I don't care why you're here now, and I won't be sad when you leave. You're selfish, Joanna. Whatever happened to you in Rome, I'm sure you brought on yourself."

Marcy climbed the stairs to her room and closed the door behind her. She refused to waste another thought on her sister.

CHAPTER 20

TWO DAYS LATER, Joanna and Gracie stepped out the door into the crisp air of a bright October Monday morning, on Gracie's first day of school.

"Ready to go?" Joanna reached for Gracie's hand as they descended the garden stairs to the courtyard.

"Don't I look pretty, Mommy? Lendard said I look pretty."

"He's right, you absolutely do." Joanna smiled at her daughter's uniform. A crisp white shirt, green plaid jumper, and shiny patent Mary Jane shoes. The uniform hadn't changed since Joanna wore it, two decades before.

Saturday's argument with her sister had cut Joanna to the core—she'd never seen Marcy so angry. Her sister never lost control like that. Not ever. After their fight, Joanna had spent the rest of the weekend avoiding her sister, so she could think. If even only part of what Marcy said was true, she'd hurt her grandmother deeply, and hadn't meant to.

"Mommy, look!" Gracie pointed to a trio of girls in green plaid jumpers. "They're going to my school, too."

Joanna nodded. "It looks that way."

"They might be in my class." Gracie's eyes widened as she considered the possibility.

"They might be," Joanna agreed.

"They don't know to be my friend yet." Gracie pulled free of her mother's hand. "I have to go to tell them. "With her blonde curls flying behind her, Gracie ran ahead to join the group.

Yes, she and Gracie could live a very nice life without Marcy.

Once inside the classroom, it didn't take long for Gracie to make friends. Joanna watched as one little girl took Gracie by the hand and led her on a tour of the classroom, reciting the rules of recess and explaining sharing time. Another showed Gracie to her cubby, which had been decorated with pumpkins and fall leaves cut from orange and yellow construction paper. When the bell rang for school to begin, Joanna wasn't entirely sure Gracie had noticed her leave, and she was delighted. Everything would be all right. She and Gracie would build a life here. Gracie would make friends in school, and Joanna would find a job, away from Palmetto Holdings and away from her sister.

She took the long way home, through tree-lined streets and cobblestone alleys, past jack-o'-lanterns and window boxes filled with autumn flowers. Maybe she'd buy a pumpkin that she and Gracie could carve. And it wasn't too late to find a costume for trick-or-treating. As she walked, she felt the tension of the past two weeks uncoil from her shoulders, and before she knew it, she was home. As she entered the garden, she heard the house telephone ring, and her breath caught.

Please, don't let it be the school calling already.

Rushing into the kitchen, Joanna scooped the receiver from the cradle and answered with a breathless, "Hello?"

"Marcy Rutledge, please."

"She's not in. Can I take a message?" Joanna dropped her house key onto the counter. Shifting the phone to her other ear, she rummaged through a drawer for a pen.

The woman snapped her gum. "This is a courtesy call from Care Angels," she recited. "We're calling to let you know that your contract with us has been voided."

"Care Angels?" Joanna glared at the phone. "Did you send someone named Flora here last week to care for my grandmother?"

The woman sniffed. "Yes."

"Well then, we need to have a discussion." Joanna dropped the pen on the counter. "Did you tell my sister that Flora had nursing experience? Because, I can tell you, she didn't."

"Flora is no longer with our agency—"

"I bet she's not."

"Please notify Ms. Rutledge that we will not be sending another home health care worker to you and we expect our bill to be paid in full within seven days." And the line went dead.

"Fantastic," Joanna muttered as she slipped the pen into the drawer and slid it closed.

No one knew that Joanna had physically removed Flora from their home on Saturday, and she'd like to keep it that way. She tapped her fingertips against the countertop as she thought, then she picked up the telephone and dialed.

It was answered on the first ring.

"Hello, Letty? Do you have a minute?"

Thirty minutes later, Joanna had the beginnings of a plan.

CHAPTER 21

"Gram, do you know anyone at the college Alumni Office?"

The first part of Joanna's plan involved finding a job that would support her and Gracie. As an alumna of the college, she was still allowed to use the office's resources to find a job, but having a letter of introduction would help.

"Gram?" Joanna repeated, before remembering that her grandmother refused to raise her voice.

Joanna filled her mug with coffee and went to the table to join her grandmother. She'd fixed Eudora's breakfast, a pot of hot tea with lemon and a slice of dry wheat toast before she walked Gracie to school, but that was at least an hour ago. It lay untouched, apparently forgotten, on the table as her grandmother stared out the window to her garden below. "Your tea must be cold by now, Gram. Can I bring you a fresh cup?"

Joanna slid into the chair beside her grandmother. "Gram?"

Eudora blinked, and her expression cleared. She'd been daydreaming again, something Joanna had noticed that

Eudora did quite a bit, but Joanna knew better than to comment.

Instead, she gently repeated the question.

Eudora nodded. "Yes, I know several people in the Alumni Office. Palmetto Holdings has been quite a generous donor to the college in years past. Why do you ask?"

For a moment, Joanna considered confiding in her grandmother about the tension between her and her sister.

In the end, Joanna took the easy way out. "I'm doing a bit of research, that's all."

Eudora gestured absently toward her office. "My address book is in my desk. You'll find the names inside."

"Can I use the computer in your office?"

"You may." Eudora rose unsteadily from her seat, with one hand pushing from the table's surface and the other gripping the arm of the chair. "Would you mind bringing a tea tray to the sunroom? I believe I'd like it better in there."

"Of course, Gram. I'll bring it right in." Joanna went to fill the kettle with water.

When Eudora was settled, Joanna entered her grandmother's office. Switching on the computer, she stared at the blinking cursor. She needed a resume but she didn't have one. She'd never needed one. The plan was for her to stay home with Gracie until she was old enough to go to school, then she'd enter the workforce slowly, with part-time jobs that she could fit in until Gracie came home. But those plans changed when Russell left them. After he left, she took whatever paying job she could find, and none of them seemed to require a resume.

Once settled at Eudora's desk, Joanna found a pen and wrote down every job she'd held since college graduation, and the list was disappointing. Bartending was first, as soon as she realized that her husband wasn't coming back, and he didn't plan to share his salary. The bartending job had seemed like a good idea, working nights while Gracie slept, but it wasn't. She went to bed late, and woke up every time Gracie did. One morning, dazed and stupid from lack of sleep, she filled Gracie's bottle with the black coffee she'd been living on, instead of with Gracie's formula. One of the more recent jobs was delivering morning newspapers to suburban residents. Which seemed like the perfect solution because she could bring Gracie with her, asleep in her car seat. But Joanna didn't count on having to keep the windows open for the newspapers, or the sleet and cold that blew past her and filled the car. After a few weeks, Gracie developed a double ear infection, and Joanna was fired for missing work to care for her. Scattered between the two was a series of low-paying jobs, each one worse than the last. Only the quarterly checks from Palmetto Holdings had sustained them, and Joanna had come to depend on the money.

That left Rome.

Twisting her hair back into an elastic, Joanna considered how to best describe her time in Rome. How to make moving there appear like a wonderful opportunity, when the truth was very different. Rome was always someplace she wanted to visit, to see the museums she'd only read about, to touch the buildings that housed masterpieces. Nicco's family was there, she'd been told. They had connections. She could work at any museum she wanted. She just had to get them there, and that meant selling almost everything she owned and starting over. But when she and Gracie arrived, things were more difficult than she ever imagined.

Joanna rubbed her fingertips across her forehead and heaved a sigh. Maybe she should start with something easier than a sad accounting of her professional life. Maybe the letter of introduction was a better place to start, but first she needed the name of Gram's contact. Pushing back her chair, she opened the top drawer of Eudora's desk to look for her address book. At first glance, Eudora's office appeared to be neat and tidy— books neatly shelved, every surface sparkling—but her grand- mother's desk was another thing altogether. The top drawer contained a wad of old crossword puzzles, half-completed and torn from newspapers, along with a jumble of dull, stubby pencils. The second drawer was stuffed with Junior League recipe books, glass marbles, and silver kitchen spoons.

"Wow, Gram. What a mess," Joanna muttered.

Closing the desk drawer, she sat back in her chair and regrouped. "If I were Gram's address book, where would I be?" Joanna's gaze swept the room.

Maybe Eudora meant the drawers in the bookcase behind the desk. Joanna swiveled in her chair and began her search. The first two drawers contained more of the same clutter, and as she leaned forward to open the bottom one, Joanna spied an oversized white envelope wedged under the desk. It looked as if it had fallen, or had been kicked under by mistake. Retrieving it from the floor, she turned it over. The return address was Palmetto Holdings, and it was addressed to company called LowCountry Trust. Joanna propped the envelope on the corner of the desk, to figure out later.

It took Joanna two hours to compose a decent cover letter. It wasn't perfect, but it would have to do. With an eye on the clock, Joanna stood and stretched.

She found Eudora still in the sunroom, dozing in her favorite armchair near the window, a woolen throw spread across her legs, and the morning newspaper carelessly tossed on her lap. The tall windows that spanned the length of the room seemed to magnify the sunlight, so this room felt hot and stuffy.

She crossed the room to open a window. As the breeze filtered in, cooling the room, and bringing with it the scent of late blooming roses from the garden below, her grandmother stirred.

"Gram, aren't you hot under that blanket?"

Eudora woke but it took a moment for the look of confusion to leave her face "Yes. Yes, perhaps I am."

"It's got to be eighty degrees in here, Gram." Joanna removed the blanket and folded it across the back of a chair. "There. That's better, isn't it?"

Eudora took a deep breath and smiled. "Please ask Letty to bring some flowers from the garden to the table tonight. Your grandfather does so enjoy the scent of my roses with dinner."

"Gram?" Joanna took a step toward Eudora.

But Eudora waved her away. "You needn't shout, Joanna. I'm right here."

But Joanna stayed where she was. "Gram, you told me to ask Letty for flowers."

"Don't be ridiculous. Letty retired years ago." Eudora frowned. "Honestly, Joanna."

Joanna regarded her grandmother. Maybe she *had* overreacted; it was hard to tell. Eudora's color seemed to have returned; her short temper certainly had. "Can I bring you anything, Gram?"

"No, thank you. I'm comfortable just as I am." Eudora leaned her head back and closed her eyes.

"Okay." Joanna turned to leave but paused at the threshold. "I almost forgot. I found this in your office. Do you know what it is?"

Eudora's brow creased as she studied the address on the front of the envelope, then she shook her head. "Where did you find it?"

"In your office, under the desk."

"No, I'm afraid I don't know anything about it."

"Okay." Joanna shrugged as she turned to leave the room. "I'll put it in the kitchen. Marcy can take care of it when she gets home."

Eudora called her back. "Let me see it, please. I'll give it to your sister myself."

"Okay." Joanna passed the envelope to her grandmother on her way to the kitchen.

～

Eudora stared at the envelope on her lap. She'd seen it before. It was important, she knew that, but she didn't know why. Something she was supposed to do, or something she wasn't supposed to do. Eudora couldn't remember.

It was happening again.

Sometimes, details came to her if she closed her eyes and relaxed, so she did. After a moment, they came to her slowly, in fragments, like pieces of a soggy jigsaw puzzle. Disjointed and fuzzy.

Her office.

A man in a business suit. Was it Brock? She couldn't tell.

And something about Marcy. Something that Eudora must keep from her.

Her head buzzed as she arranged the pieces, until gradually, a few of the images came into focus and Eudora was able to make sense of them. The image of the man in the business suit was Daniel Kennedy. And something about Joanna. Had Joanna finally telephoned? Were she and Russell coming to visit?

Letty would know.

Eudora would ask Letty.

She reached for the silver bell on the side table, but it was missing. Then she remembered that Letty was away from the house, but she couldn't remember why. She felt her body tense as a bubble of panic stirred inside her chest.

Unexpectedly, a breeze drifted into the room, bringing with it the scent of freshly turned earth and damp pine mulch, and she turned her head toward it. Her garden had always been her refuge, and it would calm her now. Breathing in, she pictured the seasons—the flowering cherry tree in the spring, the rose garden in the summer, and the gazing ball sparkling with raindrops after a winter rain. She held these images close to her heart, and her panic receded.

She'd let herself become overheated again.

When Letty returned from shopping, she would bring Eudora a sleeve of headache powder and a glass of cool water. She would be fine when Letty returned. Turning her attention to the mystery envelope in her lap, Eudora unfastened the clasp and shook out the pages. Inside were several papers that looked interesting, so she read through them. The first was a form granting Marcy permission to purchase property on behalf of Palmetto Holdings. On the bottom of the page, a series of red arrows pointed to spaces for signatures—hers and Daniel's.

Both signature lines were blank.

The bubble of panic grew, pressing against her chest, trapping her breath inside.

Surely not. Surely, she would not have forgotten to sign Marcy's paper.

The power of attorney had been a silly requirement anyway, a means of curbing Marcy's ambition until Joanna returned. Marcy resented the oversight, and Eudora was running out of reasons to continue it. Marcy was perfectly capable of running the company and had been for years. It was past time to hand over control.

Despite the pain in her head and the ache in her legs, Eudora rose from her chair and went to the kitchen to find her granddaughter. She needed to fix this, quickly, and in a way that didn't implicate Joanna.

"Joanna, I've changed my mind," Eudora announced. "I'm going to my room."

Joanna had been slicing chicken on a cutting board, a basket of red grapes and pecans nearby. She lowered the knife. "You don't want lunch?"

"No." Eudora forced a smile, despite feeling a bit queasy. It had been a mistake to spend the morning in that stuffy room. It clouded her judgment and she needed to be sharp if she was going to fix this mistake.

"Are you sure, Gram? You didn't have much breakfast."

"It's a lovely day, Joanna. Go for a walk." Eudora braced herself against the countertop, hoping Joanna would not notice. If she did, she would never leave.

"Well, if you're sure." Joanna wiped her hands on the dishtowel. "You look better, and it *is* a nice day for a walk."

The instant the garden gate closed, Eudora snatched her purse from the table and her address book from her office. She managed to lock the front door behind her, but once outside, doubt settled, and she was unsure how to proceed. Luckily, she remembered that just this morning, Brock told her that if she needed to leave the house and neither he nor the driver was available to take her where she wanted to go, she was to get a taxi from the stand near the hotel at White Point Gardens. The valet would summon a car and would send her husband the bill.

So that was where she went.

CHAPTER 22

Despite window-shopping along the entire length of King Street, Joanna was still early to pick Gracie up. She tossed her empty drink cup into the garbage and found a bench in the shade, across the street from the school. As she settled in to wait, Joanna turned her thoughts back to her job search. Several of the shops she passed on her walk to Gracie's school had help wanted signs in the windows, and Joanna could have worked in any one of them, but retail wasn't her first choice. The hours were long and unpredictable, and after what happened in Rome, she wanted to stay close to Gracie.

Across the street, the first car pulled through the line of orange cones. The deep-green finish reflected the afternoon sun, and the tinted windows and dealer plates seemed to shroud the car in mystery. When the engine turned off, the driver emerged, a deeply tanned woman in crisp tennis whites, with a blonde ponytail threaded neatly through the back of her visor.

She looked around and spotted Joanna.

"Hello." She fluttered her fingers as she called, her

diamond bracelet glinting in the sunlight. "Hello," she repeated.

She certainly was friendly. Joanna waved back.

The woman brightened and hurried over to Joanna's bench. "Would you mind watching my car?" She seemed to know Joanna, but Joanna drew a blank. The woman tilted her head and spoke with an odd lilt in her voice that Joanna couldn't place. "I won't be a minute, and I find that the carpool aides are always so strict, don't you agree?"

"I'm sorry, have we met?" Joanna asked.

The woman blinked. "No, I don't believe so. Anyway, I don't expect to be more than just a few minutes. Not long at all."

Before Joanna could reply, the woman jogged back across the street and disappeared into the school building.

"I see you've met Karen Rayburn."

Joanna turned toward the voice, raising her hand to shield her eyes from the afternoon sun,

The woman stepped to the side, using her body to block the glare of the sun. She had a kind face and an easy smile. Her dark hair was swept back into a loose bun at the base of her neck.

"I guess I have. Do you know her?" Joanna asked.

"Not well. I think her family owns real estate up north." The woman shrugged. "She's probably going to be towed again, but I don't think she cares anymore. Word is that her brother's towing company has a truck on call just for her."

"Well, that explains it." Joanna offered her hand. "I'm Joanna Reed. My daughter Gracie is in first grade. We're new this year."

"It's nice to meet you. I'm Trinity." Her grip was firm, and Joanna liked her immediately. "We've been at Santee since kindergarten. My daughter, Zoe, is fifteen now," she said with a wistful sigh, "Hard to believe how quickly the time goes."

Across the street, the school gates opened, and a woman carrying a clipboard and wearing a safety vest glared at Karen's car. With just minutes until school let out, there was a long line of cars behind Karen's abandoned car and no way to navigate around it.

Joanna glanced at Trinity, who just laughed. "Every time."

"Do you think I should go find her?" Joanna asked. "She did ask me to look after her car."

But Trinity shook her head. "No, it's okay. Karen does this all the time."

As they watched the carpool aide approach the second car in line, Trinity explained the hierarchy. "That car belongs to Amanda Buckley. She and Karen have been trading jabs at each other since their kids were in preschool."

"What grade are the kids in now?"

"Both of them graduate in June."

"Wow."

Trinity nodded. "I know."

Amanda got out of her own car and made a beeline toward Karen's. The aide reached for Amanda's arm, but Amanda shook her off and pointed at the car.

"Every time," Trinity sighed. "I wonder what they'll do when their kids graduate."

Across the street, the school bell rang.

"That's us."

Trinity stood up and brushed a stray pine needle from her khaki shorts. She pulled a scrap of paper from her pocket and wrote a telephone number on it.

"If you ever need anything, give me a call. Sometimes it's easier to figure things out if you've got help."

Joanna accepted the paper with a grateful smile.

"Thank you, I will."

A short time later, an older girl approached, dressed in the same green plaid uniform Gracie wore, but she carried it with the ease of an older student. Her blue cardigan was knotted around her waist, and the sleeves of her oxford shirt were pushed above her elbows.

Trinity wrapped her arms around the girl, in an easy hug. "This is my daughter, Zoe," Trinity let go and the girl faced Joanna. She was almost as tall as her mother, with the same long brown hair and the same kind eyes. "Zoe, this is Mrs. Reed. Her daughter just started first grade."

Joanna offered her hand. "Hello, Zoe."

"It's nice to meet you, Mrs. Reed."

Trinity slipped her arm around her daughter's shoulders. "How was your day?"

Zoe's backpack dropped to the ground with a thud. She melted against her mother with a groan. "Homework. So. Much. Homework."

Trinity retrieved Zoe's pack from the ground. "Then we should get going. You have karate today—your belt test, in fact."

Turning to Joanna, Trinity added, "It was nice to meet you, Joanna. I hope to see you again."

Back at the school, Joanna spotted Gracie, skipping toward her. She had a smile on her face and her cheeks were flushed with excitement.

Joanna peeled off Gracie's cardigan. Her shirt was damp with perspiration. "How was your first day?"

Gracie's stories tumbled out all at once, one on top of the other. She loved her classroom, had already made new friends, and was well on her way to becoming her teacher's new favorite.

Gracie pointed across the courtyard. "Mommy, did you know they're going to build a pool over there? I need to learn to swim right away because the swim team starts in fourth grade, and I have to swim fast by then."

"I'll see what I can do," Joanna replied. This is what home felt like: making plans three years ahead because you know you'll be there to keep them.

Gracie slowed, her eyebrows creased with concern. "Will we live here when I'm in fourth grade?"

"Absolutely," she said, and she meant it.

"Good." Gracie reached for her mother's hand as they walked home. "I need a 'mission slip, Mommy, and a sacked lunch."

"What for?"

"Miss Allison is taking our whole class to see the sea turtles," Gracie chattered. "We have a class turtle, too, but that's not the same as a sea turtle. Our turtle's name is Simon. You can never reach in and touch Simon without asking Miss Allison. Never." She looked up at Joanna, her expression grim. "Only Miss Allison can touch him because he has germs. He's still a good turtle, though." She added, "We will put him back in the water before winter comes because he likes to sleep under the mud when it gets cold."

"Is that right?"

"Yes," Gracie confirmed.

They arrived home, and Joanna opened the gate to Eudora's garden. Gracie turned to her mother and declared that she had already found a best friend. "His name is Jared, and he shared the yellow markers with me when Sissy Rawlins tried to keep them all for herself." Drawing her first real breath as they approached the garden steps, Gracie continued, "Jared is going to ask his mommy for swimming lessons too, so we can both join the pool team." Resting her hand on the banister, she looked back at her mother. "So, I really need them. Can I take swimming lessons with my friend Jared, Mommy?"

Joanna smiled at her baby, her heart full. "I'll see what we can do."

CHAPTER 23

As the taxi driver turned onto Meeting Street, Eudora sat in the back seat, shredding a tissue with her fingers. Brock had been mistaken. There was not taxi stand in front of the hotel by the park as he had said. In fact, there hadn't been a hotel there at all.

Eudora stood, holding back tears of frustration until a young woman came to her rescue. Eudora explained her situation in halting words that seemed to stick in her throat. The woman listened politely, then explained that hotel had closed years ago, when she was a little girl. Why would Brock want to trick her? Why had he sent her all this way? The woman called for a taxi and guided Eudora inside. As the taxi pulled away, Eudora looked out of the smudged window, watching for landmarks in a city she didn't recognize.

The closeness of the air inside the car and the heat of the day had made her queasy. Eudora used the shredded tissue to blot the perspiration that had gathered along her brow. Her mother would scold her for not having a cloth handkerchief. A lady always carried one.

"Excuse me." Her own voice sounded strange, thick.

The driver glanced at her in the rearview mirror.

"Is it much farther?" Eudora croaked.

The man mumbled something she didn't understand, but she didn't trust her voice to ask him to repeat himself.

"Ma'am?"

Startled, Eudora saw the door of the taxi open, and the driver standing on the curb. He was offering his hand. She wasn't aware they had arrived.

"Yes, thank you." Eudora's body felt strange as she exited the car. It was awkward and heavy, as if she were walking underwater. Her stomach felt queasy and her head pounded. It was the heat. She needed to get out of the heat.

Eudora opened her wallet and removed a sheaf of bills. She pushed them into the driver's outstretched hand and watched his eyes widen. How much had she given him? How much was the fare? She hadn't thought to ask.

Standing on the sidewalk, Eudora stared at the building in front of her. The Palmetto tree that Brock had planted in front of Daniel's building was taller than she remembered. The stairs were steeper, and the door was a different color. Was this Daniel's office? Had the driver made a mistake? She turned back toward the car, but the driver was gone. Why hadn't he waited? Drivers are supposed to wait.

The pain in her head tightened and her skin felt suddenly clammy, as if she were catching a cold.

Her progress to the front door was slow, awkward, as if she were a million years old instead of just eighty-three. When she was younger, she would have bounded up these stairs without a second thought. Now, she was forced to rest between each step. Tears of frustration pricked behind her eyelids, as she gripped the hand rail, but she would not yield to them.

A young woman skipped up the stairs just as Eudora had reached the top. Her hand rested on the door handle. "Can I get the door for you, ma'am?"

"Yes, thank you." Eudora's words sounded garbled to her ear. She cleared her throat and tried again, but the woman was gone, and Eudora was inside the building.

The lobby was a swirl of chaos, and Eudora's confusion grew. She had thought her only task was to present herself to the building receptionist. The receptionist would summon Daniel's secretary, as he had many times before. But nothing looked familiar. Eudora swallowed, pushing past the panic as it burrowed into her chest. She couldn't think with all this noise, and the people rushing—so many people rushing.

"Can I help you find someone?" The young man looked so like her son William, that Eudora felt dizzy with gratitude. William would make things better. He always did.

"Would you take me to see Uncle Daniel, please William?"

"Ma'am?"

Eudora turned to smile at her son, but his face had changed. His chin was sharper, and his eyebrows were drawn together with concern.

Then she remembered, and it broke her heart again.

William had been lost in Vietnam, on his very first tour of duty. This wasn't her son.

"Ma'am?" The man's eyes were kind. "Can I call someone for you?"

"Daniel Kennedy, please." The pain in her head made her wince.

"Kennedy, you say?" He had moved to a directory board, near the elevator. "I don't see a Daniel Kennedy listed, but there is a Preston, Kennedy, and Tradd on the third floor."

The elevator doors closed before Eudora realized she was

inside the car, and they opened before she was ready. Eudora approached the reception desk as beads of perspiration trickled down the small of her back. She pressed her fingers against her temple to dampen the throbbing and noticed that she had left home without her gloves. She'd been warned about that before, and this time her mother would be told. This time she would almost certainly lose a week's pocket money.

The receptionist's smile faltered, as if she had asked a question and was waiting for a response.

Another wave of uneasiness touched Eudora. The room began to vibrate, and her mouth went dry. Leaning against the desktop to steady herself, Eudora opened her mouth to ask for Daniel Kennedy, but the words would not come.

"Ma'am?" The receptionist's voice came from far away, as if she were shouting down a deep hole.

Eudora felt a trickle of perspiration run down her back. "—Mrs. Eudora Rutledge—Mr. Daniel Kennedy—some urgency."

But the sounds that came from Eudora's mouth was unrecognizable, even to herself. She felt the envelope fall from her hand and she watched it flutter to the ground.

A young man in a dark suit appeared before her, his face a blur of concern. "Mrs. Rutledge?"

She wanted to assure him that she was fine, that she was simply overheated but the words would not come.

"Ma'am, I'm sorry but Mr. Kennedy doesn't work here. He retired eight years ago."

All at once, the air whooshed from the room, and Eudora felt herself being pulled under, as if she were caught in a riptide. She heard someone call for water. She felt someone's hand on her shoulder. The edges of the room folded in on themselves. There was a humming in her ears and an explosion of light in her eyes.

The sound dimmed, and Eudora felt a warm touch on her arm and she turned toward the familiarity of it.

Alice.

Her baby had come home, and everything would be all right now.

"Alice?" Eudora spoke as if her mouth were stuffed with cotton, but it didn't matter. Alice was here, and everything would be alright. Her baby girl had finally come home, and this time, Eudora would insist she stay.

Leaning her head against the wall, Eudora closed her eyes and allowed herself to drift.

She was so very tired.

CHAPTER 24

"Can you make sure I have room in my calendar to meet with the structural engineer this afternoon?" Sliding her car into a parking space in front of her office, Marcy switched off the engine and unbuckled her seatbelt.

"Sure," Andrea answered. "How much time do you need?"

"Thirty minutes should do it. Please make sure both Pete and Skip are there."

"Okay."

"Is there anything that needs to be rescheduled?" Marcy gathered her things from the passenger seat.

"You have a meeting with Bruce Calhoun, but I can move that." Andrea no longer bothered to disguise the fact that she didn't like Bruce. Marcy chose to ignore it, for now.

"No, keep that one. The closing is in a few days. I'll call Dave Hemmingway to ask him to visit Meeting Street tomorrow afternoon—"

"Dave Hemmingway, the building inspector?"

"Yes," Marcy confirmed. "He owes me a favor. I'm on my way up." Pulling her work bag from the passenger seat, she set it on the hood of her car. "Is there anything I need to know before I get up there?"

"You know I can see you from here, don't you?" Andrea waved from an office window on the second floor. "What could possibly happen in the two minutes it will take you to walk up the stairs?"

"Any sign of Bruce?" They had had a meeting scheduled yesterday, but Bruce had canceled at the last minute. Maybe the uneasiness she'd felt had something to do with him.

"Nope."

Marcy closed her eyes. Now was not the time for him to go missing. "Find me when he calls, will you please?"

"Okay." Andrea hesitated. "Do you want me to come to the closing?"

Marcy shifted her phone to her other ear. "No, it will be quick. We're right up against the deadline, but that shouldn't matter. Everything we need is already at the attorney's office; all I have to do is sign the papers, and those warehouses are ours."

"Hurray." Andrea's voice was flat. Marcy would really have to address the tension between those two.

Marcy sighed as she crossed the lobby of her building. "Those warehouses are not beautiful, I know, but the income from them will fund projects that are. This is important, Andrea."

"Speaking of which, have you made time for Skip yet? He's got some interesting ideas."

"I'm sure he does, but it takes money to fund his ideas, and we don't have anything to spare right now."

"Can I put him on your calendar for—"

"Friday," Marcy finished for her. "End of day. Thirty minutes at the very most—I'm not kidding."

As Marcy climbed the stairs to her office, she mentally listed everything she needed to do before the closing. In three days, the warehouse would be theirs, and her time would be her own again. Rounding the corner at the top of the stairs, she collided with Andrea. Her assistant's eyes were wide, and her face ashen.

Marcy stopped in her tracks. "What is it?"

"Your sister called. Eudora's in the hospital."

CHAPTER 25

JOANNA RUSHED through the sliding doors of the emergency room, toward the nurses' station. Behind the desk, a sullen woman looked up from her work as Joanna approached.

"Excuse me, my grandmother is here. Someone called. Someone from here. Someone called about my grandmother."

"Patient's name?" The woman turned her attention to the monitor in front of her.

"Eudora Rutledge." Joanna's heart squeezed as she waited.

The woman's jaw worked a wad of chewing gum as she studied her monitor. Finally, she said, "The doctor is still with her. Have a seat in the waiting area, and someone will be out to talk to you."

"Can you tell me what happened to her?"

The woman snapped her gum. "I won't have any information until the doctor completes his notes."

"How long has she been here?"

The woman sighed and turned her attention back to her computer screen. "About an hour." She pointed to a spot across the room. "Have a seat over in the waiting room. Someone will be out."

In the waiting area, Joanna sat on the edge of a cold plastic chair. The room flickered with harsh fluorescent light, and an oversized vent pumped frigid air onto the chairs. Shifting her position, Joanna pulled the sleeves of her shirt around her hands and rubbed her arms to chase away her sudden chill.

Marcy should have arrived by now.

Joanna lifted her phone from her pocket and stared at it. When the hospital called, she had imposed on Trinity, because she didn't know who else to call. Trinity was gracious, assuring Joanna that it would be no trouble at all to take Gracie with them for the afternoon.

As Joanna fumbled through her contacts, wondering if she should call Letty, the doors whooshed open and her sister pounded across the polished floor.

CHAPTER 26

MARCY STRODE into the waiting room.

"What happened?" Marcy's words were clipped. She didn't have time for one of her sister's stories. She didn't have time for anything but the barest of facts.

"They haven't told me yet. The hospital called me, and I came right over." Joanna's response was slow, and Marcy felt her body vibrate with impatience. "They said Gram collapsed. They said—"

Marcy started the stopwatch app on her cell phone. "When did they call?"

"I've been here only a few minutes."

"What time did they call, Joanna?" Marcy insisted, her voice sharp. "How long has Gram been here?"

"I don't know, Marcy." Joanna drew a ragged breath, and Marcy knew there would be a story. Joanna always had a story. "Gram rested most of the morning. I offered to make her lunch, but she said she wanted to rest, so—"

"Have you seen the doctor yet?" Marcy cut her off, not bothering to be polite.

Joanna shook her head. "They told me to wait here, and someone would—"

"'be with you in a minute'," Marcy finished her sentence. "They always say that."

Without another word, Marcy left her sister in the waiting room and made her way toward the nurse's station. Doreen was perched behind the desk, hostile and territorial, ruling her kingdom like a miser. She'd spent all of her adult life working at this hospital, but the years hadn't softened her. Several months before Marcy had made the mistake of questioning one of Doreen's arbitrary rules in front of a doctor and she'd never been forgiven. Doreen's word was law in the ER and everyone—patients and doctors, alike—did what Doreen said because it was easier that way.

But today, Marcy didn't have time for rules.

"Doreen, I need to know the name of the physician treating Eudora."

Doreen looked up, her mouth drawn into a tight line. She glanced at her monitor. "Last name?"

"You know her name." Marcy's voice was low, a warning. "Rutledge."

Doreen stared at her computer screen long enough for Marcy to consider jumping over the desk and looking up the information herself. Finally, Doreen spoke. "There has been no update posted on the chart. Everything else, I've already told that other woman—"

"My sister," Marcy corrected. "'That other woman' is my sister."

"Whatever." Doreen shrugged. "I told her to wait over there," she pointed a stubby finger toward the waiting room, "and you need to do that, too. The doctor will be with you when he can." Doreen blinked her piggy little eyes, the merest hint of a smirk crossing her lips.

Marcy pulled out her phone and started a timer and an outline. "What is the doctor's name? The one with Eudora?"

With a sigh, Doreen turned her attention back to her monitor.

"Doreen." Marcy hissed. "This is not the time. Answer my question, immediately, or things will not go well for you."

Doreen looked at Marcy and narrowed her eyes.

"I'm not kidding, Doreen."

"Genrhett," she muttered, finally, giving up. "Dr. Genrhett. He's the attending."

"When was she admitted?"

"About forty minutes ago."

Marcy nodded her thanks and turned from the desk to join her sister in the waiting area. As she walked, she used her phone to search for Dr. Genrhett's credentials.

"I'm sure they're doing their best," Joanna began, but Marcy ignored her.

Marcy had been at this hospital before, too many times to count. At night when Eudora wandered the house, calling for a cat that didn't exist. The day Eudora insisted that Brock was at work but was refusing to take her calls because he was having an affair with one of her bridesmaids. And the time Eudora's blood pressure spiked so high that Marcy didn't trust herself with the short drive to the hospital, and called an ambulance. It was the longest twenty minutes of Marcy's life. She drove behind the ambulance, even through the red lights, terrified that they wouldn't make it to the hospital in time. Last month, Dr. Hadley had given Marcy a list of symptoms to look for and a protocol to follow if Eudora displayed any of them.

Marcy swiped to her contact list and tapped Dr. Hadley's number. The call failed. Cell phone reception in this part of the hospital was notoriously spotty. Marcy hurried to the window where the signal was stronger. One weak service bar flickered to life on the screen.

Dr. Hadley's assistant, Kelly, answered the phone. "Kelly, this is Marcy Rutledge. Eudora is in the ER, and I need to speak with him right away."

"I'm sorry, but Dr. Hadley is in with—"

"Interrupt him. Now—right now." They were losing time. Dr. Hadley had stressed how vital the first sixty minutes would be to Eudora's recovery.

"What are you doing? What's wrong?" Joanna whispered. She'd moved from her place on the chair and was standing behind Marcy.

Marcy turned away.

"This is Dr. Hadley."

"Yes, hello, Dr. Hadley." The connection crackled, and Marcy was afraid the call would drop. She moved to the parking lot, where the connection was stronger. "Eudora's been taken to the ER. My sister said that Eudora collapsed."

"How long ago?" His voice was terse. She heard him scribble notes.

"No one has been able to tell me for sure, but my best guess is close to an hour."

Dr. Hadley sighed. Marcy heard the scribble of a pen on paper. "Who's the attending?"

"Genrhett."

He paused. "I don't know him. Has he ordered a CT scan yet?"

"I don't think so, but I don't know for sure." Marcy

pressed the phone to her ear. "Doreen won't tell me anything."

"Hang on a minute." Dr. Hadley's voice was muffled as he called to his assistant. "Kelly, I need you to find out the neurologist on call at Charleston General right now. Track him down and get him on the other line right away." Directing his attention back to Marcy, he continued, "I can't come up there right now, but we'll make sure Eudora is taken care of until I can." He muffled the phone for a moment as he spoke to someone else, then returned to Marcy. "Kelly said that John Plyer is the neurologist on call and that he might be there now, on rounds. His assistant is trying to reach him. One of us will call you as soon as we can."

"Thank you."

Marcy returned to the waiting area, where Joanna was speaking with a doctor whom Marcy didn't recognize.

He frowned at Marcy, as if he were annoyed at the interruption. "I am Dr. Genrhett. I understand you're looking for me?" Short and spray tanned, the man smelled of peppermint gum and arrogance.

"Yes, we are. Eudora is our grandmother and one of your patients. How is she?"

His face hardened. "The reason you had me paged is to ask how she is?"

"Yes," Marcy answered. "There are extenuating circumstances—"

"Which I am happy to discuss when I am free." Dr. Genrhett folded his arms in front of his chest. "I believe you were instructed to wait for me, that I'd—"

"We were told to wait, yes. And we have. But Eudora's condition requires immediate intervention."

Extracting a chart from the stack he carried, Dr. Genrhett

opened the cover and glanced at the contents. "As I suspected initially, your grandmother is suffering from simple dehydration."

"Where is she now?" Marcy pressed.

The doctor closed the folder. "Resting comfortably in a quiet room. We're administering IV fluids. She should be ready to go home in a couple of hours."

"What time was she brought in?" Marcy pulled up the notes on her phone. "You must have a time stamp on her chart. What does it say?"

"Now, girls. I know this must be frightening, but there really is nothing to worry about. Dehydration is common among our older population, and the weather in recent months has been unseasonably—"

But Marcy would have none of it. "I understand that symptoms of dehydration are similar to those of a stroke and I'm sure you're aware that time is critical in the early stages. Have you ordered any tests? A CT scan? Have you consulted a neurologist?"

The question hung in the air, unanswered.

Dr. Genrhett stiffened. "Now, see here, young lady, we're doing everything we can to care for your grandmother. We don't have the facilities to care for every ache, real or imagined."

"Have you checked on her since she arrived?"

Dr. Genrhett matched Marcy's glare with one of his own. "I have a full schedule of patients, and your grandmother is one among many. If you believe my treatment has been in some way lacking—though I can assure you that is not the case—you are welcome to follow up with your personal doctor when my patient is released.

"I've already done that. Dr. Plyer is the hospital's chief

neurologist. He's on his way. He'll want to see my grand-mother's chart and, I'm sure, will have questions about the treatment she's been provided so far."

"Very well. I'll be on rounds. Dr. Plyer can have me paged." With a curt nod of his head, Dr. Genrhett turned on his heel and disappeared down the hall.

Joanna sank to the chair. "What is going on? What's wrong with Gram?" Joanna's voice quivered. "Marcy, please tell me."

"I will." Marcy drew a deep breath. "But first, I need you to tell me everything that happened this morning, as quickly as you can. Did Gram seem disoriented this morning? Was the health aide with her when she left the house?"

"Gram wanted tea and toast for breakfast. She read for a bit in the sunroom, then—"

"Did she drink her tea?" Marcy interrupted.

"What?"

"Did she drink anything this morning?" Marcy repeated. "Could Dr. Genrhett be right? Is it possible that Gram was dehydrated?"

"I don't think so." Joanna's brow creased as she thought. "She seemed fine when I left. A little tired maybe, but fine."

A nurse in a soft green cardigan approached them, the soles of her white sneakers squeaking across the tile floor.

"Ms. Rutledge?"

Marcy rose from her chair.

"Dr. Plyer is with your grandmother now." She produced a slip of paper card from her pocket, with a telephone number scribbled on it." "In the meantime, he asked that you store this number somewhere safe. It's his cell number, in case you have questions."

"He's giving me his direct number?"

The nurse shrugged, then offered a smile. "I might have told him how you'd been treated—at the front desk and by Dr. Genrhett. We're not all like that."

The paper crinkled as Marcy's fingers curled protectively around it. "Thank you. I'll put this in my phone right away.

Only when the nurse walked away did Marcy allow herself to sink into a chair. Tipping her head against the back of the chair, Marcy closed her eyes and exhaled fully for the first time since Andrea met her on the stairs.

"Marcy." Joanna interrupted her thoughts. "What is going on? What's wrong with Gram?"

Marcy opened her eyes and looked at her sister before answering. She had been dealing with Eudora's deteriorating health for the past several years, but it was new to Joanna. Eudora's most recent health scare occurred during a garden club meeting, four months ago. Marcy had forced her grandmother to go because she had been spending too much time alone, in the house. Eudora fainted at the meeting, and they called an ambulance. Marcy got there just as the ambulance pulled away and she remembered every detail: the flashing red lights on the ambulance, the terrifying drive to the hospital, a delayed diagnosis, and the threat of lasting damage. For the next four days, Marcy waited.

For tests.

For doctors.

For a diagnosis.

No matter how she wheedled, bullied, or pleaded with someone to fix her grandmother, they all said the same thing: it would take time. And the only thing she could do was wait. She was alone and scared, and now, Marcy recognized the same fear on her sister's face.

Slower, and with a bit more compassion, she explained

everything Joanna had missed in the years her sister had been away. She watched her sister's eyes widen, but she didn't interrupt.

When she finished, Marcy leaned back in her chair, exhausted.

"Who is Dr. Hadley?"

"He's a specialist I found after Gram's last appointment with her regular doctor. Her cholesterol is dangerously high. Dr. Hadley has prescribed medication and exercise to lower it, but Gram won't do anything he says."

"Can't Letty help? She always listens to Letty."

"Letty did help, and for a while it seemed that Gram was getting better. But Letty's own doctor forced her to retire because she refused to slow down. When she left, it seemed as if Gram gave up, and her health deteriorated pretty quickly. In the beginning, Letty would come over to visit, because Gram refused to leave the house. But that couldn't go on forever. Letty is almost as old as Gram, and she's got her own health issues."

Marcy remembered the day she told Eudora that Letty would have to leave. The look on her grandmother's face still haunted her, even now. "Gram was—" Marcy searched for the word, before settling on one that didn't even come close, "distraught when I told her that Letty had to retire—her diabetes was getting worse because she wouldn't rest while she was here." Marcy drew a deep breath, tamping down the guilt that would not leave her. "Gram spent a week in her room, crying. When she finally emerged, she was like a different person, withdrawn and sullen. She hasn't voluntarily left the house since Letty retired. She doesn't see her friends. She's stopped going to garden club altogether."

"But she loved garden club. Wasn't she a founding member?"

"She was." Marcy smoothed crinkles from the scrap of paper. "Remember the walks Gram used to take us on, along the seawall?"

"To see the sailboats. I remember."

"As far as I know, Gram hasn't even looked at the harbor since Letty left. And I know for a fact that she hasn't eaten a single apple."

"Apples?" Joanna blinked. "What about apples?"

"Gram hates them. Carrots, too. Dr. Hadley wants her to change her diet pretty drastically. She's supposed to eat apples, carrots, and oatmeal," Marcy waved her hand in the air as she recited the list she'd memorized long before. "But Gram won't touch them. She insists that she's old enough to eat what she wants."

"What does she eat?"

"I caught her eating pimento cheese the other day." Marcy scoffed. "She paid an aide to get it for her."

Immediately after the checkup with Dr. Hadley, Marcy had ordered fancy apples, directly from an orchard in Washington State because she'd thought they were the best. Surely Eudora would appreciate the taste of heirloom apples. But a month after the box arrived from the grower, Marcy found the gardener hauling the entire box to compost, the apples still wrapped in red paper.

"That's why you hired health aides? To get Gram to eat properly?"

"To get her to eat, to take her medication, and if not walk every day, to at least go outside and sit in her garden. She's been getting so pale lately." Marcy pushed a lock of hair behind her ear. "We've been through three agencies, and Eudora has hated every person they've ever sent. In the beginning, I arranged my schedule back at work, so I could at least come home to check on her, but I can't always leave, and Gram doesn't seem to notice."

"Why didn't you tell me any of this? I could have helped."

"I couldn't find you." Marcy rested her head against the back of the chair and closed her eyes. Everything she'd been trying to hold together was unraveling. She was utterly exhausted.

"I'm so sorry, Marcy." Joanna's voice was soft.

Marcy opened her eyes and looked at her sister. "What?"

"I'm sorry," Joanna repeated, her voice stronger this time. "I'm sorry for leaving you with everything. I didn't know."

Marcy turned to Joanna, knowing that if she didn't say this now, she would never have the nerve again. Maybe her sister arriving when she did was a good thing. "None of this is your fault, Joanna. It's just easier to blame you, I guess, for leaving me here to deal with everything by myself."

Thankfully, Joanna's phone vibrated, and she turned her attention to the screen. She flicked open the screen with her thumb. "Gracie. That's the alarm for the end of school. I have to pick her up."

After silencing the alarm, Joanna asked. "Can I borrow your car?"

Marcy blinked. "My what?"

"Your car. I need to go pick up Gracie from school. If I have to wait for a taxi, I'll be late."

"Don't you own a car?"

Joanna shook her head.

"How can you not have a car? How have you been getting

around?" Digging into her bag, Marcy extracted her keys. "Never mind, don't tell me. Here. Go."

Marcy closed her eyes again and listened to her sister's footsteps receding down the hallway.

She was alone, again.

CHAPTER 27

THE AIR WAS FILLED with the scent of hothouse flowers and beeswax, and hummed with the nervous twittering of debutantes eager to make a good impression. The fireplace mantel had been draped with Christmas garland; it sparkled with silver ornaments and tiny fairy lights. In the hearth, a slow fire burned. The warm light reflecting the polished brass on The Citadel uniforms, as if it were stardust.

Eudora tightened her grip on her father's arm as she approached the table, though she knew it was a breach of etiquette to do so. After months of instruction, Eudora knew every rule by heart. When it was their turn, Eudora's father gave his name to the hosts while Eudora arranged a serene expression on her face and surveyed the room. They were one of the last to arrive, and Eudora suspected it had been purposeful. Despite his pedigree, her father thought the St. Cecilia Ball was outdated and hadn't wanted to participate. It was her mother who had unexpectedly persuaded her father to accompany her because she knew how much it meant to Eudora.

Someone handed Eudora a dance card, the trailing ivory-colored ribbon exactly matching the shade of her gown. She slipped her hand through the loop and hoped it wasn't too late to find partners to fill it.

"Eudora." Her father's voice broke into her thoughts

"Sorry, Daddy," she murmured, allowing her father to slip the gardenia corsage onto her wrist.

Before entering the ballroom, the debutantes were required to curtsey before their hosts. Eudora held her breath as she sunk into a deep curtsey, effortlessly, as she'd been taught.

Eudora stood by the dance floor alone, waiting for someone—anyone—to ask her to dance. Her palms perspired through the soft fabric of her gloves, and she fought the urge to run. Surely, everyone in the room could see that her card was empty and that she didn't belong there.

"May I have the next dance, Miss Gadsden?"

Eudora turned, relieved that she had found her first partner and looked into the handsome face of Cadet Brock William Rutledge. With smoldering dark eyes and wavy auburn hair, he looked just like Burt Lancaster, and just thinking about him made Eudora's cheeks flame. They had been formally introduced at a tea reception at The Citadel two weeks before, but she never dreamed he'd remember her. Especially because Peggy Ravenel claimed Cadet Rutledge for herself, telling all the girls that he was hers.

"Yes, of course." Her fingers shook as she printed his name on her dance card.

The dance was a blur, a collection of moments she held close to her heart, to relive again and again. The press of his hand against her back, the smell of his cologne, the way her breath caught when he looked at her.

And it was over before she knew it.

When he escorted her from the dance floor, it was all she could do to not ask him for another dance. But of course, she couldn't do that. Her mother was watching. Instead, Eudora bowed her head as she'd been taught and thanked Cadet Rutledge for the dance. But as she watched him walk away, a single thought took hold and would not let go:

She was going to marry that man someday.

That night, as she prepared for bed, Eudora let her mind wander, indulging herself in daydreams of a spring wedding. The azaleas along the far wall would be flowering, Rows of tulips and beds of daffodils in the perennial garden would scent the air, and in the far corner the big dogwood would be in bloom. She imagined wearing her grandmother's bridal veil made from antique Brussels lace under the canopy of dogwood blossoms. After a wedding that perfect, no one could say she didn't belong. Not even Peggy Ravenel.

A sudden, icy draft, blew through the room, though the windows were closed, and a fire burned gently in the hearth. Reaching to secure her woolen robe tighter around her shoulders, Eudora felt herself shiver.

CHAPTER 28

"SHE'S COLD." Marcy pulled a blanket from the end of the bed and tucked it around her grandmother. Tubes and wires from her grandmother's body connected to a machine by the side of the bed, measuring her life in sharp, rhythmic beeps.

"I'll get a blanket from the warmer. I'll be right back." The nurse was kind, and Marcy should have thanked her, but she was gone before Marcy could find the words.

As she stood beside her grandmother's bed, Marcy noticed the IV tape on the back of Eudora's hand. Whoever had started the IV had missed the vein. More than once.

The nurse returned with a warm blanket and laid it over Eudora. "This will make her feel better," the nurse said as she smoothed the edges.

"Thank you." Marcy's voice caught, so she cleared her throat and tried again. "Thank you."

"Let me know if you need anything; I'll be right outside."

Marcy pulled a guest chair closer to the bed and sank into it. The first memory Marcy had of her grandmother was from the back seat of her mother's station wagon. They'd been fighting again, Alice and her second husband, but this time there was the sound of breaking glass and crying. Marcy and her sister shared a room at the time, and Marcy remembered watching her sister, asleep in the next bed, and praying she wouldn't wake up. Joanna always got so scared when Alice and her husband fought.

Eventually, the house quieted. It seemed safe enough to fall back to sleep, so Marcy recited her multiplication tables for a math test the next day. She was almost asleep, when Alice snapped on the bedroom light and hissed at the girls to get into the car. There was just enough time for Marcy to help Joanna find her shoes and button her coat before they left.

They drove the rest of that night, and part of the next morning. Alice cried and chain-smoked cigarettes, and the girls looked out the window, wondering where they were going, but too afraid to ask. At last, they pulled into a drive-way, and Alice tapped a code into the security box. Marcy's first thought, as the heavy iron gates slid open, was that she and Joanna would be safe here, in a house surrounded by iron.

Eudora appeared at the garden gate, almost immediately, smiling and waving a greeting. She wore a sun hat and garden gloves, and she carried a wicker basket of flowers over her arm.

Marcy's vision blurred as she remembered. The three of them, Alice, Joanna, and Marcy, lived with their grandparents for three years, not nearly long enough.

Marcy leaned closer to her grandmother and whispered, "Please get better, Gram. We need you here with us."

A fumbling behind the closed door startled her. Straightening in her chair, she swept the smeared mascara from under her eyes.

Joanna shouldered the door open, carrying a large bag and a tray of drinks in her hands. "Can you take this?"

Marcy rose to help. "What are you doing?"

"Letty's watching Gracie—" Joanna interrupted herself with an apologetic shrug. "I know we're not supposed to call Letty, but I thought she'd want to know what happened to Gram."

Marcy took the tray and set it on the table. "No, you were right to call her. She's Gram's closest friend."

Joanna set the other bags on the table and began unpacking. "Letty sent these."

The first thing she pulled out was a cobalt-blue teapot and a matching cup, Eudora's favorite. It had always seemed strange to Marcy, that the Spode remained in the butler's pantry while her grandmother chose to drink from this cup. Marcy ran her finger along the handle. The cup and the saucer were unremarkable, really. Ordinary ceramic, white with a faded blue pineapple printed on the front and not especially well-made. Eudora had at least two other sets that had been in her family for generations. She used them for special occasions but always chose this one for herself. Marcy had never understood why.

Lifting a thermos from the bag, Joanna placed a spoon on top and offered both to Marcy. "Letty sent something hot for you. I think it's soup."

Marcy sat back in her chair and cradled her hands around the thermos, welcoming its warmth.

Reaching into a duffel, Joanna pulled out a wool cardigan. "She sent this for you, too. She said the hospital is cold at night."

"It is. Thank you." Marcy slipped her arms into the sleeves. "Is Letty staying the night?"

"No. Gracie can be a handful at bedtime, and I can't leave Letty to deal with that." Joanna dragged a chair across the floor and sat. "So, I can only stay a little while, I'm sorry it can't be longer." She pointed to the thermos Marcy had put on the table. "Letty said to eat your soup while it's hot."

Marcy unscrewed the lid from the thermos and breathed in the rich scent of Letty's shrimp gumbo. "I can't believe she remembered." Marcy swallowed past the lump in her throat.

"Remembered what?"

"Do you remember the first day we arrived at Gram's house in Charleston?"

"Not much—I was only six years old. But I remember pieces of that first year, and more of the years after." Joanna propped her elbow on the arm of her chair and rested her chin in her palm. "What does that have to do with . . . ?"

"It's not soup," Marcy corrected. "It's gumbo. Letty made it the day we arrived, and after that, she made it anytime I was worried about something. It's her way of telling me that everything will be okay." Marcy stirred the rice with her spoon.

"What happened the first day?"

Marcy put down her spoon, surprised that Joanna didn't remember. "Just after we arrived, Mom had one of her 'episodes.' She locked herself in her room, crying and pacing. While Gram was upstairs, Letty put us to work making gumbo. Your job was to wash and peel the vegetables, mine was to clean the shrimp and chop the onion. Letty kept us busy, telling stories and teaching us to cook." Picking up her spoon, she scooped the gumbo into her mouth and tasted okra, green pepper, and soft rice. Hot and spicy, it tasted like home.

"I miss Letty," Joanna said.

"I do, too," Marcy agreed.

They passed some time in comfortable silence, Marcy eating her gumbo and Joanna sitting nearby. And Marcy felt better.

Too soon, an alarm from Joanna's cell phone beeped, and she reached into her pocket to turn it off. Standing, she gathered the empty bags. "I'm sorry, but I have to go." She paused and regarded her sister. "Will you be alright for a while? Should I come back?"

Marcy shook her head, her mouth filled with gumbo. She swallowed and called to her sister just as Joanna reached for the door. "Joanna?"

"Yes?"

"Thank you."

Joanna smiled. "You're welcome."

CHAPTER 29

THE NOISE WOULD RUIN her wedding reception.

Piercing and insistent, it sounded as if an alarm clock had been left untended. Eudora glanced at her new husband to see if he had heard it too. He was in the corner garden, and Peggy Ravenel was giggling and clutching his arm, hanging on his every word. Brock looked up and swept his bangs from his forehead; his new wedding ring glinted in the sunlight. He caught Eudora's eye and winked as if they shared a secret, and Eudora felt herself blush. That man could always make her blush.

In the distance, someone called her name.

The voice sounded familiar, but Eudora couldn't place it. The sunlight in the garden shifted, but none of the guests seemed to have noticed. The voice repeated her name, louder this time. Eudora frowned; her body felt as if it were floating, away from her wedding.

"Mrs. Rutledge, can you open your eyes?"

The wedding guests and her new husband receded into shadow as Eudora tried to do as she had been asked. Trading one dream for another, it felt as if her head were filled with cotton wool, and her body ached as if she'd fallen.

"Mrs. Rutledge, please open your eyes."

A bright light shined in her eyes, and Eudora winced.

"That's right. Wake up, please."

Eudora struggled to do as she was asked.

All around her was chaos, people talking, giving orders, but she couldn't understand what they wanted. She opened her mouth to explain, but no words came out. She tried to move, but her body felt weighted. Tears of frustration welled in her eyes as she struggled.

Slowly, the room came into focus, but Eudora recognized nothing in it. A tangle of wires encircled her arm. Her skin was mottled and laced with bruises. Had Brock hit her again? She couldn't remember.

Her heart began to thump in her chest.

Shifting her gaze, she looked toward the windows, toward the garden. She would find comfort in her garden, just as she always had. But it wasn't there. Instead, there was a field of asphalt, a bright sun, and a shimmer of reflecting heat.

Eudora closed her eyes. It would be a small thing to surrender now, to return to her new husband and her wedding reception.

"Mama. Mama, I'm here."

Eudora's eyes snapped open. She recognized the voice.

Alice.

Her baby girl, in the chair beside Eudora's bed, sitting quietly amid the chaos of her room.

"Oh, Alice," Eudora whispered, "Alice, you've come."

Her daughter smiled, radiant and beautiful. And in that moment, Eudora didn't need anything else.

Turning her head away from the clatter of the room, Eudora closed her eyes and drifted into a peaceful sleep, a smile on her face.

CHAPTER 30

"WAS THAT ENOUGH?" Marcy asked. "Was she conscious enough for you to tell if the stroke caused any lasting damage?"

"We know she heard us, that she understood and that she tried to wake up." Dr. Plyer sighed as he clicked his penlight and slipped it back into his front pocket.

"But she said 'Alice,'" Marcy insisted. "I heard her."

"I heard something, too, but it would have been better if she had engaged, spoken with someone in the room."

"Dr. Hadley said her next stroke would be a big one. Was this it?" Marcy braced herself, expecting the worst but not wanting to hear it.

Dr. Plyer looped his stethoscope across his neck "Her test results are encouraging. The scan we ran last night showed no signs of hemorrhaging in the brain. That usually means there will be no lasting damage, but I can't say for sure until she is awake and alert."

Marcy's breath felt tight in her chest. "What happens now?"

"We'd like to keep her a few days longer, to run a few

more tests. Make sure we haven't missed anything." Dr. Plyer's smile was kind, reassuring. "Your grandmother is in good hands, Ms. Rutledge. You should go home and get some rest yourself. The nurses tell me you've been here for three days already."

"I'd like to stay a little longer."

"Okay." Dr. Plyer reached for the door, then turned. "One more thing." He pulled a card from his pocket. "Dr. Hadley mentioned that you've been having trouble with health aides, and I think we might be able to help. My office keeps a list of private nurses that we've already screened. You might have better luck with one of them."

Marcy accepted the card and murmured her thanks.

Before he left, Dr. Plyer glanced around the room, then back to Marcy. "I'll see about getting a cot wheeled in for you."

Sleeping in a cot would be a nice change from spending the night in the guest chair. "Thank you."

CHAPTER 31

On the fourth day at the hospital, Marcy remembered the closing.

She rushed out of the hospital and into the waning afternoon. The attorney's office closed in less than an hour, which left just enough time to swing by her office first. Sliding into the driver's seat, Marcy considered checking her messages, but she was so close to the office that it would be quicker to have Andrea summarize everything when she got there. She tossed her bag onto the passenger seat, snapped her seatbelt, and pulled into traffic.

As she pulled up to the first traffic light, Marcy imagined her calendar for the next several months. Eudora would need supervised care, better quality than visiting nurses could provide. There would be doctor visits and probably physical therapy. Transportation would have to be arranged but Marcy wasn't sure she trusted anyone but herself to drive Eudora to the appointments. Things would need to change at home, as well. Dr. Hadley would almost certainly change Eudora's diet again. There might be vitamins and more timed medication.

Someone would need to be with Eudora to make sure she complied.

Somehow, Marcy would have to find the time.

After the closing, decisions would need to be made and plans would need to be finalized—new access roads and new construction, all would require permitting. She'd been so focused on acquiring the land, she hadn't realized the amount of time her little strip mall would require.

She realized, with a start, that it might take twelve to eighteen months to finish. Much longer than she wanted.

The other day, one of the social workers had casually suggested Eudora be moved to an assisted living facility, so Marcy could "get on with her life." The idea was horrifying, and Marcy had flatly refused to discuss it. Eudora's health *had* been fragile lately, ever since Letty left. Marcy thought Eudora simply missed her friend and that the solution would be a matter of scheduling.

She was wrong.

But she'd figure something out; she always did.

As she pulled into her parking space, Bruce rushed to her car, his face stern, his Hawaiian shirt billowing behind him. "Marcy, where have you been? Didn't you get my text messages?"

"I had a bit of an emergency—"

Bruce cut her off. "I need to talk to you before the closing."

"Can it wait?"

Bruce shook his head. "'fraid not."

"Okay." Marcy stifled a groan. "Come with me."" Marcy led the way to her office, trying to shake off the irritation she felt for Bruce. In the past several weeks, he had cancelled several of their regular appointments and had been unresponsive to her email. Whatever problem he brought to her now, would have to wait until she had time to solve it.

As soon as they entered her office, Bruce settled into one of her guest chairs and began his explanation.

Marcy switched on her desk light and tried to remember where she'd left her closing packet. It was in the top desk drawer the last time she saw it.

"The owners like you, so they're willing to push it back until tomorrow, but twenty-four hours is all the time they'll give you."

"Push what back? The closing?" She opened the packet and glanced at the contents.

"Yes."

"Why do we need to push back the closing?" She found it in the top drawer.

Bruce leapt to his feet. "Marcy, didn't you read *any* of the texts I sent?" He dug his hands into his pocket and began to pace. "The owners, Marcy. They've got other offers, solid offers that will give them more cash up front than we will." He stopped in his tracks, and turned to gape at Marcy. "I told you all of this."

"Cell reception at the hospital is terrible." Marcy reached for her phone and pulled up a list of fifteen text messages, all from Bruce, all marked *urgent*.

Marcy abandoned the closing papers and dropped to her chair. "Start from the beginning and tell me everything."

He dug his fingers into the back of his neck. "There's only one thing to tell, and it's big. We're missing documents for the closing. Specifically, the power of attorney authorizing you to buy property on behalf of Palmetto Holdings. We can't close without it."

"But I have it. It's one of the first things Eudora signs."

Marcy shuffled through the pages in the packet, then stopped when she remembered the conversation with Eudora and Daniel Kennedy in Eudora's office. Marcy sagged in her chair as the realization hit her: that must have been why Eudora went to Daniel Kennedy's office.

"Don't worry; I fixed it." Bruce held up his hand.

"How could you possibly have fixed this?"

He paused, as a smile of triumph spread across his face. "I offered the owners a little something for their trouble"

A shiver of warning brought goosebumps on Marcy's arm. "What did you do?"

"I told you: I fixed this problem." A shadow of anger crossed his face, but disappeared so quickly that Marcy almost didn't see it. "I offered the owners an incentive for delaying the closing for twenty-four hours, and they took it."

"What *kind* of incentive?" She laced her fingers together, giving him her complete attention.

Bruce shrugged, unconcerned. "A bonus. A little more cash up front. An extra ten percent of escrow, a bonus. It's all in the texts I sent you."

"Bruce," Marcy bristled with anger, but tamped it down. Now was not the time to lose her temper. "For something as important as that, I would think you would do more than *text* me. You don't have the authority to speak for this company. And you certainly aren't authorized to spend its money."

Bruce raised his chin. "I was doing you a favor."

Marcy stiffened at the lie but didn't address it. "If we were in this much trouble, why didn't you call Andrea? She always knows where I am."

Bruce shrugged as he flicked something from his shirt. "Andrea and I don't exactly see eye to eye." He straightened, and Marcy could see the deception in his eyes. This is why

Andrea didn't trust him. Why didn't Marcy see this before now?

"Look," Bruce continued. "I think you're missing the point here. There are competing offers, but for some reason, the owners want to sell to you, and they're willing to wait an extra day. That almost never happens." Bruce chopped his hand into his palm. His eyes were bright. "We still need a signed power of attorney, but at least we have another day to produce it."

"Bruce, Eudora is in the hospital, unconscious. She can't sign anything, today or tomorrow."

Andrea entered the office carrying a tray laden with food and fresh coffee.

Bruce palmed a cornbread muffin from the basket. "We can work round that."

Andrea frowned and offered Marcy a mug of coffee. Marcy cradled it between her hands, breathing in the rich smell of strong black coffee.

"She doesn't need to actually *sign* anything." Bruce spoke with his mouth full of cornbread. "Attorney friend of mine— a fishing buddy—you might say. He specializes in," Bruce curled his fingers into air quotes, "'difficult situations' just like this one. If Eudora is truly incapacitated, he can file an emergency motion to get a judge to recognize you as the legal head of Palmetto Holdings. You won't need Eudora, then. You could do anything you want." His eyes widened as his face flushed with excitement. He stood, and a shower of muffin crumbs fell to the floor. "My friend can probably be at the courthouse before the close of business today, so we can get this taken care of right quick. I'll call the owners and tell them we're on our way." He fished his cell phone from his front pocket and began to dial a number. "A'course we'll have to stop at the bank to withdraw that incentive, but I don't think the owners will mind waiting. The owners are going to want a cashier's check, and my buddy prefers cash."

"Put that phone away."

"What?" Bruce looked up from his screen.

"I'm not doing that—not *any* of it. I'm not using your sleazy attorney friend, and I'm not paying any kind of bribe to the owners."

Marcy shook with anger, but most of the anger was directed at herself. For months, Marcy had thought the warehouse property was the most important thing in her life. She offered more money than the company could afford to pay for the property. She hired Bruce to secure tenants for the new strip mall, ignoring whispers about his reputation, and Andrea's warnings. Worst of all, she neglected her grandmother's health.

All at once, she saw Bruce for what he was: an opportunist who didn't care at all for her company.

"It's your choice." He shrugged as if he didn't care, but his good-ol'-boy manners didn't fool Marcy. Not anymore. "There is one final option, but it has to be done today, and there isn't much time."

"What is it?"

"You must have Eudora's signature on file somewhere."

"I do." Marcy knew what he wanted. She waited to hear him say it.

He chose a pen from her desktop. "Print a new letter and add Eudora's signature to the bottom. We'll bring it to closing, and they'll have to honor it. Done deal."

"You mean forge it?"

"Well." He must have mistaken her demeanor for acceptance because his voice turned jovial again. "It's not really *forging*, is it?" Bruce offered a wide smile. "I mean, you know she *wanted* to sign the paper; she just didn't get to it."

"Absolutely not."

"That would be a mistake." Bruce's eyes narrowed. "You know the potential in that property, and the only thing preventing us from getting it is a signature on that power of attorney."

"I've just told you that my grandmother is in the hospital, and the doctors aren't sure what's wrong with her. And you're suggesting first thing we do—the most important thing—is to forge her signature so we can steal her company from her?"

Bruce leaned forward, his eyes were like granite. "You can't let this deal slip through your fingers. The land alone will be worth a fortune in a few years."

She pressed her hands around her coffee mug to keep them from shaking.

Bruce misunderstood her silence for acceptance, and he smiled. He wiped his mouth and crushed the napkin in his hand. "I'll call my attorney buddy. I'm sure we can get this taken care of." Bruce pulled out his phone and tapped a message.

"That's enough." Marcy set her mug on her desk, and called for Andrea. She appeared almost immediately, which meant she had been listening at the door. "Andrea, call Scotty and Jason from downstairs, please. I need to see them now."

Andrea moved aside, and the two stonemasons entered the office. "I already did. They're here."

As short and as solid as a cannonball, Scotty spoke first. "Something you need doing, Ms. Rutledge?"

"Yes, thank you." With her gaze fixed on Bruce, Marcy held out her hand. "Give me your keys to the office, Bruce. You're fired. Gentlemen, please escort this man from the building."

A moment of stunned silence hung in the air, but Bruce was the first to recover. He rose to his feet and took a step toward her, his hands fisted at his side. "You can't be serious, Marcy. We had a deal," he spat. "What about my commission? You owe me at least that, and I'm gonna hold you to it."

"I am deadly serious." Marcy's voice was granite. "Consider yourself fortunate that I haven't called the police for what you suggested today." Nodding at Scotty and Jason, Marcy said, "Please escort him out the front door. Don't stop at his desk, and don't let him talk to anyone or take anything from the building."

They approached Bruce, but he shook them off. "I know enough about this company, and about you, to *ruin* you. Think about what you're doing, what you're losing."

Marcy rose from her chair. "You forget how much I know about *you*, Bruce. I suggest you leave town while you still have the chance."

She nodded to Scotty, who placed his hand on Bruce's shoulder. "If you try to re-enter this building, you will be arrested."

Marcy dropped into her chair and glanced at Andrea. "How did you know?"

"That he was stealing clients? I've suspected that for a couple of weeks, but only found out for sure two days ago," Andrea answered.

"Stealing clients?" Marcy repeated. "What do you mean 'stealing clients'?"

"I thought you knew—I texted you." Andrea blinked. "If you didn't fire him for that, what *did* you fire him for?"

"It doesn't matter now." Marcy pressed her warm coffee cup against her temple to ease the pounding. "We've lost the North Charleston property."

"Good." Andrea took a seat in front of Marcy's desk. "I've never understood why you liked it. Developing strip malls is not what we do."

"We had to branch out, Andrea. You know we're not making the same money we used to."

"You'll figure it out," Andrea was confident. "You always do. This just isn't the way."

"I'll have to figure it out later." Marcy set her mug on the desk and rose from her chair. "If you need me, I'll be at the hospital."

"Hang on a second." Andrea disappeared from the office, returning a moment later with a large paper bag. "Thousand Island or French?"

"Excuse me?"

Andrea lifted the bag she carried. "On your salad. Do you want Thousand Island or French?" The bag crinkled as Andrea set it on the desk. "Joanna called and asked me to get you something to eat. She said you probably wouldn't want it, but to give it to you anyway." Andrea smiled. "I like that sister of yours." Andrea lifted up a bottle of each and jiggled them. "So, what will it be? Thousand Island or French?"

Marcy laughed, and it felt good. "Thousand Island."

"Great." Andrea slipped the bottle into the bag and folded it closed. "One more thing." She held out her hand. "Let me have the prescriptions. I can fill them."

"Prescriptions?" Marcy repeated, stupidly. She'd stuffed them in her pocket and had forgotten them.

"Yes." Andrea confirmed. "When my Aunt Irene went into the hospital for heart surgery last year, there were about a dozen things we needed to do before we could take her home. I can take what you have to the pharmacy and pick them up when they're filled." She offered a reassuring smile. "The transition will be easier if the little things are in place before Eudora is released."

Marcy dug into her bag and handed Andrea the pages. "Thank you, Andrea."

"You know, there are a lot of people willing to help you. All you have to do is let them. I'll text you when I've got them." She turned to leave, then stopped, a wide smile on her face. "—oh, wait. You don't get reception at the hospital." She flashed a smile on her way out the door. "I'd say that was pretty lucky this time."

CHAPTER 32

JOANNA'S HEAD was swimming with details, but they weren't even close to being finished.

The social worker handed her another printed page. "This is the referral for speech therapy. Dr. Plyer wants you to schedule speech therapy for your grandmother right away— every day to start. Then probably dropping down to three times a week, depending on her progress. Add this page to the packet of things I already gave you."

Joanna wished she could remember the woman's name. Tall and competent, the woman wore a black pencil skirt and a cream shell blouse, but her name tag was obscured by her scarf. Bright blue reading glasses hung from a silver chain around her neck, and a stack of silver bangles sparkled against her dark skin.

After the paper came a dense booklet marked "Aftercare." The woman tapped the cover. "These are referrals for nutritionists and physical therapists, organized by area they serve. Check with your insurance company to see if they're in your network. Do you have any questions?"

"Um, not right now." Joanna took the booklet, wishing she had absorbed enough to ask a question.

With a quick nod and a brief smile, the woman continued. "Dr. Plyer is going to want to see your grandmother, for a follow-up, after she's released. I can get the insurance process started now, to save you time." The woman looked at Joanna, expectantly. "Do you have her information?"

"Insurance information?"

"Yes."

Eudora must have insurance, but Joanna had no idea what kind, what it covered, or which company issued the policy. "Not with me. Can I get back to you on that?"

"That's fine, but please don't take too long. Some companies can be sticky about preauthorization, so you'll want to start that process as soon as possible." The woman's bracelets tapped against her clipboard as she scribbled a note.

Just as Joanna was about to confess that she knew nothing about Eudora's care. That Joanna had, in fact, forgotten almost all of what she'd been told, and could she please start over. the door to Eudora's room opened, and Marcy entered.

Joanna smiled.

The cavalry had come.

The woman clipped her pen to the board and offered her hand. "You must be Marcy."

"I am. Marcy Rutledge." Marcy set her things on the chair and shook the woman's hand. She offered an apologetic smile. "I know we've met before, but I can't recall your name at the moment."

"LeShawnda Miller. I'm a social worker, here at the hospital." The woman smiled. "And it's okay. I know you both have a lot on your mind. I was just going over some last-minute details with your sister about your grandmother's aftercare."

"Aftercare?" Marcy's eyebrows raised. "We have a release date?"

"No, nothing definite. Dr. Plyer's office asked me to coordinate a few things now, to make it easier later." She gestured to the envelope she'd given Joanna. "His information is in the packet, and I've added a few things of my own. Options you might be interested in."

Marcy took it and opened the cover.

LeShawnda leaned her shoulder against the wall. "You know, you're lucky you have each other. When my Grammy West got sick, it was just me left to take care of her. I was in grad school at the time, and let me tell you, I would have given a lot to have a sister to help. Not that caring for my Grammy wasn't a blessing, it was. She was the best woman I ever knew." LeShawnda pushed herself from the wall and continued. "You're going to need our insurance codes for the referrals. I can coordinate with you—"

"You can take this one back right now." Marcy had pulled a brochure from the packet, and her expression had changed. "We're not doing this. We're *never* doing this."

Joanna glanced at the picture on the cover. It seemed innocent enough, a white-haired older woman, about Eudora's age, dressed in a soft cardigan and flanked by two younger women, who looked like daughters. One of the daughters had her arm lightly draped around the older woman's shoulders, and they all smiled encouragingly. It looked, to Joanna, as if they were going on vacation together, and that didn't sound like a bad idea. A weekend away would be something for Eudora to look forward to, and they could even invite Letty.

"That's okay. It's just an option." The woman soothed. "You might reconsider later."

"We don't need it, thank you," Marcy repeated as she thrust the brochure back.

"That's fine." LeShawnda slid the brochure underneath the other, on her clipboard. "Some families like to have the option, but no one is pushing you."

"We've been presented with that before, and I've refused. I haven't changed my mind. Eudora will stay where she is." Marcy was firm.

"I understand."

LeShawnda reached for the door. "I'll check back in a few days. If you have questions in the meantime, my card is stapled to the inside front cover."

The moment she left, Marcy dropped to the chair and closed her eyes. She looked utterly exhausted.

"What is in that brochure?"

"First tell me if there's any news about Gram. Has she woken up yet, or spoken?" Marcy spoke without opening her eyes.

"What happened to you?"

Marcy opened her eyes. "What do you mean? I'm fine."

But she wasn't. Joanna looked closer at her perfect sister: Marcy looked as if she would shatter at the slightest touch. Her eyes were ringed with deep circles, her mouth was drawn with worry and the collar of her suit was twisted. Joanna wished she had thought to bring Marcy a change of clothes.

Marcy straightened in her chair and reached for the envelope of referrals. "There is a lot to do before Gram is released, especially if we plan to keep her home."

"I can help—" Joanna offered, then stopped. "Wait. What do you mean 'if we plan to keep her home'?"

Marcy sighed and dropped the envelope onto the table. It landed with a thud. "It has been suggested—strongly suggested—that we move Gram to assisted living. I've refused, but now that she is starting to wander, we may not have much of a choice."

"That's what that brochure was? "Joanna asked. "Assisted living?"

"There's a place on James Island. It's nice. I've been there. But it didn't seem right."

Joanna couldn't imagine Gram's house without Gram in it. "So, what happens now? What can I do to keep Gram at home?"

"We need to find help." Marcy dug into her bag and produced the card Dr. Plyer had given her earlier. "We need a qualified nurse who has experience with older patients. Dr. Plyer's office has a list of nurses they've vetted. You can start there."

"No problem," Joanna promised.

"It's not as easy as you think," Marcy warned as she leaned her head back and closed her eyes again. "Gram doesn't like anyone who isn't Letty."

"I'll start now." Joanna gathered her things. "I'll meet you at home."

CHAPTER 33

MARCY SPENT THE NIGHT, and most of the next day, at the hospital by Eudora's side. Joanna came and went when she could, bringing food from home and a change of clothes. It was Dr. Plyer who told Marcy to go home, offering his personal cell number and promising to call if there was even the slightest change in Eudora's condition.

But instead of going home, Marcy went to work. She spent the day trying to salvage the damage she'd done to Palmetto Holding by trying to acquire the North Charleston property. Andrea told her that the property sold right away, for more than Marcy offered. When she called to congratulate them, she asked them to return her escrow. But they refused, pointing to the section in the standard contract that allowed them to keep it.

Marcy turned off the engine and rolled down the car window. She closed her eyes, leaning into the evening air, feeling the breeze cooling her face. To fix what she'd done, Marcy would have to steer Palmetto Holdings in an entirely different direction, with limited funds and no safety net. And she had no idea how to do that.

"Aunt Marcy?"

Marcy opened her eyes with a start. Her niece, whom Marcy had spoken to exactly twice since she'd arrived, stood before her, wide-eyed and dressed in a yellow and black striped leotard, her chubby cheeks smeared with chocolate. Around her waist was a cloud of yellow tulle, and on her head, a gold crown pasted with an assortment of rhinestones the size of half-dollar coins.

Marcy offered a tentative smile. She had no idea how to talk to children. "Hi, Gracie. Are you out here all alone? Does Jo—does your mother know where you are?"

Gracie nodded, her blue eyes solemn. Taking a step forward, she whispered, "She said I could wait for you, to give you something."

"What is it?" Straightening in her seat, Marcy couldn't imagine what Gracie had for her, especially because they were virtual strangers.

Gracie dug into her pocket for something and pushed her chubby arm through the open car window. When Marcy held out her hand, Gracie dropped half a dozen warm chocolate candies into her palm.

"Mommy said you were sad," Gracie explained, "so I saved my best party candy for you."

Marcy blinked. The shells of the candy were cracked, and some of the soft chocolate oozed from underneath. "Your party candy? You went to a party today?"

Gracie nodded as she dug into her skirt pocket for more. Popping them into her mouth, she answered through the crunch. "Hall'ween. I had the best costume, even though stupid Tara Wilkins said it didn't count because I wasn't a real thing. But Miss Allison said I was the best Spelling Bee she ever saw."

Marcy examined her niece's costume. Clearly, the yellow and black stripes were bee-related. As Gracie smoothed the yellow tulle of her skirt, a streetlight reflected the gold in her crown, and Marcy saw it. The rhinestones pasted on it formed letters, making Gracie a Spelling Bee.

Marcy's snort turned to laughter as she saw the look of delight on Gracie's face. "Miss Allison is right: you are the best Spelling Bee."

Straightening her crown, Gracie's smile spanned the width of her dimpled cheeks. "Are you happy now? You can come inside now if you're happy. Miss Letty said to let you in only when you got happy."

"Miss Letty is here?" Marcy asked as she pushed open the car door.

Gracie nodded, enthusiastically. "She's making dinner, and there's chocolate cake for dessert."

"You really like chocolate, don't you?" Marcy said, with a smile.

"It's my favorite thing," Gracie confirmed.

Marcy gathered her things and followed Gracie through the courtyard and into the garden. The garden path was one she hadn't taken in years because it always seemed to be an unnecessary detour, a waste of time. As her hours at work became longer, it was easier to just park the car and use the front door. But now, as she walked the slate path, with flowers and plants on either side, she wondered why she hadn't come this way more often.

It was pretty. The air was fresher here, and Marcy felt herself beginning to relax.

On the stairs to the piazza, Gracie slowed. She turned, her face troubled. "Aunt Marcy? Please don't tell Mommy that I ated the chocolates. She told me not to."

"It will be our secret," Marcy promised easily. "But you'd better wipe your chin before you go in, though. Melted chocolate is a dead giveaway."

After a quick swipe, Gracie scrambled up the stairs and pushed open the door to the kitchen. Her words came out in a rush. "I found Aunt Marcy, Mommy. She's happy now."

Joanna pulled a dishtowel from the hook and dried her hands. "Good job, Goose. Now go wash up for dinner..." Joanna's brows knit as her words trailed off. She held her daughter by the shoulders and looked deeply into her eyes. "Why do you smell like chocolate?"

Gracie stiffened as the color rose in her cheeks.

"She gave me some party candy that she'd saved, when she met me outside." The lie fell easily from Marcy's lips, and she didn't feel the least bit regretful. In fact, it felt good to share a secret with her niece. "It was a little melted, but it was good—just what I needed at the end of the day. Thank you, Gracie."

Gracie sagged with relief, and Marcy turned away to smother a smile.

"Nana, can I borrow the keys to your car? We need special laundry soap, and I think Piggly Wiggly by the hospital carries it."

"Amina?" Marcy ventured. Amina was Letty's grand-daughter. She and Marcy used to play together in the summers but her family moved away years ago, and they'd lost track of each other. Looking at her now, the resemblance to Letty was unmistakable. She and Letty had the same kind, dark eyes, the same warm smile. Both were tall and dark skinned, but where Letty had always worn her hair short and natural, this woman seemed to celebrate her hair with a cascade of thin braids twisted with beads.

The woman drew Marcy into a tight hug. "Marcy! It's been forever."

Marcy's words were muffled against her friend's shoulder. "I didn't know you were visiting."

"Not just visiting." Amina held Marcy at arm's length, her eyes dancing with excitement. "You won't believe the news!"

"We had an idea—" Joanna began.

But Letty cut her off. "Oh no, honey. We didn't think of this. This was all you and you should be proud of yourself."

"Fine." Joanna smiled and held her palms up in surrender. "My idea. We need a private nurse and Amina needs a place to stay while she finishes her Masters' degree—in Nursing. She can stay here and take care for Gram when she comes home. She's qualified to supervise meds and we can give her permission to contact Gram's doctors if we need her to." Joanna's voice trailed away as she searched Marcy's face.

Letty turned to Marcy, her eyes narrowed in warning. "Tell your sister what do you think of her idea?"

If Letty thought Marcy would reject the idea, simply because it came from Joanna, she would be mistaken. It took too much energy to be stubborn and it was a waste of time.

"I love it." Turning to Amina, Marcy added, "I'm glad you're back and delighted that you're going to stay with us. Congratulations on your Masters'. That's tough to do."

Amina laughed. "I don't have it yet."

"You're well on your way," Letty admonished. "You be proud, little girl."

Joanna flapped her hands. "There's more. Letty's going to live here too, as part of the family. She's chosen the blue guest room, and we can move her things in next week."

"I get to be near my grandbaby, every day," Letty said. "It's a happy time for me."

"I can monitor her diabetes since I'll be close. Nana's doctors will be happy about that," Amina volunteered. "The problem we're trying to solve is that Joanna said you need someone full time. I can cut back my class load, but I can't manage full-time here."

Marcy remembered what LeShawnda had told her about it being a privilege to care for her grandmother. "I'm sure we can work something out. Joanna and I will be happy to help. Whatever you need."

"Well, you best get started," Letty directed. "There's a lot to do." Letty dropped a set of car keys into Amina's palm. "Get some grapefruit while you're out. Miss Eudora likes to start her day with a glass of fresh juice, and she likes grape-fruit best. If they don't have that, I suppose orange will do, but she won't be happy about it."

Amina hesitated. "Maybe we should talk to Miss Eudora's doctor before we buy any juice. Citrus can interfere with medication."

Marcy could count on one hand the number of times anyone had contradicted Letty's instructions, and she watched, with great interest, to see what Letty would do, but Letty seemed not to notice.

Letty frowned. "Okay then, but you be the one to explain to Miss Eudora, and I don't envy you that. Miss Eudora is set in her ways."

"A, B, C, D..." Down the hallway, in the little bathroom, Gracie began to sing the alphabet—loudly, and with great enthusiasm.

Letty flicked her gaze toward the bathroom and back to Joanna. "That child do love the water. I b'lieve she's part fish."

Joanna sighed. "The school nurse told Gracie's class to

sing the alphabet while they wash their hands—the entire alphabet. Gracie likes to practice. A lot." She called down the hallway. "Gracie, that's enough. Time for dinner."

Gracie skipped into the kitchen, her hands dripping water, humming the alphabet song. She stopped in front of Marcy. "Aunt Marcy, are you picking me up from school tomorrow?"

"I haven't asked her yet, Gracie." Joanna turned to Marcy. "I have an appointment tomorrow, near the hospital, and I'd like to visit Gram afterward. If you have time, I was hoping you could pick Gracie up at three o'clock. If you're busy—"

"Sure. I've got time tomorrow." Marcy had nothing but time until she figured out how to restructure her grandfather's company. Picking Gracie up from school might be a nice distraction from work. How difficult could it be?

"Well, that's fine." Letty stood and reached for her apron. "All the world's problems solved just in time for me to get dinner started."

Joanna moved toward her. "You're a guest here, Letty. I can cook dinner."

Letty snorted as she pulled the apron over her head. "I have seen what you cook, little missy, and I don't want any part of it." Tying the apron strings, she gestured to Marcy with her chin. "And I haven't seen you do anything in this kitchen, other than flick a switch on the coffee brewer, in years." Reaching for a second apron, Letty slipped it over Gracie's head. "No, ma'am. Y'all two sit and visit. It's past time for someone to teach little bitty to cook, anyway. At least one of you Rutledges should be able to do something besides read a menu and dial for takeout."

Marcy frowned. "I thought you were a guest, Letty. You promised not to do this again—you know what happened last time. Gram will never forgive me if it happens again."

Letty scoffed. "I can make one dinner. It's that, or we'll all starve." She gestured to Gracie. "At least until this baby learns to cook. She's my last hope for this family."

When dinner was over, and everyone had gone to bed, Marcy turned off the lights and set the house alarm. That night, for the first time in months, Marcy slept peacefully, without waking in a panic, without nightmares of things left undone. She still needed to address the problems she'd created at Palmetto Holdings, but that could wait until the morning. Right now, Eudora would live at home, surrounded by her friends and family.

Everything else could wait.

CHAPTER 34

"ARE you sure you can pick up Gracie from school?" Joanna tugged at the waistband of her sweater. Acrylic and ugly, it stretched across her hips in exactly the wrong place. She didn't have money yet for new clothes, so she had borrowed the sweater from Eudora's closet. Something told her this one wouldn't be missed.

Marcy didn't look up from the spreadsheet on her laptop. The table in front of her was spread with papers. "Yes. I've got it scheduled on my phone."

"You know where her school is?" A swipe of lipstick and Joanna was ready. Coral wasn't exactly her color, but shades of coral were all Eudora had on her vanity.

"Of course, I do. We went to school there, remember?" Marcy finally glanced up from her work and stared. "What in the *world* are you wearing?"

Joanna felt her cheeks burn as she covered her stomach with her palms. She knew what she looked like, but this was the best she could do. She already owed Eudora a substantial amount of money for Gracie's uniforms and tuition. She didn't want to ask for anything more.

"The sweater just doesn't seem like something you'd wear. I was surprised, that's all." Marcy had put down her pen and offered an apologetic smile. "Do you want to borrow something?" She rummaged in her bag and produced a credit card. "Or: buy yourself something new. You might like the shops off King Street. Here, use this."

Joanna shook her head, feeling the rough acrylic against her neck. "I'll be fine." It was tempting to take Marcy's card, to have her big sister fix everything. But Joanna wanted to find her own way this time. Swinging one of Eudora's cast-off purses over her shoulder, she turned to leave the room. "Thanks for picking up Gracie. Call me if you need anything."

"Got it." Marcy waved her away and returned to her work.

Once outside, Joanna crossed the street to the seawall along the Battery, almost without thinking. She'd always been drawn to the water. A fishing boat chugged out to sea, and a trio of sailboats raced across the harbor. The water shimmered in the sun, and the crisp air had finally made it feel like fall.

Mindful of the time, Joanna flagged down a rogue taxi as it drove along East Battery. As it rolled to a stop, she opened the door and gave the driver the address. As an alumna, she still had access to job listings in the college's placement office, and that seemed as good a place as any to start.

CHAPTER 35

As THE SCHOOL BELL RANG, the youngest students lined up behind their teachers and walked from the classroom to the carpool. Even from four cars away, Marcy spotted her niece right away, a ball of energy trying to walk carefully behind her teacher. She dragged behind her the same regulation school bag that Marcy remembered, black with a yellow crest. But Gracie's bag overflowed with drawing paper and over-sized picture books. Like Joanna's did when she was that age.

Marcy showed her driver's license to the aide with the clipboard. Her name was checked off the list and she was instructed to pull forward. Gracie skipped to the car, her blonde hair bouncing against her shoulders.

"Hi, Aunt Marcy." Gracie climbed into the back seat. "I had a great day!" Turning to the aide for confirmation, Gracie asked, "Wasn't it a great day, Mrs. Bollman?"

"Yes, it was, Gracie," the woman agreed as she buckled Gracie's seat belt. She added, "See you tomorrow," before closing the door and starting the process again with the car behind them.

Marcy glanced at her niece before flicking on her blinker and pulling into traffic. "How was school today?" Marcy asked, automatically, before remembering that Gracie had already told her.

"Good," Gracie answered, before returning her attention to the library books she had stuffed in her bag.

During the short drive home, Gracie read random passages aloud from her collection of books. After a while, Marcy allowed her attention to drift between her niece and the problems at work. The fallout from what she'd done to her family's company would be too big to hide, and she was dreading the conversation she'd have with Eudora. Her grandmother would either be furious with her, which Marcy could handle, or disappointed in her, which she couldn't.

Eudora would have no choice but to demote her. But Marcy hoped that she would at least listen to her ideas for the company. A new direction, a brilliant solution to what she'd done.

But first, she'd have to think of something.

When they pulled into the courtyard, Gracie put down her books and looked around, confused. "Are we going to the park?"

"What park?" Marcy glanced at her niece through the rear-view mirror. Her sister hadn't mentioned a park.

"We go to the park all the time on Tuesdays," Gracie explained. "I show Mommy my drawings and my spelling words, and she pushes me on the swing. Then we watch the sailboats after that."

"What sailboats?"

"The ones that go to the big castle." Gracie pointed to the harbor.

"What big castle?"

"The one on the island—Fort Summer."

Marcy glanced toward the harbor. "Do you mean Fort *Sum-ter*?"

"That's what I said—Fort Summer. Then Mommy tells the story of the long sailboat race to there."

A sailboat race to the fort. Marcy had no idea what Gracie was talking about. She couldn't possibly mean the annual Labor Day Regatta. Joanna hadn't been allowed to watch because their mother said she was too young. The year Marcy competed, the weather had been horrible and everyone except Brock stayed home. The entire day had been a miserable experience for Marcy, one best forgotten. Why would Joanna describe that day to her daughter? How would she know about it?

"What did your mother say about the race?" Marcy twisted in her seat.

Gracie turned the page of her book. "That you were the best winner in the whole club."

The year Marcy competed, she was entered into the "twelve and younger" division and she planned to use the same little boat that she'd practiced in all summer long. For some reason, her grandfather had persuaded the team's coach into entering her in an upper division, with kids three to five years older than she was. Kids who had been sailing their whole lives, not just one summer. The course for her division was different than that one she'd practiced. It was five miles long, instead of two, and the boat she had to use was considerably bigger, and one she had never sailed before. By the time her race was called, the wind had changed, kicking up whitecaps in the harbor under a darkening sky. An unexpected flood tide washed in from Fort Sumter, forcing Marcy to navigate an unfamiliar course and an aggressive current.

But none of that mattered to her grandfather. He expected the best, always. Anything less than first-place was unacceptable. And to Marcy's horror, he had boarded the judges' launch, just to watch her race.

Frayed nerves caused a false start, her boat crossed the starting line before the gun went off. It was an inexcusable error. Marcy fought back tears of frustration as she tacked the boat around the marker to restart her race, handicapping herself by several boat lengths before she even started. The race was terrifying. At times, she let the sails flutter while she bailed water from the boat, ignoring her grandfather's shouts to continue.

In the end, she placed fifth in a division of fifteen, a significant accomplishment, all things considered. But she watched the storm brewing in her grandfather's face as the judges announced the winners, and she knew what was coming. She tied off at the dock and abandoned her boat, running home to Letty.

She and Joanna and Alice left early the next morning for Pensacola, back to their stepfather, and only Letty was there to say goodbye. Marcy carried the weight of her failure and her grandfather's disappointment for the entire car ride home, and for years afterward.

But her sister couldn't possibly have known about any of that.

"How do you know this story?" Marcy asked.

"Because Mommy saw you. She used nock-u-lars to watch, and she crossed the busy street by herself to watch." Gracie's voice dropped to a whisper. "But she got in trouble."

"Got in trouble? What do you mean 'got in trouble'?"

Goosebumps rose on Marcy's arm. That phrase meant something very different in the Rutledge household, especially when it was their grandfather who was angry.

"I don't know." Gracie tugged the seatbelt on her booster seat. "Can we go now?"

"Wouldn't you rather read your books?" Despite working all morning, Marcy still hadn't been able to untangle the finances at work. She'd hoped Joanna would be home by now, so she could get back to work, but the house looked empty.

"Books comes after dinner, at bedtime," Gracie explained.

"I didn't know you were such a stickler for details," Marcy said, as she unlocked her car door. There didn't seem to be a way out. "I guess we're going to the park." Then an idea came to her and it made her smile. "Unless you want to go the yacht club and look at the sailboats?"

Gracie's smile dimpled her cheeks. "Yes!"

"Leave your stuff in the car," Marcy instructed as she held out her hand. "We can walk from here. It's not far."

Gracie slipped her hand into Marcy's, and they crossed the street to the harbor. As they walked along the seawall toward the yacht club, Gracie chattered, changing topics as quick as a hiccup.

"I have a friend at school, Aunt Marcy. She's older than me, but she comes into my classroom sometimes to help Miss Allison at craft time. My friend's name is Zoe, and she likes all the things I like. She likes horses, and soccer, and blue glitter." Gracie held up an index finger to correct herself. "Only the *blue* glitter and not yellow, because yellow glitter is always dried up, and red glitter is for boys."

"Girls can have red glitter, too, Gracie," Marcy said automatically because it seemed like the right thing to say. But really, she wondered why red glitter was reserved for boys.

Marcy entered the code at the gates at the entrance and led an excited Gracie down the path to the clubhouse. Overhead, the burgees snapped in the breeze, bright primary colors against a clear blue sky. Perfect sailing weather. The thought surprised her because, despite being founding members of the club, Marcy never ventured beyond the clubhouse, not after the regatta. It made her sad, suddenly, to think of what she'd lost. She had loved the water.

At the top of the stairs, Marcy held the door open as Gracie slipped inside.

"So pretty," Gracie breathed as she saw the vase of flowers on the entrance table. Orange, yellow, and burgundy mums were arranged in a tall crystal vase engraved with the club's crest. To the side was a pyramid of knobby squash, and a glass dish filled with chocolate pumpkins wrapped in foil. Gracie's eyes lit up the moment she saw the chocolates. "Can I have one?" she breathed.

"Sure." Marcy's attention was drawn to the sailing trophies in the display case. She wondered if they still held the Labor Day Regatta.

By the time she had turned her attention back to Gracie, it was too late. Gracie had reached for the dish of chocolate pumpkins, but somehow her foot tangled on the edge of the tablecloth, and she lost her balance. The cloth pulled away, and the crystal dish teetered on the edge of the table before falling to the floor and smashing against the tile.

"Gracie, no!" Marcy shouted, and lunged for her niece. She grabbed for the girl's shoulder, hoping to shield her from the shattering glass.

But Gracie recoiled the moment Marcy touched her. She dove under the table and disappeared.

Marcy dropped to her knees beside the table, her mind racing. "Gracie, wait—what's wrong? Did I scare you? I didn't mean to. I was just trying to keep you away from the broken glass."

From under the table, Marcy heard Gracie whimpering, and the sound triggered a memory. She lifted the tablecloth, her senses heightened. "Gracie, are you hurt? Please, let me see. Please, come out." Marcy softened her voice as if she were trying to coax a kitten from a tree branch. "Take my hand." Marcy slowly reached under the table. She held it there, steady, as her own memories assailed her.

The touch on Marcy's hand was slight, a kind of test, and Marcy didn't move. After what seemed like an eternity, Gracie's head appeared under the edge of the table. Brushing the tablecloth to the side, Marcy pulled her niece onto her lap. It was a long time before Gracie's trembling stopped. Gracie's reaction seemed familiar, and Marcy prayed that she was mistaken.

Marcy's voice was soft, barely a whisper. "You have to tell me what's wrong, Gracie. I can't help you if I don't know."

"I broke the glass." Gracie's body stiffened.

"I saw. It was an accident."

Marcy adjusted her position, so she could see Gracie's face. As Marcy moved, the collar of Gracie's uniform shirt dipped below her shoulder blade, and Marcy saw the bruise.

Her heart skipped.

She was right: She and Gracie shared a secret that Marcy wouldn't wish on anyone.

Marcy swallowed. Everything in her told her to run from this, but it was her niece, and she couldn't. "Gracie, that bruise on your shoulder looks like it hurts. Did you get that at school?"

Gracie froze, her eyes widened. Her face paled, and the trembling began again.

Marcy smoothed Gracie's hair. Gracie flinched, and Marcy stopped. "Was somebody mean to you? Because that's not okay. No one should ever hit you."

Even as she asked the question, Marcy realized the bruise couldn't have come from school. The mark was yellow already, too old to have happened recently. And it was in a place that would be concealed, covered by clothing. Marcy felt bile rising, burning the back of her throat. Only adults knew how to hit so the bruise would be hidden.

"Gracie, who did this to you?"

Gracie looked away, her voice barely audible. "Nicco."

That name meant nothing to her. "Who is Nicco?" Marcy asked.

"Mommy's friend. He's mean."

"Does your mother know about this?"

Slowly, Gracie nodded. "She took us away."

Marcy drew a deep breath as she scooped Gracie up from the floor and into her arms. "I promise you, Gracie, that man —Nicco—will never touch you again. You're safe here."

As she turned to leave, the door of an office opened, and a woman walked toward them. She stopped when she saw the tablecloth and the broken glass. Her expression turned to concern.

Gracie lay limp against Marcy's body, her head resting on Marcy's shoulder. Her breathing was peppered with hiccups and shudders. Marcy stroked Gracie's back as she spoke to the woman, "I'm afraid we've had an accident. I've broken the dish."

"Is anyone hurt? I have a first-aid kit in my office." The woman approached, and Gracie flinched.

Instinctively, Marcy shielded Gracie's body with her own. "Thank you, we'll be fine. I just wanted to let you know."

As Marcy walked up the path, she wondered what to do next.

CHAPTER 36

"COME ON, AUNT MARCY." Gracie raced along the garden path and pounded up the stairs to the kitchen door, practically vibrating with excitement.

The past three hours had been a blur—her head buzzed. The din of the shops still bounced in her head. The look of joy on Gracie's face every time she had been handed a toy, picked out a dress, or tried on a pair of shiny shoes had salvaged the afternoon. Marcy switched the bags to her other hand and stopped to rub her palm against her thigh, hoping to bring feeling back to her fingers.

"I'm right behind you." As she climbed the stairs, Marcy dug into her purse for her house key. When she reached the piazza, she eyed the wicker chairs with longing. What she wouldn't give for an hour with nothing to do but watch Eudora's garden, to avoid the discussion she was about to have with her sister.

Marcy unlocked the door and held it open as Gracie rushed into the house, a ball of energy. "Mommy! Mommy! You can't believe it! What we did, you just can't believe it!"

"I'm over here, Goose." Joanna folded her newspaper as

she rose to greet them. As Gracie chattered, Marcy slid the packages and Gracie's school bag onto the table.

Joanna glanced at Marcy, then did a double take. "What happened to you?"

Marcy pinched the fabric of her T-shirt and held it away from her body. The smear of chocolate across the college seal was from the ice cream sundae she and Gracie had shared right after the incident at the yacht club. The knees of her jeans were flecked with sand where she had knelt on the beach as Gracie dug for treasure, and the snag on her sleeve was probably from the swing at the park.

Marcy shrugged as she dropped into a chair. "Gracie happened."

Gracie grabbed her mother by the hand and dragged her to the table. "Presents, Mommy! Presents for me!"

"What do you mean, 'presents'?" The paper crinkled as Joanna peered into one of the packages. She eyed them with an expression Marcy didn't understand.

Pushing herself from the table, Marcy made her way to the refrigerator. "We had quite a day, didn't we Gracie?"

Gracie danced in place, her new sneakers squeaking against the wood floor as she upended the shopping bags. "So many things, Mommy! You can't believe it." She laughed as she pulled a plastic tub from the bag. "We got markers, Mommy. So many markers, and I don't have to share. Yellow's in here, right Aunt Marcy?"

"I would bet it is," Marcy confirmed as she twisted the cap from a bottle of water.

Gracie went to the next bag, and the next, each time exclaiming over a treasure she didn't remember buying. And when it was all over, when the floor was littered with torn bags and tissue paper, Gracie stood in the center of the wreck-age, her face wreathed in a dimpled smile.

"Looks like you both have had a full day." Joanna's voice was tight, her expression shadowed.

Except for a few dresses, and the sneakers Gracie had insisted on wearing out of the store, what they bought had been mostly toys. After the incident at the yacht club, Gracie had been alarmingly detached. What brought her back was a trip to The Toy Shop, and instructions to "pick out anything you want." It wouldn't be a final solution, of course, but it made her niece smile. And for the moment, that was enough.

Marcy held a glass against the ice dispenser; the cubes clinked into the glass. "Gracie knows exactly what she likes." Did her sister know about Gracie's bruise? She must have—Gracie said they'd left Rome because of Nicco, so Joanna must have known. Why hadn't her sister said anything?

"This is for me, Mommy! It's all for me." Gracie's eyes widened as she gazed at the cache spread across the table.

It did look like a lot. Every kid's dream Christmas.

"I think you missed something." Marcy pointed to a forgotten bag propped against the back of a chair.

With a gasp, Gracie lunged for it and pulled out a wooden box. Inside, like jewels from Aladdin's cave, was a collection of glitter glue tubes, in an astonishing array of colors.

Staring at the contents with a deep reverence, Gracie breathed, "Look, Mommy—*two* reds."

If all it took was a trip to the toy store to make her niece forget what had happened to her, Marcy would do it every week. Scooping an empty paper bag from the floor, she laid it flat and smoothed out the wrinkles. "Apparently, red glitter glue is a very hot commodity in first grade," she said, idly.

"Stupid Tara Wilkins hogs it all," Gracie declared, her

brow creased with the righteous indignation reserved for six-year-olds.

"Don't say 'stupid,' Gracie. It's not nice," Joanna's voice was flat

Gracie clutched the box to her chest and breathed, "Lendard—I have to show him. Can I show him, Mommy?"

"Of course," Joanna replied.

The moment Gracie pounded up the stairs, Joanna crossed her arms and glared at Marcy. "*Why* did you do this, Marcy? All I asked you to do was pick Gracie up from school. That's it. You didn't need to do all this. I didn't *want* you to do all this."

Marcy struck back. "It's a few markers and toys. Gracie doesn't appear to have brought much of either."

"I can take care of my daughter." Joanna stiffened, and she turned away, but not before Marcy saw the redness coloring her face.

It was on the tip of Marcy's tongue to retort that Joanna, in fact, had *not* taken care of her daughter. She wanted to point to the bruise on Gracie's shoulder and question what kind of mother allows someone to do that to her child, but she didn't. She looked at her sister and saw someone who was doing the best she could. Joanna had come to Charleston with her daughter and nothing but the clothes they had on. She must have known she wouldn't have been warmly received. But she came anyway.

She came home to start over, and that took courage.

If Marcy wanted to find out what Joanna was running from, she would have to change her approach. "We should talk," she said, finally.

Gracie pounded down the stairs, Lendard under her arm,

and the box of glitter glue still clutched to her chest. "Lendard wants to see the glitters, Mommy."

Steering Gracie toward the counter, Joanna pulled a barstool from underneath the island and patted the seat. "Hop up, Goose. I'll put Lendard right here. He can watch." Spinning the drawing pad around, she popped open the cover and positioned the tub of markers within easy reach.

Marcy pulled a cold bottle of chardonnay from the refrigerator and glasses from the cabinet. This would be a difficult conversation, and she still didn't know how to approach it.

"Aunt Marcy and I will be just outside," Joanna said.

"Okay, Mommy." Gracie popped the cap off a marker and began to draw.

They settled into the wicker bistro table in the corner of the piazza. There was no easy way to approach this, so Marcy decided to be direct. "I saw the bruise on Gracie's shoulder."

The color drained from Joanna's face. Her fingers curled around the edge of the seat cushion. "She showed you?"

"Not on purpose. Something happened today, at the yacht club. It's the reason I took Gracie shopping."

Marcy filled one of the wine glasses and pushed it toward her sister. Joanna ignored it.

"What happened?"

"Gracie broke something by accident, and her reaction was...familiar." Marcy caught her sister's gaze and held it. "When our stepfather came after us, armed with his belt buckle and his rage, you hid under the bed to get away from him, the same way Gracie did today."

Marcy paused. She let her gaze wander to Eudora's garden, wishing that she didn't have to ask. The answer Joanna gave would change everything. Whatever the answer was, Marcy would help. Whatever needed to be done, she would do, because Joanna was still her sister.

As the shadows fell in the corners of the garden, Marcy gathered her strength. Finally, she turned to Joanna. "I need to ask you: Did something like that happen to you and Gracie in Rome? Will someone come here, looking for you?"

Joanna shifted her weight in the chair, fidgeting with the corner of her seat cushion.

"Mommy! Come look at my picture!" Gracie called from inside.

Joanna stared across the garden, seeming not to have heard her daughter call. Tears slid down her cheeks, and she let them fall, unchecked.

"I'll go." Marcy rose from her spot, her thoughts racing. Would whomever Joanna was running from find them here? Was he dangerous enough to threaten Eudora or Amina or Letty? Was Joanna stupid enough to go back to him? If she did, Marcy would take Gracie from her, just as someone should have taken them from their step-father? Was there time to sue Joanna for custody of Gracie? At the very least, Marcy would need a lawyer. For the briefest of seconds, Marcy wished she had kept the name of Bruce's fishing buddy. Honesty wouldn't matter to her if the fishing buddy could keep Joanna and Gracie safe.

Somehow, she managed conversation with Gracie, even as her mind shifted through possibilities to find a solution. When she returned to the piazza after looking at Gracie's glitter pictures, Joanna was staring across the garden, her attention far away. Her arms were crossed as if protecting her body from something physical.

Finally, Joanna sniffed, swiping at her nose with the back

of her hand. "You know that story of a frog in a pot of water? The one Letty used to tell us?"

Marcy took her place at the table.

Joanna continued as if she were speaking to herself. "I never understood that story. At the time, I thought it was stupid, but it turns out, I've been living it." She took a ragged breath. "She said that if you drop a frog in a pot of boiling water, he'll jump right out because he recognizes the danger he's in. But if you put him in a pot of cool water and you gradually increase the heat, the frog won't see what's happening. Even when the water boils, the frog stays put because he doesn't remember that he once had a choice to leave."

Joanna's voice was wooden, disconnected, as if she were narrating someone else's life. "I hated Chicago. I knew it was a mistake to move on the very first night, but Russell was my husband and aren't I supposed to do what he says?"

Marcy didn't answer. She didn't need to. She knew they were both remembering every time their mother pulled them out of school to move somewhere else. Their mother always did whatever her husband said.

Joanna scoffed. "Anyway, it didn't last. Russell decided he didn't want a family and he left us. He left me the apartment and five hundred dollars in a savings account. It didn't last long."

"I met Nicco last winter, and he said all the right things. He made me feel like I mattered, Marcy, and after four years of being a single mother, I needed to hear that. I'd just lost another job. Gracie was sick, and we were broke. I hadn't gotten my check yet from Palmetto Holdings, so money was tight." Joanna turned to her sister. "It was the winter I called you at work, in the middle of the day."

Marcy remembered that phone call. She'd been furious

because it had been the first time Joanna had called in years, and she called to ask for money. Eudora had stopped going to garden club meetings, stopped meeting friends, and spent her days wandering the house instead, never more than two rings away from any extension. Marcy had been livid.

"If you needed your quarterly checks so badly, why didn't you tell me?"

"Tell you what, exactly, Marcy? That Russell left me?" Joanna's voice was flat, as if she felt utterly defeated, and it broke Marcy's heart. "You never liked him, and I didn't need to hear you say, 'I told you so.'"

"I didn't 'not like' him," Marcy lied. "I just didn't think he was good enough for you."

The truth was that Marcy had loathed Russell. They were both business majors in school, though Russell was a year behind Marcy. She'd refused his invitations to dinner or drinks because she didn't like his type—slick and arrogant. She knew he fabricated evidence for his case studies and that he paid graduate students to write his research papers. Two weeks before she was to graduate, he proposed marriage. He wanted to start an investment firm, he said. Their families, the Rutledges and the Reeds, were two of the oldest in Charleston, and combining them would practically guarantee his company's success. Marcy had been repulsed, and told him so. Russell began dating Joanna a week later and had proposed within a month.

Marcy never said a word. Now, she wished that she had.

Joanna pulled her arms tighter around her chest and shivered. Marcy reached into the basket for a woolen blanket and draped it around her sister.

"I wish I had known, Joanna," Marcy began. "I wish I had known you were buying food with the dividend checks."

"What did you think I was doing? *Shopping*? *Lunching with my friends*?" Joanna spat. "Guess what, Marcy? I didn't *have* any friends. Every one of them left me when Russell did." Joanna closed her eyes. When she opened them again, she seemed calmer. "Gracie and I were barely living, Marcy. I stood in line at the food bank more times than I can count, praying they would give me enough diapers and formula to last the week. I turned the heat off at night to save money and brought Gracie to my bed to keep her warm. Do you know why I can't bear the smell of peanut butter? We ate so much of it that the thought of it literally makes me want to vomit."

"I didn't know, Joanna. I didn't know things were so bad for you. That's why you didn't call us. I should have picked up the phone, and called you myself. I'm sorry I didn't. I'm sorry I was so stubborn."

Joanna didn't answer, and Marcy didn't expect her to. Their relationship had always been complicated, a series of misunderstandings and power struggles that pushed them further apart. It had to change. Marcy wanted it to change. She wanted her sister back.

In the garden below, the light had changed to the deep blue of twilight, with a breath of salt water coming from the harbor.

After a moment, Marcy broke the silence with the question that had been tugging at her since her sister's return. "How did you end up living in Rome?"

Joanna shifted in her seat, folding her legs underneath, and drawing the blanket tighter around her shoulders. The wicker creaked as she moved. "I was so stupid." Joanna voice was a whisper, as if she were speaking to herself. "I believed everything that man told me, and he was very good. He said that his family would welcome Gracie and me, that he could find me a job working in an art museum, that Gracie would have cousins to play with, and that we would be happy there."

"I didn't know that you were unhappy." Marcy's voice was soft against the cool night, but Joanna startled, as if she hadn't realized Marcy was there.

Joanna pulled her legs up underneath her and shivered. "Things were bad after Russell left. I never could seem to get ahead, no matter what I did or how I worked and last winter was the worst. Gracie was sick, and I'd just been fired from another terrible job."

Marcy reached for the blanket and spread it across her sister's lap. In the kitchen behind them, Marcy could hear Gracie chatting with Lendard about colors and glitter.

Joanna tucked the blanket around her legs and continued, still looking out over the garden. "In the beginning Nicco was perfect. He cooked us dinners and made sure we were okay. He brought books for Gracie and flowers for me. It was nice." Joanna snorted. "A lie, but I wanted to believe it, so I didn't look too closely."

He said he wanted to marry me, but he couldn't bear to be so far from his family." Joanna drew a deep breath and tracked a beetle across the floor. "So, I paid for us to move—I sold the apartment in Chicago. Pulled Gracie from school and moved her away from her friends. I promised her that I'd always be there when she got home from school and that I'd be there to tuck her in at night."

"Just like Mom used to promise us, every time we moved."

"I guess so." Joanna replied. "But as soon as we arrived, it was like Gracie and I didn't exist. I never met Nicco's mother, his family, or any of his friends, and he never mentioned marriage to me again."

"Does he know where you are? Will he come find you?"

"The money's gone and he's back in Rome now." Joanna looked up from the floor with the saddest expression Marcy had ever seen. "I don't have anything he wants anymore."

"If he wants you back?" Marcy pressed. She hated herself for asking, but she needed to hear the answer. "Will you go to him?"

"He hurt my child, Marcy." Joanna's eyes snapped with fury. "Of course I won't go back to him."

"Why didn't you say something when you arrived? We could have helped you."

"I told Gram everything the first day, during afternoon tea in the garden. But she doesn't remember. I tried to tell you, too, that night I waited up for you. But you didn't want to listen."

Marcy leaned back against the wicker. "Joanna. How could you—"

"How could I what?" Joanna turned on Marcy with an unexpected fierceness. Her eyes blazed with anger. "I know what you think of me, Marcy, what you've always thought of me. My whole life, I've always been less than you—fatter, uglier, stupider. You're going to tell me again that I got what I deserved, or that I'm a bad mother. Well, I don't want to hear it."

Marcy reached for her sister, but Joanna pulled away. "That's not what I was going to say, at all. I was going to ask how could you imagine that you couldn't come to me with something so important? Despite things being sticky between us right now, I'm still your sister, and I'm still going to help you. No matter what." Marcy sighed. "Letty told me that you and I had lost track of ourselves. That we are sisters and we should start acting like it."

"I miss Letty in the house."

"Me, too."

In the silence that followed, Marcy watched a bead of condensation slide down Joanna's wine glass. A thought occurred to her. "Did you sell your pearls, too?"

"Which pearls?"

"The strand Gram gave each of us when we turned sixteen. She took the double strand her mother had given her when she debuted and had two single strands made." Marcy held her breath. "Joanna, did you sell Gram's pearls to pay for your move to Rome?"

"No. I didn't sell them. I took them with me. They're hidden in the apartment in Rome, but I won't go back there." Joanna shook her head. "Not ever."

"You won't have to, Joanna. Give me the address, and I'll figure out a way to get them for you." Marcy leaned forward and held her sister's gaze. "That necklace is a part of you, Joanna. It represents your family and your history, and a man that hurts you doesn't get to keep them."

But Joanna wouldn't consider it. "That part of my life is over, Marcy. I want to forget I was ever that stupid."

In the distance, a sailboat passed, tiny white lights spanning its length and winding around the mast. The laughter of the passengers echoed across the water and drifted into the garden. On the bow, a bride posed for pictures, her veil floating in the breeze, the sunset behind her.

When the boat passed from sight, Marcy turned her attention back to her sister. "Letty told me, one time, that your twenties are for making mistakes, big ones. So, in some ways, I envy you."

Joanna scoffed as she finally reached for her wine. "You don't make mistakes, Marcy. You never have."

"Maybe I would have liked to," Marcy countered as she reached for her own glass. "I've always done exactly what's expected. I run Grandpa's company—or try to. Two hundred people, all of them depending on me. I take care of Gram, and Letty, too, sometimes, and I manage this house. My life has been running the same course for years. Nothing changes. But what if I wanted it to? What if I want something different, something else? Not counting the time we lived in Pensacola, I've never traveled more than three hundred miles from this house in my whole life. And I've always wanted to."

"Really?" Joanna sniffed and swiped her nose with the back of her hand. "You never said."

"Oh, I'm not finished." Marcy slapped at a mosquito. "It gets worse. I've had three relationships in the past five years, each one ending as soon as they saw how committed I am to the company. I have a few good friends who know me and a million acquaintances who think they do. I didn't choose this life, Joanna, I fell into it and I don't want it anymore."

Marcy hadn't realized how resentful she was, until she said it out loud. The truth was that she felt trapped in a life that she had no control over. She managed the house and the company, and took care of Eudora because there was no one else to do it. What she really wanted was to travel. She would have loved to have the courage to pick up and move to Rome, like her sister did.

They sat in silence for a bit, listening to the hum of the crickets outside and Gracie coloring with Lendard in the kitchen. The air had cooled, and it was almost time to go inside and start dinner.

"I'm sorry, Marcy," Joanna said, abruptly. "I'm sorry I left you with everything. I'm sorry for both of us, actually."

"I'm sorry for us, too." Leaning her head against the back of the chair, she closed her eyes and listened to the hum of the frogs in the garden.

After a moment, Joanna's voice broke the silence. "What do we do now?"

Marcy answered without opening her eyes. "We stick together, and we figure it out."

CHAPTER 37

"MIND THE WALLS, NOW." Letty followed the movers back up the stairs, clucking like a wet hen. "Miss Eudora will have something to say if you scuff them walls."

Behind her, the movers balanced Eudora's box spring on the landing, pausing to catch their breath. Marcy tried to slip by unnoticed.

"And where do you think you're going, missy?" Letty asked.

"To work, Letty," Marcy said.

But Letty would have none of it. "You know Miss Eudora coming home tomorrow. I'd think you would want to help us get this house ready." She pointed to the stairs. "G'won down there, and see can you give your sister a hand packing up that room." Next, Letty shooed the movers from the stairs. "Break time's over. We ain't paying you to loll around."

It had been Amina's idea to convert Eudora's sunroom into a bedroom. The reasoning was that the sunroom was closer to the kitchen, and Eudora would feel less isolated downstairs. When Letty found out, she had been horrified. "What are you all thinking?" she had said. "Miss Eudora spent the past two weeks in that hospital, doing her therapies, thinking that when she was finished, she'd have her own room again, and things could go back to normal. Here you go making up a sick room and putting her in it. Don't you know that's exactly the wrong place? Miss Eudora ain't sick."

So, movers had been summoned back, and everyone spent the rest of the morning packing boxes and dragging furniture back up the stairs.

Marcy entered the sunroom, as she'd been instructed, and found Joanna packing the last of Eudora's things. "Letty sent me," Marcy said. "What do you need me to do?"

Joanna pointed to a collection of silver-framed pictures on a table. "Can you wrap those up? The frames are so old and fragile that I'm afraid the silver will scratch."

"Sure." Marcy balanced on the edge of an armchair by the window and spread a tea towel across her lap. Since their conversation on the piazza the other night, their relationship had been less strained, less formal. It was as if they had gotten a glimpse of the reality of each other's lives, and they didn't need to pretend anymore. It wasn't perfect, but it was a start. "I still think Amina's idea to convert this room is a good one. Gram's always liked this view of her garden, and she's close to the kitchen. We can hear her if she needs anything."

Joanna bent down to plug the vacuum cord into the wall socket. "Maybe. But I think Letty's got a point. Gram might be happier in her own room."

Smoothing the wrinkles from the towel, Marcy reached for a frame and laid it on her lap. The photograph inside was cracked and faded but it always had a place in the collection on Eudora's bedside table. The picture had been taken on Eudora's wedding day, more than six decades ago, just before she and Brock left for their honeymoon. Dressed in a powder blue traveling suit with a white corsage and a veiled hat, Eudora's smile was radiant, hopeful. By her side was her new husband, dressed in his military uniform, fresh from graduation at The Citadel.

Marcy felt Joanna over her shoulder, looking at the picture.

"They look happy." Joanna pointed to a small tree in the background of the picture. "Is that the big cherry tree in the corner of the garden?"

"It is. And there's a story behind it, too." Marcy had heard the story from Eudora a thousand times before. "She met Grandpa at some kind of reception at The Citadel. He was a cadet there, a senior, and very handsome. Apparently, Gram and one of her 'friends' had been vying for his attention, and the friend thought she'd won him over. So, Gram was more than a little surprised when he asked permission to walk her home, which was a huge breach of etiquette, by the way: a man escorting a woman anywhere unchaperoned. Anyway, on the way home, Gram happened to mention that pink cherry trees were her favorite. On the day he proposed, Grandpa planted a cherry tree and knelt beside it, joking that she'd better say yes because he'd already planted the tree."

"How romantic," Joanna breathed.

Marcy snorted as she covered the picture with a towel. "He had a mistress."

"What?"

Marcy nodded as she reached for another picture. "It's true. Gram never said a word, but he did, for years. I think she was Gram's friend, the same one from the dance where she met him." Stacking the picture with the others, Marcy added, "Their affair lasted forty years and only ended when the woman died."

"Did Gram know?"

"Of course. She and the woman were in the same garden club."

Joanna leaned against the edge of the chair. "But she and Grandpa seemed so happy."

"This family has a lot of secrets." Marcy reached for another picture, then hesitated. It still bothered her that Joanna had left everything behind when she left Rome and that she seemed to have no interest in retrieving any of it. Setting the picture on her lap, she tried again. "Joanna, are you *sure* you don't want to go back to Rome, to get the things you left?"

"I'm sure."

"But he has your *pearls*, Joanna," Marcy persisted. "Pearls that belonged to Gram and should one day belong to Gracie. I can get them for you. He'll never know who I am."

Joanna's expression was hard. "Marcy, no. Nicco doesn't know where we are now. And if the price to keep him out of our lives is a string of antique pearls and an apartment in Rome, then that's what it costs." Joanna turned and clicked the release on the vacuum. The subject, apparently, was closed.

Marcy scooped up the stack of pictures and headed for the stairs. As she passed through the kitchen, her cellphone buzzed with a text message from Andrea. *Skip wants to see you. What should I tell him?*

Sighing, Marcy typed a reply. *About Meeting Street?*

Andrea's answer came quickly: *Yes.*

Marcy still had hopes of persuading the original owners to refund at least part of the escrow, but until that happened, she had some hard choices to make. One of them involved selling the Meeting Street property. The most obvious solution was to flip the property, but it wasn't her first choice.

Marcy typed an excuse: *I can't see him today. Maybe next week.*

Putting Skip off a third time was a coward's way out, but at least it gave her a few days to come up with a plan that didn't include selling that property.

CHAPTER 38

EUDORA HAD BEEN home for almost a week when Marcy realized that she couldn't put off the conversation any longer. No matter how she had arranged the numbers on the spreadsheets, they were always the same. Unless Palmetto Holdings changed direction immediately, it was headed for a disastrous year. The expansion she'd hoped for was out of the question, and she was out of ideas.

Dropping her work bag near the table, she asked, "Is Gram still awake?"

Joanna filled a glass with ice cubes and opened the refrigerator. "She just went upstairs, but I don't think she's asleep."

Upstairs, Marcy knocked softly on Eudora's door, almost too softly. Truthfully, she hoped Eudora was asleep because she dreaded the conversation that would follow.

"Come in." Eudora was seated in her favorite chair near the tall doors leading to the piazza, reading the evening newspaper. A breeze blew in from the harbor, carrying with it the smell of rain and damp earth. A yellow pashmina wrapped her shoulders, and a cup of tea sat on her side table.

"You look comfortable, Gram. I'm glad you're home now."

Lowering the newspaper, Eudora removed her reading glasses. Her gaze swept over Marcy. It missed nothing; it never did. "Marcy...what...a pleasant surprise."

Since her stroke, Eudora's words had slowed, coming in bursts, with a frustrated hesitation between. Letty had been the only one brave enough to insist that Eudora continue therapy no matter how much she complained. Conversation with Eudora took some getting used to, for both the cadence of her words and for the hesitation in between.

"Come. Sit." Eudora pointed to the ottoman at her feet. "Tell me...what...is wrong."

Marcy sat, tucking her hands underneath her thighs. "It's about work. Palmetto Holdings."

Eudora nodded for her to continue.

Marcy looked away, focusing on the scrollwork of the mirror across the room. She couldn't meet her grandmother's eye. She was about to tell her grandmother that she'd ruined the family company by bidding on a property they couldn't afford and then losing a sizable escrow because she didn't have all the paperwork at closing. It didn't matter that Eudora hadn't signed the power of attorney or that Joanna hadn't delivered it. The ultimate accountability was Marcy's, and she had failed.

Pushing her palms into the fabric of the ottoman, Marcy drew a breath. "Gram, do you remember the property I wanted to buy? An industrial property, by the airport. Warehouses and land."

"Yes."

But Marcy couldn't do it. She couldn't burden her grandmother with her own failings. Dr. Plyer had said that because they didn't know what caused Eudora's stroke, they weren't sure what would trigger another. Stress, certainly, and this news was definitely stressful. She would go back to work and figure something out.

Pushing against the cushion, Marcy rose to leave. "It's nothing, Gram. I'm sorry I bothered you."

But Eudora motioned for her to sit. "Did I ever tell you… how your grandfather…built this company?"

"Many times, Gram."

Eudora's face reddened as she forced the words. "Now… let me tell you what…really happened."

It took a full hour for her grandmother to explain, and when she had finished, Marcy sat in stunned silence. Everything she'd been told about her family's company had been a lie. Her grandfather bought the first building, not by saving his salary, but with the money he and Eudora had been given by her parents to pay for their honeymoon. And instead of the honeymoon in Paris that he'd promised, he took Eudora to Augusta, Georgia to spend the weekend in a dingy hotel and had pocketed the rest of the money. The construction crew he had hired, the one Marcy had assumed was filled with craftsmen dedicated to preserving Charleston's unique heritage, was mostly a group of college buddies whom Brock paid under the table, to avoid taxes. They worked at night to avoid code inspections from the city. When the money ran out, Brock continued to write checks, and every one of them bounced.

"But Gram, Palmetto Holdings is—"

Eudora drew a labored breath and gathered her words. "Palmetto Holdings thrived…in spite of your grandfather…

not because of him...I chose...the buildings... He...told everyone...they were his idea."

Outside, Marcy heard the swish of car tires on the wet road and muffled shouts as a group of college kids called to each other in the rain. A breeze from the harbor ruffled the sheers drawn across the open windows. For as long as she could remember, Marcy had been trying to live up to the legend that was her grandfather's legacy. It was the reason she'd chosen to study business in college. The reason she had pursued her MBA. And the reason why her best efforts never seemed good enough.

"Marcy Elizabeth...Rutledge, I am...speaking to you."

"Yes, ma'am." Marcy's response was immediate, a reflex. Her grandmother's voice, however fractured, still commanded respect.

Marcy turned her attention back to her grandmother, who cradled her favorite teacup in her palm as gently as she would hold a rose blossom from her garden.

"I asked...if you knew...why this teacup is my favorite."

"No, I don't, Gram. You never told me."

Eudora touched the outline of the pineapple on the front of the cup. Her voice softened as if she were narrating a memory. "One of the properties...your grandfather... acquired was a storefront...on King Street." After a moment, she continued. "I wanted...to open...a tea shop there. I had... I had these cups made..."

Marcy pictured Palmetto Holdings' portfolio in her mind —every property they'd ever owned, and every building they'd ever flipped. A tea shop on King was not among them.

"You might be mistaken, Gram," Marcy soothed. Dr. Plyer had said that Eudora might become confused if she allowed herself to get overly tired. Marcy glanced at Eudora's bed, wondering how to persuade her grandmother to nap.

Eudora slapped her hand against the seat cushion. "Don't patronize me...Marcy...I am...not stupid." She drew a ragged breath and continued. "Your grandfather...bought the building...I wanted but...sold it...to buy...another. Said...my teashop...was...silly idea."

In the silence that followed, Eudora's color slowly returned to normal, though her face was etched with fatigue. "You...idolized your...grandfather...and...you were...the apple of...apple of...his eye."

The newspaper drifted from Eudora's lap and fluttered to the floor. Marcy retrieved it and set it on the table.

"And...I doubt very much...that anything...you have to tell...me is worse...than what...he did...to me."

Encouraged, Marcy began. Slowly at first, until she realized that Eudora might not be as fragile as Marcy had thought, then Marcy told her everything. How she had found the property and described her business plan to develop the strip mall on the vacant land. How she had made the mistake of hiring Bruce Calhoun to fill the mall with tenants, even though she didn't really trust him. She left out the unsigned power of attorney, saying only that she had missed the closing and had been forced to forfeit a sizable escrow.

When she was finished, she looked up. Eudora's eyes sparked with interest, and Marcy understood. It was her grandmother who loved Palmetto Holdings, not her grandfather. If Eudora had lived in another time, maybe she could have claimed the company as her own, instead of standing behind her husband. What a team they would have made, Eudora and Marcy, if only it had occurred to Marcy to ask for help.

"Which...family?"

"The one who was selling the property?" Marcy asked.

When Eudora nodded, Marcy answered. "Rayburn."

Eudora's brow creased as she thought. "Evelyn... Ray...Rayburn?"

"Yes, that's the one. But it was my fault, Gram, not theirs. I missed the deadline for the closing. If they had returned the escrow, it would have made things easier for us. Technically, they weren't required to, but the property closed on the same day for twice as much as we had agreed to, so they actually made money by *not* selling to us."

"Bad family...greedy. Always have...been." Leaning back with a sigh, Eudora closed her eyes. "I find I'm in need of a rest...after all."

"Of course, Gram. Let me help you." Rising from her place, Marcy helped Eudora to her bed. After plumping the pillows, Marcy unfolded the quilt at the foot of the bed.

As she reached to turn off the bedside lamp, Eudora stilled her hand. "Not finished yet."

Marcy sat and waited for Eudora to catch her breath. When she did, her voice seemed stronger. "I should have given you...control of the company...years ago... I was wrong not to. You are the brightest...woman I've ever known. You remind me...of me." A papery laugh escaped Eudora's lips. "I have every...confidence...that you will do...remarkable things...with this company...no matter...the challenges."

Marcy swallowed past the lump in her throat, but she was unable to speak.

"Rest...now." Eudora's voice was ragged.

Marcy kissed her grandmother's cheek, something she rarely did and now found herself wondering why not.

"Do you want me to close the doors, Gram?"

"No. I like...to hear...the people outside."

Marcy rose from her place. "I'll be back in an hour or so. Amina said you're not allowed to eat on a tray in your room anymore. From now on, you have to eat meals with the family."

Eudora closed her eyes with a sigh. "She's worse...than Letty."

CHAPTER 39

WHEN EUDORA WOKE, the shadows of the day had softened, and the light from the window was fading. This time, she didn't have to ask. She knew Alice was nearby. She could feel it.

"Thank you, Mama." Her daughter's voice was a whisper.

"For what, baby girl?" Eudora held her breath. She didn't want to break the spell.

"For bringing my girls together. For giving them the home I couldn't."

"I always…will. I promise."

Eudora felt a brush against her cheek, as soft as a whisper, and then as quickly as she'd arrived, Alice disappeared.

CHAPTER 40

EARLY MONDAY MORNING, Andrea leaned against the door-frame, waving a sheaf of papers. "Here are the latest projections for Meeting Street."

Marcy looked up from her spreadsheet, confused. "Is that for my meeting with Skip?"

"Yes." Andrea entered Marcy's office and deposited the papers on her desk. "I've already rescheduled twice, and you need to meet with him. At least put him out of his misery." She flipped to the printed spreadsheet and pointed to the bottom. "The numbers look good. Skip's used the latest construction costs. Pete told me that Skip called him last night, just for the most recent numbers."

Marcy looked at the numbers, then glanced at Andrea. "Have you seen the renovation?"

Andrea smiled as she walked toward her desk to answer the phone. "It looks amazing. You're going to love it."

The building on Meeting Street had been abandoned, boarded, and forgotten in a weedy gravel lot behind a chain-link fence. The selling agent had marketed the lot for land value only, reasoning the building was unsalvageable. The listing even contained an estimate to raze it. But the first time Marcy saw it, she heard her grandfather's voice, whispering that the house had good bones, so she bought it on the spot. But with her attention on the North Charleston project, she hadn't seen updates for Meeting Street in quite a while.

Pulling up her email, she scanned her inbox for the latest information from Pete, the construction manager. The report from two days prior contained no less than twelve attachments, pictures of detail work the craftsmen had completed in the last week, and a few candid shots of workers celebrating. Curious, Marcy clicked one of the pictures and marveled at the transformation. Pete's crew had restored the original heart pine floors to a warm honey-gold. Warped sheetrock above the front entrance had been removed to reveal framing for transom windows. And the interior had been painted a cool gray with bright white trim.

Impressed at the transformation, Marcy called to her assistant. "Andrea, this is amazing."

Andrea appeared in the doorway. "I know. Pete gave us a tour yesterday."

"Are they finished?"

"He said they would be, by the end of the week."

"Do we have anything planned for them?"

"You mean like a party?" Andrea arched an eyebrow as she planted her hand on her hip. "I thought we were watching expenses."

"Here." Marcy slid a personal credit card from her wallet. "Use this. Invite everyone who worked on the project, including their families." Handing the card to Andrea, she added, with a smile, "Something better than cake in the breakroom, but not too much better."

Andrea beamed as she turned to leave. "I know just what to do."

"Tell Skip he can come in," Marcy called after her.

A few moments later, Skip entered her office with a laptop under his arm and the price tag peeking from beneath his crisp, blue tie.

The stack of papers he carried landed on Marcy's desk with a thud, and he reddened instantly. "Sorry," he mumbled.

Marcy pushed back from her desk and pointed to her conference table. "Why don't we work over there? There's more room to spread out, and the light's better."

Scooping his papers from her desk, she said, "I just saw pictures of the restoration on Meeting Street. It's exceptional, Skip. Very well done."

"Thanks." Skip reddened as he opened his laptop. "But that's not why I came. I have something else to show you." He tapped a few keys and swiveled the screen, so Marcy could see.

As Marcy peered at the screen, her breath caught. She pointed. "Is this information current? When did it come on the market?"

Skip straightened in his chair and adjusted his tie. "Well, it's not *officially* on the market yet. The owners signed an agreement two days ago, but I wanted you to see it before anyone else did."

One of the perks of working for Palmetto Holdings was that anyone in the company could bring a listing to the sales office. When it sold, they received a referral fee from the agent. If the property had renovation potential, the agent would bring it to Marcy's attention after they listed it. For Skip to bring the information to her now, before it was public, meant he was losing money.

Marcy flicked through Skip's pictures, her interest growing. "This is near the college."

"Yes," Skip confirmed.

"We've never done a renovation this far north."

"It has enormous potential."

"I see that." Marcy looked up. "And these buildings are being sold all together—you're sure?"

"Yes."

"Zoned commercial, permitting already in place?"

"Yes. That was all done before the builder went out of business." He removed a page from his folder and slid it across the table.

As Marcy glanced at the letterhead, her eyes widened. "He's secured approval from the Historic Commission?"

"Yes, and he's willing to include the approval with the renovation plans."

"Show me an aerial view."

A few keystrokes later, and Marcy was looking at a plat on Upper King Street. A set of three buildings that appeared to be retail on the first floor, and living space above. The property was close to the college and a residential district. Goosebumps rose on Marcy's arm.

Leaning forward, she squeezed her hands together. "Skip, how long can you give me to put together an offer before you show it to anyone else?"

"Well, I don't know," Skip pondered. "It's already been two days, and I don't want to get in trouble with the owners."

"Can you give me until five o'clock?" Marcy heard the excitement in her voice. This could be the answer she was looking for. "You're absolutely right. This property is a treasure, and I want to make an offer, but I need a couple of hours to get everything together."

"Maybe we can work something out." He leaned forward, an unexpected gleam in his eye. "If you want to buy them, that means you want to renovate them. If I wait for your offer, will you let me manage the restoration?"

"The restoration? Of all three buildings? That's kind of a big job."

But Skip pressed her. "I have proven that I can do the work. Meeting Street— you've seen the results I get, and you said you like them." Skip shifted in his chair, eager for a chance. "I want to do that again, with another property. There is something about bringing an old building back to life that —" He paused as he searched for the words.

"Skip," Marcy began to let him down gently. "I agree. You *have* done an outstanding job on Meeting Street, but managing three buildings at one time is something else entirely. And you've seen the condition they're in. The owners expected the buildings to be razed; which means they've given up on them. I'm not sure anyone can manage this project by themselves."

"I don't mind sharing the work," Skip countered. "But I want to be the one in charge, answering only to you."

Marcy nodded slowly, her mind racing with possibilities. "Okay, I'll give it serious consideration. Just give me until five o'clock."

The moment Skip left her office, Marcy picked up the phone and dialed a number. "Pick up. Pick up. Pick up." She muttered.

"LowCountry Trust, how may I direct your call?"

"Seth Hinkley, please."

"One moment, please."

On the fourth ring, he answered. "This is Seth."

Keeping her voice light, Marcy replied. "Seth, this is Marcy Rutledge."

"Marcy, how are you?" His voice was oily, and Marcy cringed. She didn't like him, but at the moment, she needed him. She counted on him being sloppy enough not to check for updated financials, like other banks would.

With her elbow on the edge of her desk, she rested her forehead on her palm and closed her eyes. Word choice would be crucial. "I have a business proposal for you. A good one."

"Shoot."

"I've decided to transfer the loan from the industrial property to a better investment. One that just now came on the market. It's a much better opportunity, and most important: it's not on the market yet. All the permitting is in place, and we're ready to move on it, immediately. The reason I'm coming to you is because you already have our financials, and it would be nothing at all to transfer that information to the new loan."

"Well, now," he drawled, "You of all people ought to know you can't transfer loans just like that. It's a complicated business we're in. We have to start fresh with a whole different application, and that takes time. You know that."

"Not this time, Seth. This closing is time-critical, but it will mean a healthy profit for both our companies."

Then she held her breath, and waited.

If Seth refused, Marcy was prepared to call in every favor she'd ever extended in the entire city of Charleston. Somewhere there had to be money enough to buy these buildings.

"Well," he drawled, finally. "We might could work something out. Come to my office, and we'll see what we can do."

"I'm on my way."

Andrea, who had been lurking in the doorway during the call, entered the office, her eyes blazing with anger. "Marcy, you cannot go back to that vulture for money. He's just one step above a loan shark. There has got to be another way."

"I know. He's awful, but this property is incredible, and we need to move on it right now. At the moment, he's all we've got."

"He's going to squeeze you for a huge down payment."

"It will work out. I have an idea." Marcy assured her.

What Marcy didn't say is that she planned to use her own money for a down payment. And she would use the rest— her savings, her investment accounts, her retirement— as collateral against the loan. With that much at stake, she'd be able to negotiate a lower interest rate and payments would be manageable.

She had a feeling about that property, a really good feeling.

CHAPTER 41

GRACIE POUNDED up the stairs in a tornado of energy and excitement, slamming the door behind her. "Mommy! Mommy!"

Joanna closed her notebook and went to her daughter. "Shhh! Gracie, you're going to wake Great-Gram."

Gracie frowned. "But you said you'd take me to see the sailboats, and I've waited *all day*. Can we go now?" Gracie shifted her weight from one foot to the other impatiently.

Joanna pulled an apple juice from the refrigerator and looked at her daughter. Gracie's cheeks were flushed, and her face glistened with perspiration. "Where have you been?"

"Playing soccer with Zoe. She's the best soccer player ever, and she said I have good kick." Peeling off her hoodie, Gracie let it drop to the floor.

"Pick up that sweatshirt, please, and put it in the laundry room."

"After that, can we go?" Gracie was relentless.

"I have to finish this first."

Gracie moved closer to look at the pages spread across the surface of the table. "What is it?"

"I'm thinking about going back to school, and that's the spring schedule."

Gracie's eyes widened as she sipped her juice. "My school?"

"No, honey." Joanna closed the course catalog. "College." But she hadn't really decided yet. Going back to school seemed like starting over, and Joanna didn't want to start over. She loved her Art History degree; she just couldn't find a job using it.

The soft creak of footsteps on the stairs caught Joanna's attention. It had to be Eudora—Marcy was at work, Letty was at home, and Amina hadn't yet returned.

Joanna rose from her place and rushed to the hallway. "Gram, you should have called me. Let me help you."

But Eudora waved her off. "Nonsense Joanna...I am fine. I have lived in this house for more than half a century...been up and down these...stairs a thousand times."

Eudora's speech seemed to be less hesitant when she was rested, but Joanna wouldn't make the mistake of bringing that to Eudora's attention. Eudora hated being coddled. Still, as her grandmother navigated the stairs, Joanna's hand hovered underneath Eudora's arm.

Eventually, Eudora noticed and shook Joanna off. Her recovery was slower than she wanted, and it wasn't unusual for her to become frustrated and snappy. "If you insist on helping me, I could use a nice cup of tea."

As she moved down the hallway, Joanna noticed Eudora's walk seemed to have improved; she shuffled less. Dr. Plyer insisted on maintaining her physical therapy three times a week, even though Eudora had wanted to quit after the first week. For encouragement, Marcy and Gracie had secretly decorated a pair of bright white sneakers with red glitter glue and stickers for Eudora to wear to her therapy. Joanna noticed that Eudora wore them to every session.

Joining Gracie at the table, Eudora offered a rare smile. "Would you like to join me for a...cup of tea, young lady?"

"A tea party?" Gracie put down her juice box. "A real one? Like the ones you have with Aunt Marcy and Mommy?"

"Yes." Eudora folded her hands in her lap, and Joanna smiled. Her grandmother's posture was still arrow-straight, a perfect three inches from the back of the chair.

"Can I wear a pretty dress?"

Eudora eyed Gracie's grubby shirt and arched an eyebrow. "I would insist upon it."

Gracie turned to Joanna, her face bright with excitement. "Can I, Mommy?"

"Go pick out your dress, and I'll help you with the shower."

As Gracie bounced back up the stairs, Marcy and Amina both entered through the kitchen. Amina set grocery bags on the counter and shrugged off her coat.

Marcy stood in front of her sister. "I'm glad you're here, Joanna. I'd like to show you something. Do you have a minute for a quick errand?"

Joanna hesitated, glancing at Eudora. "I promised to make Gram a cup of—"

Eudora waved her away. "Go with your...sister. Amina... can help me."

CHAPTER 42

TWENTY MINUTES LATER, Marcy parked her car in the front of the property on Upper King. A chain link fence surrounded the buildings, two facing the street, and one in back. Sliding the key from her pocket, she slipped it into the lock and entered the building.

"Come on," she urged.

"Is this legal?" Joanna whispered.

"Not entirely, but we should be fine." Marcy glanced at her watch as she pulled a flashlight from her bag. "Just hurry."

Marcy closed the door behind them, flicked on the flashlight, and swept the beam across the room, feeling a tingle of anticipation for what this building would become. It did have good bones. Original floors, built-in shelving, and a leaded-glass window above the front door. In the back room, sheets of wallpaper, yellowed with age, lay crumpled beside a rusty steamer and a stack of empty buckets.

"Marcy, what are we *doing* here?"

She'd add an inspection to the offer, of course, and would insist on reviewing all permitting before closing.

Moving to the window, she glanced at the gravel parking lot shared by the buildings. She pictured a commercial dumpster there, something big enough to service both buildings.

"Marcy." Joanna's voice was sharp, and Marcy turned, surprised to see her sister. In her excitement, she'd forgotten Joanna was there.

"What are we doing here?" Joanna repeated. "Are we trespassing? Because it feels like we're trespassing."

Marcy flicked off her flashlight. "We're going to buy this building."

"Well, that's great, Marcy, but I'm not sure why you needed to show it to me."

Marcy corrected herself. "Joanna, I want *us* to buy this building. And renovate it."

Joanna stared. "What do you mean?"

"This building, and the ones on either side," Marcy pointed out the back window, "are all being sold together. Skip brought me the listing, and I need to make an offer in the next two hours, or he puts it on the market. If he does, we'll probably lose them. It's an amazing opportunity. You can't find anything like this anymore."

"I'm happy for you," Joanna began. "But what does that have to do with me?"

"I want you to work on this project, too, with Skip. Together, you can bring this building back to life. He's really good, Joanna, and you can learn a lot from him."

Joanna wandered the room, letting her fingertips graze the plaster walls and looking at the crown molding. She tugged on a strip of wallpaper, and it fluttered to the ground.

"You can use your Art History degree," Marcy offered.

"That's not how Art History degrees work." Peering

inside a bucket, she poked a rag with her finger. "All three buildings? Really?"

"Yes. I need someone who appreciates the beauty of these buildings, someone who will work hard to bring that beauty back." Marcy bit her lip as she glanced at her watch. "Look, Joanna—"

Joanna looked at Marcy and laughed. "Are you *kidding*? This room is beautiful now. After restoration, it will be magnificent. I'd love to help."

"Good. Let's go. I have to write up the offer."

CHAPTER 43

THE BUILDING DIDN'T HAVE electricity or running water, so the reception inside wasn't entirely legal. But the party was important, a new project kickoff for the crew and a new direction for the company. All the pre-construction clutter had been cleared from the room, and the floors had been swept clean. Most everyone stood, though there were a few small tables near the front. Someone had put together a trestle table by laying a door between two saw-horses and covering it with what looked like one of Eudora's damask tablecloths. A makeshift buffet had been laid out on top, with bottles of champagne in buckets of ice. The ribbon she'd cut earlier that afternoon to officially open the building to construction fluttered in the late afternoon breeze, a flash of red brushing against the rough bark of the palmetto tree planted the week before.

"These buildings are amazing. I can't believe anything like this still exists in Charleston." Andrea approached with a pair of champagne flutes in her hand and offered one to Marcy. "What did Eudora say when you told her what it was going to be?"

"We haven't told her yet." Marcy watched her grand-mother, seated at a table near the front of the room, whis-pering and laughing with Letty and Amina. Their friendship seemed to have taken up exactly where it had left off before Letty retired. Her grandmother's health had improved in the last few months, though her speech was still fragmented when she got tired.

"Doesn't she recognize it?" Andrea pointed to shelving that carpenters had finished just the day before. Skip and Joanna had translated Eudora's vague descriptions and frag-mented memories into something that looked as if it belonged. Beside the shelving, a spattered drop cloth obscured a far wall.

"Not yet, but she will."

"When is the grand opening?" Andrea asked.

"That's up to Skip and Joanna. Work begins on Monday."

Andrea sipped her champagne. "They work well together."

Marcy spotted her sister across the room and smiled. Joanna had changed so much since she'd first arrived. Relaxed and confident now, she seemed to have a good working relationship with Skip and the crew. Saturday morning meetings were fully catered now, and that seemed to be key. Attendance was up, and she'd heard that some staff even looked forward to them.

Joanna approached with a folder of papers in her hand and a smile on her face. She'd come into her own style, as well, different from Eudora's or Marcy's. She wore a gray tunic over a pair of black leggings and boots, with a vintage silk sari scarf tied casually around her neck. "We're almost ready to start." Joanna looked expectantly at Marcy.

But Marcy shook her head. "This is your project—yours and Skip's. You go up there."

Joanna drew a breath so deep that Marcy saw her sister's chest rise. Joanna nodded once but was interrupted when Gracie appeared, red-cheeked and breathless.

"Mommy, can I go with Zoe now?" She pointed toward the back of the room. "Zoe and her mommy are right there."

"I almost forgot." Joanna hooked a blonde curl behind her daughter's ear, and dropped a kiss on the top of her head. "Yes, you can go. I'll be there later." Joanna watched her daughter run to Zoe, and she waved to Trinity as she shepherded the girls out the door.

Marcy felt herself smile. Her niece had changed from the tentative, shy child she'd been just six months before. She was a ball of energy, with a lot of friends. She would be seven years old next month, and Marcy planned to surprise her with sailing lessons at the club. It was time. For both of them.

"Marcy, are you listening?" Joanna asked.

Marcy startled. "No, I'm sorry; I wasn't. What did you say?"

"I asked if you were going to dinner with Dr. Plyer tonight?"

"Dinner? You mean like on a date? Of course not." Marcy felt herself blush. "I mean, he did ask if I was free after this, but it's not a date."

"Of course, it's a date. He's interested in you, Marcy." Joanna laughed. "Haven't you wondered why he comes to the house so often?"

"He comes to check Gram's progress."

But that made Joanna laugh harder. "Doctors don't make house calls, Marcy. Especially the Chief of Neurology at Charleston General."

"Fine." Marcy waved her hand in the air. "He asked if I was free for dinner after the reception, but I haven't given him an answer. I have a lot to do here."

Marcy had issued the invitation to the construction party casually, not expecting Dr. Plyer to accept. But he did, and she'd been on edge for days. He arrived with a bouquet of flowers for Eudora and bottles of champagne for Joanna and Skip. Marcy had introduced him to everyone and noticed that he was equally at ease with both office staff and craftsmen. At the moment, he stood in a group of women from accounting, his cheeks dimpling as he smiled. She noticed, too, that he glanced at her and smiled.

"You're not managing this project, remember? So, you've got nothing to do here," Joanna pointed out. Skip motioned for her to join him, and Joanna touched Marcy's arm. "Remember what you told me on the piazza that night. Now's your chance: go get what you want."

As Joanna threaded her way to the front of the room, Marcy went to find Cecily. "I'm glad you're here, Cee."

"At the beginning of your new empire?" Cecily squeezed her arm. "I wouldn't miss it for the world. These buildings are amazing."

"Wait until you see what we do with them."

Cecily moved closer and lowered her voice. "To answer your question from before: Yes, my passport is still current. You going to tell me what this mystery trip is?"

Marcy smiled and played along. "You've been chosen for a very important mission. Be packed and ready to go, passport in hand. I'll tell you everything—later."

Cecily groaned at the sketchy details, as Marcy knew she would. But it would have taken longer than the few minutes they had to explain where they were going and why it was important.

Cecily heaved a resigned sigh. "Just tell me this: is it legal, what we're doing?"

Marcy arched an eyebrow. "Mostly."

The conversations in the room stilled as Skip and Joanna took their place at the front of the room. The drop cloth was directly behind them, with a rope securing it at the corner.

"Thank you all for coming," Joanna began, her voice clear "I know it's unusual to have a pre-construction party, but this is a unique circumstance." As Joanna walked across the room, her posture straightened and Marcy smiled. Her little sister was a natural public speaker. "Today, we're celebrating a commitment to Charleston's history. I'm so proud to join the fight to save and restore these buildings.

"But today, we're also celebrating family." Joanna paused and stood in the center of the room, all eyes on her. "Before we go any further, I have to tell you how proud I am of my sister. I've always looked up to her—she doesn't know it, but I still do. Several months ago, Marcy saw an opportunity to give back to a city she loves. She bought this property because she could look beyond the chain-link fence and the boarded windows, and see something beautiful."

Joanna held Marcy's gaze and her smile widened. "My sister looks past what's broken and sees possibility. And when she's behind a project, you know it will succeed."

Joanna moved toward the drop cloth.

"In keeping with the commitment to Charleston's history, we have one more thing to celebrate: a corrected mistake. Sixty years ago, it was my grandmother's dream to open a tea shop. She'd chosen the perfect location, selected the inventory, and ordered custom-designed tea services. But the circumstances weren't right—and she had to abandon her dream. Now it's our turn to give back to her.

"You are all officially invited to the grand opening later this summer, but until then, ladies and gentlemen, Palmetto Holdings proudly presents..." Joanna reached for the cord and gave it a gentle tug. The sheet fell away to reveal an exquisite navy and cream-colored sign:

King Street Fine Teas

During the dedication, Marcy stood next to Cecily and watched her grandmother's reaction. At first, Eudora seemed confused. Marcy's gaze cut to John Plyer, but he shook his head. Eudora was fine. Letty leaned toward Eudora and whispered something. Eudora pressed her fingertips to her mouth and stared at Joanna.

"She thinks this shop is Joanna's idea," Cecily observed.

"I know."

"But it wasn't."

"I know that, too."

"You should tell her." Cecily was a champion of fairness. "This was your idea, too—you've been planning it for months."

"It doesn't matter who gets credit." Marcy shrugged. "What matters is that Gram gets her shop."

Cecily stared at her in mock horror. "Could it be that your Grinch's small heart grew three sizes today?"

Marcy arched her eyebrow. "Pretty brave talk for someone who might be going to Rome with me."

"Rome?" Cecily squealed. "Is that where this mystery trip is going? When do we leave?"

"Sooner than you think."

Before long, the crowd thinned, and the caterers cleared down the buffet. Outside, the streetlights blinked on as twilight deepened, and parents gathered their sleepy children. Construction was slated to begin early the next morning.

Joanna tapped Marcy on the shoulder. "I came to tell you that Dr. Plyer—John—wants to move the party to the River Rock. He's opening a tab and says that everyone's welcome."

Marcy shook her head, automatically, though her excuses sounded weak, even to her. "I need to make sure Gram gets back and rests." She glanced at her watch as if to demonstrate how busy she was. "She needs to take medicine in about thirty minutes."

"I'll take her home," Amina offered. "I have studying to do anyway."

"Are you going, Joanna?" Marcy asked.

"I have to pick up Gracie at Trinity's new gallery. I thought I'd stay a while, see her new exhibit."

Marcy turned to Cecily. "That leaves you, Cee. Are you coming?"

Cecily snorted. "Forget it. I know what a third wheel looks like."

John Plyer wandered over. "I don't seem to have any takers for the River Rock, but I refuse to take it personally."

Cecily bumped Marcy's shoulder with her own. "Marcy wants to go."

He brightened. "Do you? Well, if it's just us, I think we can do a little better than the River Rock. How about dinner?"

Marcy felt her stomach flutter as she accepted. Maybe her sister was right: maybe this was the beginning of something.

AS THE NIGHT DEEPENED, the evening breeze shifted, bringing cooler air in from Charleston Harbor. Joanna slid her arms into her cardigan. The house was quiet, and Joanna sat on the piazza overlooking her grandmother's garden. An empty pie plate sat on the table in front of her, and a warm woolen blanket covered her legs. It felt like spring would come early this year. The azaleas were already beginning to bud, and she looked forward to seeing them blossom. She and Eudora had taken pad and pencil in hand and had redesigned the annuals bed, readying it for the Spring Garden Tour. They'd hired a new housekeeper, one that could cook, and even Letty had approved. Marcy and John Plyer were out on their third official date, though Marcy still refused to call them "dates," Even so, it was nice to see her sister happy.

The open windows behind her drew the evening breeze from the harbor, scenting the piazza with a touch of salty air. In the garden below, as the afternoon melted into evening, the bustle of the day yielded to the hum of crickets and the croak of frogs. She'd forgotten how much she loved this time of day when the afternoon light faded to gold. In Rome, the pace of the city never slowed. One kind of chaos was traded for another, and it was something she had never gotten used to, and even her life in Chicago was a world away from the civility her grandmother had created right here. Afternoon tea was served in the garden, and she had been encouraged to spend whole summer days on the piazza with a good book and a cold glass of sweet tea.

After so many years away, she had finally come home.

And she wasn't ever going to leave.

THANK YOU

There are so many people who have encouraged, inspired, and helped to shape this story. I'm grateful for all of them.

To Sandy Esene, Bridget Norquist, Heather Stewart McCurdy, Ann Reckner, Laurie Rockenbeck, and Liz Visser: Your insights and encouragement have helped me more than you can imagine. Thank you for talking me down from the ledge when I needed it and for laughing at all the absurdities of this profession. I am truly fortunate to call you guys my friends.

And a special thank you to Laurie Rockenbeck, who let me lean on her all the way to the finish line.

To Cherry Adair, Diana Gabaldon, Susanna Kearsley, and Sabrina York. Thank you for your guidance, and for answering my questions with grace and patience.

For CMR: I miss you every day.

One of the talents that Heidi's most proud of is the ability to walk and read a book, without running into anything. She loves bookstores and public libraries and is delighted to have been to both Powell City of Books in Portland, Oregon, and The Strand Bookstore in New York City.

She started writing because she loves to read. All her novels have a happy ending, though it may take some work to get there. She writes about imperfect families, forgiveness, and second chances, combining humor with human frailty to create strong characters you will remember long after their journey is over.

Heidi and her family divide their time between the stunning natural beauty of the Pacific Northwest and the rich history of the Maryland coast. They visit the beach on both coasts every chance they get because you never know what will inspire a great story.

Heidi loves to hear from readers and answers all her own email. Connect with her at www.HeidiHostetter.com, or find her on Facebook.

ALSO BY HEIDI HOSTETTER

The Inheritance

If you like the Gilmore Girls' Stars Hollow, you'll love Inlet Beach. When three sisters arrive to claim the oldest house in town for themselves, you can bet the residents of this tiny beach community will have something to say about it.

The Inheritance is filled with the quirkiness of a small town, the craziness of an imperfect family, and the hope of a second chance.

Pacific Northwest Writers Association 2015 Literary Contest Finalist.

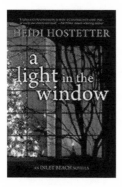

A Light in the Window

At Inlet Beach, storefronts are draped with garland, sprinkled with fairy-lights and dusted with Christmas magic.

But things are not as perfect as they seem.

As a blustery Pacific Northwest Christmas draws near, can the community of Inlet Beach help a boy with a shattered past find a home for the holidays?

A Light in the Window is a heartwarming tale of community, family, and second chances.